the program

the program

a novel by

hal niedzviecki

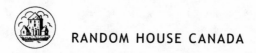
RANDOM HOUSE CANADA

Random House Canada and colophon are registered trademarks
of Random House of Canada Limited.

www.randomhouse.ca

Library and Archives Canada Cataloguing in Publication

Niedzviecki, Hal, 1971–
    The program / Hal Niedzviecki.

ISBN 0-679-31305-2

        I. Title.

PS8577.I3635P76 2005   C813'.54   C2004-905502-X

Jacket and text design: Leah Springate

Printed and bound in the United States of America

10   9   8   7   6   5   4   3   2   1

For my brother Orie. The bro! The brother!

You Press The Button.
We Do The Rest

—KODAK SLOGAN, 1888

part 1: **morphology**

DANNY CRAMS POTATO CHIPS into his mouth.

Hey, Maury says. Give me some of those.

Danny turns the bag upside down, shakes it into the grass. Powdered bits drift out, empty crumbs. The boy crunches, swallows, smiles. All gone.

You little . . . Maury says. He ruffles his son's hair. I didn't even get any.

Danny smiles again, shows teeth. All gone, he says. All gone. *Ha.*

Sure, rub it in, Maury says. The boy is ten but sometimes talks, Maury can't stop himself from thinking, like he's five.

Otherwise, the moment is perfect—commercially vibrant, Maury's marketing colleagues might say. Not that they would be caught dead in the forest. The night all around. Maury keeps eyeing the woods. There's nothing out there, he tells himself. And hey, here's something else to keep in mind: there's nothing wrong with his son. He's trying to keep that in mind. Haven't the experts examined? Weren't tests run?

Maury pictures a test—an examination—jogging down the halls of a hospital, doctors and experts chasing after, white coats fluttering, stethoscopes bobbing. Ha ha. All gone. It's not funny. If they don't know, who knows? They can sink into his son, go past the point where Maury gets stuck: Parental longing. Need. Desperation. Did it happen, or didn't it happen? *My brother.* One day, Maury thinks, he'll pay for what he did.

What did he do?

Danny fidgets, floats a hand across his face. All gone, he says in a simpering voice.

Yeah, I know, Maury says. I know.

Danny stares at the fire. Makes to throw the bag into flames, looks to his father.

Okay, Maury sighs. We shouldn't, but just this once. Bad for the environment. The ozone.

Danny flicks his wrist. The chip bag dances, settles, shrinks from green to purple, flames creeping over it.

Cool, Danny says. He leans his head against his father's shoulder.

Maury puts an arm around him, is relieved about something out of proportion to what just did or did not occur. He swallows the lump in his throat, blinks. Through the woods, on the other side of the lake, wolves howl. Maury thinks: Kodak moment. Time for a Nescafé. You deserve a break today.

But it's not like that at all; the sound is instant and collective, the opposite of some force-fed jingle. Necessary. Like air.

Daddy?

Just the wolves, Maury says. He holds his son tighter. Glances, again, at the furtive night concealed in the looming woods. Just the wolves, he says again. They don't mean any harm.

Wolves are cool, Danny says.

Danny used to be afraid of the dark. Ha! What a baby. Afraid of the dark! He's ten now. He's not afraid of anything. He can stay up all night. Even alone—I'm not—alone in the woods. Sure, could— Wolves out there. Won't hurt me. Could—

Danny wants to be alone. He wants the dark, the woods. That's what he's discovered. A revelation, though he doesn't know the word. Have fun, his mother said. Have fun with your father. She said it like she didn't really believe it. Danny picks up on things like that: back-of-the-throat tremors and vibrato inflections; the way his parents say things they don't mean as if they think they can make a lie true by giving it words.

Danny doesn't trust words. His father heaves himself to his feet, throws a handful of branches complete with rusting pine needles on top of the dwindling blaze.

Woosh. The heat peaks, flames curling toward Danny.

Careful, Maury says. Step back.

Danny extends his palms. Feels his skin singe. Words are what people say. *Have fun with your*

5

father. Careful. Step back. Danny prefers silence. Prefers feeling.

Pain on flesh.

—hot—oww! Too close—

Things happen. What do words do? They don't happen.

Just as quickly, the flames recede.

Danny sits down again. The dirt under him. Cold. His arms burning. His face damp. His eyelids heavy. He'll sleep soon. Won't be able to stop himself.

Maury's body jammed deep into a sleeping bag. Sunlight through the roof of the tent. He's in a tent. In a tent in a forest with his son. It's so simple. But there are complications. The wind blowing past places you'll never go. There are factors, possibilities. Things that could have been different. Things that might not have changed. What he did. What he knows he did. Knowledge is elusive, slippery. That's what makes us civilized, Maury thinks. That's what makes us human. He doesn't fight with his wife. There's nothing wrong with his son. What happened might not have happened. That can't ever be taken away.

Where is he now, Maury wonders. My brother.

Danny squirrels out of his bag. I'm *hungry,* he says.

He's hungry. Maury's got his hands behind his head. He's staring up at the belled dome of the tent. It's morning—so what? The boy's hungry.

Breakfast, Danny explains. He licks his little lips like a calf. Daaaad . . . I'm hungry.

Maury blinks. Sits up. He's got a hard-on, has to piss.

So how about a good morning? he says.

Hungry.

So okay. Get some water from the lake in the pot. Wait—put something on before you go out. A sweatshirt or something. It's chilly in the morning. We'll have oatmeal. The kind you like. Those little packages with the chunks of fake maple syrup in them. You know, the fat guy on the rocking chair. You love that shit, right?

Danny grins. Don't say shit, Dad. Slips out of the tent. Mitch Moose pyjama bottoms. No top. Tan back. Green forest. Smooth water.

I said put on a shirt or something. Maury crosses his arms under his head, wishes he had someone to tell him what to do, where to go. When to piss.

They hike through the woods, follow the twisting path up the hill to the ranger station. It takes an hour. Longer with Danny. He stops. Looks at a toad.

C'mon, Maury says, though he's secretly glad of the boy's interest, wants to have clever things to tell his son: the names of the trees and fungi; the puzzle fit of interlocking lives in this particular swath of semi-wilderness; what lives and what doesn't get to live; what can be seen without being seen.

Maury wrote a book once. Now he's lost in the woods. Not really. It's a marked trail. Still. Maury keeps glancing behind him, feels like someone else is

7

coming down the path. There's no one there. Eyes on him. In between the dark boughs of the trees. What kinds of trees? He has no idea. Maury has to resist the urge to make things up, doesn't want the boy to find out one day, think his dad was a liar. One day he'll write another book. In the meantime he's no worse off than anybody else. He has responsibilities, pays experts when needed. If, god forbid, they should be needed. You can be an expert in certain things, Maury figures, it's not impossible, it's not like there can't be experts. There are experts in forests, experts in lakes, experts in propane camp stoves. Maury's an expert himself. Only, he wonders what he really knows. He used to think he could make anyone buy anything. Used to? I can still—

Danny stoops, picks up a grey bone. Shows it to Maury.

Some kind of wing, Maury suggests. Hawk, or falcon, maybe?

It looks like a drumstick—but he doesn't tell the boy that. What's the point in telling him that? Sure, it's a bird bone. Chicken. Somebody's picnic. Danny picks up a rusted pop can. Coke, Maury says. It's quiet in the forest. Danny turns the bone in his fingers. Most of the sounds we can't hear, Maury thinks. Like ordering off the English menu in a Chinese restaurant.

Danny runs ahead, skips in and out of his untied running shoes. Maury doesn't notice. The boy could fall, trip, graze a knee, skin an eyebrow. Maury sometimes wants to argue with his wife. Danny's not as fragile as he looks. They walk. That feeling again. Like he's the girl in the horror movie, watched through binoculars, stalked for some deviously nonsensical reason. Maury knows he's just being paranoid. *Woods! There's just too much in them!* Not much of a slogan. Seriously, though. They're always twitching and creeping. Maury doesn't like to think about what may or not be in the woods. Details annoy him. He prefers to take the long view, to see things expansive and hazy like the sky touching the crest of the path, forest into a layer of melting cloud, the ends of things looking a lot like beginnings.

Well hello there, the Ranger says.

Danny blinks, tugs on the man's khaki sleeve. Mister?

Maury stops where he is, keeps back.

Danny holds the bone up. A serious child with a serious father. The Ranger crouches down.

Maury fans at his fat wet forehead, feels the back of his hand knock a fly.

Well well, the Ranger says, what do we have here? He reaches. Danny steps back.

Danny, Maury says.

It's all right son, the Ranger says, you hold on to it. I'll look from here. The Ranger rolls his eyes, squints in mock inspection. Danny giggles.

Hmm, could be porcupine. Or marmot. Unusual to locate those kinds of remains just lying around. You find it in the path?

Danny and Maury nod.

Well good for you, the Ranger says. There are all kinds of creatures in the forest you can't even see.

Maury moves closer, sees the leathery lines under the Ranger's eyes. He's old, Maury thinks. Older than he looks. They'll cut it all down one day. He'll be dead by then.

Here, the Ranger says, let me show you something. He hooks his finger into his belt, strides into the cabin, returns in seconds. Found this yesterday in the upper west quadrant. The Ranger snaps the pair of jaws in Danny's direction.

Cool, Danny says, showing the gaps where his teeth are growing in. The Ranger crouches. Danny runs a finger over a yellow fang.

What's it from? Maury asks.

Wolf. Not full-grown. But no baby either, as you can see. Found it at last year's summer lair.

Cool, Danny says.

We heard wolves last night, Maury says.

You want to see them? How about you, son, you like to get a look at a real live big bad wolf?

Danny's eyes are wide reflections. He jerks forward, trips on a lace, falls into the Ranger's thick legs.

Danny, Maury says, tie your shoes.

That's all right, the Ranger says, putting a big hand on the boy's shoulder.

Danny wriggles out of his grasp, stoops down, pretends to tie his shoes. It's not something he's good at. He's a bit behind in that aspect, lacks, maybe, the combination of dexterity and motor skills generally expected of someone his age. Becky wanted to get him Velcro. But Maury refused, thought to himself: what's next? a bib to catch his drool? He should call his wife, now, before she goes out, goes wherever she goes.

I'm taking a group tonight, the Ranger is saying. It's rare, but sometimes, like this summer, we know where the wolves are and we have relatively decent access to their temporary camp. Can't guarantee you'll see them. But you'll hear them all right. Can you meet back here at nine, in your car? About ten others will be joining us. We'll be carpooling if that's all right, cut down on noise and emissions when we drive through the centre of the park. It'll be something. The first public wolf howl I've led in eight years. The Ranger's eyes: earnest as moonlight.

Danny's got his laces in loops, is trying to fit them together like pieces in a jigsaw.

Maury looks away, looks anywhere.

Here, the Ranger says. Let me give you a hand, son.

The air around him greying, going fuzzy and granu- lated. But it's more than that. It's a feeling; night com- ing to life.

Soon, Danny thinks.

What the Ranger told him: there are things in the forest you can't see. Danny squints, imagines he *can* see them. Sure, why not? Revelation. Everything revealed. He crouches in a copse of trees and becomes one of those things—evening entity, tiny furry creature

with bleary eyesight and a survival instinct as fero-
cious as it is unlikely. Danny read about survival
instinct in a book. A book about animals. Jungle cats.
Crouching down, Danny imagines himself as a baby
night creature, invisible and unafraid even as a pan-
ther prowls through in search of dinner.

And Maury in the distance: Danny? Where are you?
It's time to go!

Closes his eyes. The darkness on him. Why is he
here? Because the darkness keeps calling him.

Danny? Goddammit! We're gonna be late.

He doesn't stir. He's on the edge of the forest.

—big—thousands and thousands and thousands of
miles big—

He isn't afraid—babies are—

Peeks out through the cracks of his fingers.

Darker every minute.

—big—

Danny you get over here right this second or you
can forget about the wolf hunt howl hike thing—
whatever the fuck it is!

Danny creeping up behind.

You said the f-word, Daddy.

Maury, startled. Whirling around. Hands in fists.

Better let him sit up front, Maury says to the fat man.
The man looks dubiously at the cramped back seat.

Maury shrugs. The boy won't sit in the back.

C'mon Stuey. A woman in a halter top tugs the fat
man's sleeve. Danny stands in the shadows. Maury

knows he's disturbed by Stuey, frightened by volume, by excess, by the ampleness of flesh. He's shy around strangers. But it's more than that. What is it? Maury can't figure out how to say it. The boy won't sit in the back seat.

Will you come on? the woman says again. She's small and buxom, looks young, looks young enough to be Stuey's daughter.

Up ahead, the Ranger fires the engine of his Jeep. Maury hurries into the driver's seat, fits the key in the ignition, pauses. The car shivers to life.

Get in, he says, motioning to Danny. In the pale night wash of headlights, the boy looks like a ghost. The Ranger's Jeep pulls away, followed by the other two cars. Maury's old hatchback in the rear. The engine rumbles, but it works, Maury thinks, fifteen years old and no problem. Becky wants him to get a new car. This one runs, Maury likes to point out. Doesn't this one run? It isn't the money. He can afford a new car. It isn't about the money.

Hey kid, Stuey says, voice muffled and cramped, get in the goddamned car.

Danny blinks, shifts from foot to foot. Maury swallows. That fat fuck, he thinks. Danny, he sighs. Get in this car.

They wind up a dirt road, a private road for park personnel only. Maury imagines they're trespassing, likes the excitement. They probably have permission. They must have permission. Permission to trespass, he says to himself, to Danny. He likes the sound of it.

Well now, breathes Stuey, that sounds like a real nice movie, don't it son? Some kinda thriller. Whatdaya say sonny? *Pee-mishion to Treee-sss-passs.* Danny doesn't even blink. By the by, I'm Stu—Stuey— and this here's Jeanette.

Hi, says Jeanette.

Maury nods, listens to the spin of gravel against rubber, thinks they're from somewhere though he can't say exactly where. They must be from somewhere. Everyone is from somewhere.

Maury, he finally says. And this is Danny, my son. He ruffles the boy's head, strokes his hair, he doesn't have anything to prove to these people, won't ever see them again. *Pee-mishion to*— Danny doesn't move. Breathes. Stares out the window.

Maury catches up with the column of cars, has to slow right down as the road gets rough. After the introductions there doesn't seem to be anything else to say. Jeanette asks Danny how old he is, and the boy stays silent. Maury leaves it alone, concentrates on the way the slow gliding turns of the overgrown road conceal plunges into dense obscuring thicket.

Oh-kay, Jeanette drawls, not sure if she should be insulted.

Stu puts his arm around her. She squirms in his embrace. Maury watches: rustling shadows in the rear-view mirror.

They go up, the trees thin out, then the track dips into a grove of firs. Abruptly, the column stops. The lights of the cars switch off one after the other. For a minute, everybody sits. Then Danny opens his door, slips out.

Hey, Danny, Maury shouts. He struggles with his seat belt.

The Ranger's got the boy.

You better hold his hand, the Ranger says. Don't want him getting lost in the woods.

Maury gropes through the gloom, secures his son's wrist.

Now the dark is truly alive.

His dad's fingers gouging his soft arm.

Danny is alone.

What is this thing over him? He knows it as an urge, an inevitable destiny; his heritage, his inheritance: to be—

un-born.

It's time, the woods whisper. It's time to disappear.

The Ranger: *Don't want him to—*

Danny squirms, pulls at his father's grip. Then Danny stops fidgeting, thinks of the book, jungle cats, the way they sneak to the edge of the forest and wait. Just wait.

It's so dark.

—doesn't scare—

Feet scuffing on the dry leaves covering the narrow dirt path. And other sounds: scampering, sniffling. Night sounds, Danny thinks, disappearing sounds.

The lady doctor asked him once: What do you

want? Danny shrugged. What does he want? Now he knows. He wants to undo himself, start again, step into the ancient immortal shroud of the night and emerge.

Unborn.

Even if there were words to describe such a thing—the feeling of it happening, like the feeling of wind through trees before a storm—Danny wouldn't be able to say them.

He doesn't believe in words.

What is it to get lost? It's to be found.

—don't fall—shoelaces, tied!—walk—good—

Danny keeps his head down and watches his feet step carefully.

Eventually, Maury will let go.

He always does.

Maury thinks about Becky. What would she say about this? A wolf hike! Ha! Now THAT's father–son activity. Now THIS is manly bonding. He should have called his wife from the ranger station, but he didn't feel like answering her questions, putting the boy on, keeping up a cheery demeanour, convincing her everything is fine, everyone is having fun. Danny's lilt: wolves, Mommy, *wolves*. Becky suggested this trip, it was her idea, she thought it would be good for them, close the widening gap, heal the wound, foster a better relationship. Not that he hasn't tried to be a good dad.

They trudge up the steep path. The fat man breathes loud enough for everyone. Stu, Stuey, two names, both sound like food. Shtetl meals, Maury thinks. Potatoes and beans and onions, the greasy poverty his mother talks about to this day. Stu breathes. A helicopter landing would be quieter than that guy, Maury thinks. It was Becky's idea. His mother said: To the woods? What in god's name is in the woods? Now he's pulling the boy up through the black night. Can't believe how dark it is. A crack behind foliage, like a misplaced step. Then stillness.

Maury peers. What if there *is* someone watching him. He's flattering himself. My life isn't that interesting. Maury's stalkers wear ties and pocket protectors, wield hardcover foreign-language editions of his book, follow him into convention centre elevators. There's no one—I'm not— Think calm thoughts. Like what? Calm thoughts. There *is* someone. Someone who could be— *No.* Maury stops shining the flashlight into the dark boughs of the passing trees. Directs the beam forward, illuminates Jeanette's tight buttocks.

They walk, Maury staring.

You okay, Danny?

Danny doesn't speak. He's scowling at the ground in front of him.

I asked you a question, Maury says.

Danny, plodding forward.

You have to be patient. Big deal. You've seen it before. Give him something to do. Help him occupy. That's what the therapist said. Boys need tasks, distractions.

Here, he says, want to hold the flashlight? Without looking up, the boy holds out his free hand, wrist thin like a branch. Maury glances at the forest gloom surrounding them on both sides. He hesitates. He shouldn't have offered, but he offered. Okay, here it comes, he says, as if the boy is blind, can't see for himself the progress the flashlight is making to his sticky kid fingers. Here it comes, Maury says, trying to sound comforting and practical and normal. Why not? What's the big deal? He wants the boy to be happy. He wants the boy to have a fun time.

Danny closes his fingers around the flashlight.

Don't drop it, Maury advises. The Ranger leads the way, his own light cutting through the trees like a saw.

The path levels out. Maury asks: You okay, Danny?

Danny nods.

Maury's tired of talking just to fill the silence between them. He's tired of hearing his own voice. Other boys are always going on about computer games and stupid TV shows and whatever else they have to talk about. You can't shut them up.

We're almost there, he says.

This is something the boy will remember, he reminds himself. This is the kind of thing we'll talk about when he's all grown up, when we're sitting around the kitchen table, late at night, surprise visit, last-minute business right here in town. Thought I'd drop in, it's a little late, hope you're not mad, just got lonely for the old homestead. Hey Dad, remember when—?

18

Maury looks at his son. The boy walks jerkily, like a rusted robot.

The wolves pose no danger to humans, the Ranger says. They feed on deer, primarily. The deer population of the park has declined because of moose occupying their habitat, so the wolf population is down. Just two hundred left in the park, down from five hundred ten years ago.

Maury peers into the night, squints. The Ranger has switched off his light. It's all gloom and shadows. Danny draws circles on the rocks with a weak beam. He's happy to have the flashlight, hasn't dropped it, hasn't complained about the walk, been all in all pretty good. Did the right thing giving him the flashlight, the boy needs a little responsibility.

Why don't the wolves eat the moose? Maury wonders out loud. He can feel the group turn to him, groping for his shadow form with their eyes.

Stuey laughs like something funny just happened on TV.

That's a good question, the Ranger says. A moose is a lot bigger than a deer. Wolf just can't take one down. To the best of my knowledge, a pack of wolves has never succeeded in killing a full-grown moose.

Maury looks uncertainly at the forest behind him. Who knows? Who really knows what can eat what under cover of night?

My brother, Maury thinks. Escaped lunatic. No—

Once our eyes fully adjust, the Ranger continues,

with this moon and clear sky we should be able to make out the pack. They're mostly nocturnal, so they'll be up, playing, fighting, the males might even lead the cubs on a fake hunt, stalking a rock or a bush.

Maury closes his eyes, opens them, thinks he does see something.

A wolf will always answer the howl, the Ranger explains. They discovered that in the sixties, in the golden age of parkland research. Even if it's a human howl, they'll still howl back. Why do they do it? Nobody knows for sure. There are theories about the connective force of language, the necessity of primitive speech as a form of collective action within the pack. Part of breaking down the hierarchy, keeping the pack stable. I think personally there's a simpler explanation. It's so that the lone wolves, the rogues or pups who got lost or left behind, can join up with the pack. But we use the howl to study them, locate the pack, keep an eye on the park population. Wolves have been living in these hills for thousands of years.

Jeanette slaps at her shoulder, curses, mosquitoes landing on her bare skin. Maury peers through squinted eyes. Danny dances the flashlight beam off boulders and down the cliffside.

You'll see better if you shut it off, Maury says.

Danny follows the light, diffusing and disappearing.

It's not the sharp drop Maury thought it was, but a rough, not too precipitous slope down into the valley, into the summer lair. The wolves could easily climb up here if they wanted to, he figures.

Now, the Ranger says, if we can all be absolutely still, I'll see if we can get the wolves to howl.

In the pitched night, the Ranger's hands seem huge, ancient, primal like a ram's-horn shofar.

The Ranger bellows. What lives inside. What can't be seen. Danny keeps his flashlight angled down into the jumbled rocks and stunted diagonal trees. This is something he'll remember, Maury assures himself. You don't see this every day, this isn't marketing bullshit, though you could lead tours, make a fortune, thirty a pop, free for kids under ten, price includes one complimentary alcoholic beverage back at the lodge—one, ha!—who ever has just one? Maury's not even going to think about the gift shop.

The Ranger's howl sounds awkward, weak, blocked by his cupped hands. But it spreads down into the valley, takes on a velocity of its own. Maury's mind stops jabbering. Suddenly he listens, really hears, stands amazed at the consumptive capacity of pure sound. One by one the wolves prick up their ears, paw against the solitude of the temporary earth, consider joining the answering chorus.

Then they do.

Danny leans through the animal evening. Dark. He feels himself pulled forward into recognition. It's like he's drowning, though of course he isn't because he knows you can't drown in the night.

He moves to the edge. The night. Rising. Up to his knees, his chest, his soft pale neck.

21

Wolves down there. Danny squints. Wolves are his friends. He's not afraid. Why should he be afraid?

—can't drown—ha!—

A few more steps.

Into wet. Into darkness.

The group behind him. His father. The Ranger. The fat man whose breath reminds him of . . . something.

He closes his eyes and wills himself forward.

Where?

A few more steps.

The flashlight succumbs to the gloom, slips out of his grip. He strides after it, into the inevitable elegy of the wolf howl, into the darkness he finally recognizes: familiar.

IT RAINED DURING THE BUS RIDE IN, narrow high-way turning to dirt road turning to muddy track through dense wood. Cal had never been to the country, didn't like the way the trees folded into each other. He shifted closer to his brother Maury. Their knees touching. Maury pinched him and moved away.

A young man with thick glasses hunched in the driver's seat of the bus, worked the gas pedal. He was singing. Camp song. Shouting the chorus. The bus lurching forward. Suddenly he lifted his hands off the wheel. Raised them over his head. Clapped a few beats. Kids cheering wildly. The bus veering into the trees.

The camp was called Camp Gesher. Gesher, the kids shouted, Kadima Gesher. Gam by layla gam ba boger Geeeesher. Maury leaned into Cal, said: *Gesher* means bridge in Hebrew. Cal pictured the bus creaking over a wood bridge, logs slipping out under thick rubber tires. Camp Bridge. He looked out the window, tried to see behind him. The road was gone. Leaves shimmering. The smell was sun on vinyl. The smell was chewing gum. Hubba Bubba. Bubblicious. Bazooka. The bus turned sharply. Cal again leaned into his brother.

The man driving the bus is your counsellor, Maury told him. His nickname is the Mad Zionist. The Mad Zionist had a bushy head of hair and a sparse patchwork beard covering up the zits on his chin.

What's a Zionist? Cal asked.

Toby was a fat kid, the son of an orthodox rabbi whose wife died suddenly in a car accident. An act of god, the rabbi always said. But people were uncomfortable in the presence of a holy man with bad luck. Congregants began to grumble about his long, rambling and supposedly incoherent sermons. Not six months after Toby's mother died, Toby's father was replaced. An unemployed holy man. He quickly went broke. God's will, he told anyone who was willing to listen. Jewish Aid offered to send Toby to camp. But only the Zionist camp accepted campers at a reduced rate. Toby's father explained to Toby that Zionism was evil, because only the one lord above who ruled over all could bring about the Messiah and the return of the Jews to the holy land. Nevertheless, he would allow him to go to the camp. But what, Toby asked, if they want me to learn about Zionism? Toby's rabbi father shrugged and turned away. Just eight weeks, he muttered.

How many times that summer did Cal catch himself glancing at Toby? The folds of his tubby face; his weight on him like a winter coat in summer; the fact that he had no mother. Cal couldn't stop himself from staring. What does it look like? Does tragedy show?

If nothing else, Toby had Cal and Cal had Toby. They had each other. Wolfitz was alone. Wolfitz became the bunk loser. Wolfitz was thin and pale and least funny when he tried to be funny. Their bunk had a hole in it and the boys called it the Condemned Cabin. Wolfitz slept next to the hole. Mosquitoes flew through the hole and the boys burned green chemical coils all night to keep the insects at bay. The smoke lodged in their throats. Their voices went harsh and dull, which they liked. The floor was splintering off. You had to be careful jumping from a top bunk, you might end up with a splinter wedged in your heel. Wolfitz had grandparents for fuck's sake. Wolfitz had a mother and father who loved him. They came on visiting day.

There was also a girl. Her name was Moira. She had buck teeth.

Moira was in the Chaverot, slept on the other side of the camp, hidden away in the girls' bunk, nexus of mysterious giggles, wafting spicy scents Cal sometimes caught in the air when he and Toby plodded through the back paths during lazy summer afternoons.

Cal and Toby and Wolfitz were Chaverim. Maury, Cal's older brother, was part of the Bogrim, the counsellors-in-training. Cal smelled the scent of pines, heard birds chattering, saw the sun on rocks dappled with green algae. Things he never saw so clearly again. How to describe them? For certain sensations, certain impetuous moments, there is nothing that approximates, no description that comes close.

When Cal stepped off the bus and breathed in the air, he forgot all about himself, how he was. There was a photo his mother kept in a special album. She took it from his grandmother's dusty apartment after his grandmother died. A snapshot of a huddled group of Yiddish peasants. The colour was grey. There was no colour. My father, his mother once explained to him, your Zadie. Indicating a young man, blond, smiling. Then she pointed her finger to the wall just behind his shoulder. That's where they shot him.

The breeze tickled Cal's nostrils, air made intangible in its inexhaustible openness. They learned the names of the birds, the bugs, the trees. But he didn't care. This thrush or that rush. Words without feeling. Names uttered knowledgeably as if to fill the wide open spaces.

He ran away several times intending to get lost in the forest, die a death of poison mushrooms and rough moss. He imagined dying alone, in a clustered grove of trees, leaning against a dead crooked trunk. He wanted the mosquitoes to feast on his polluted blood. Nobody noticed he was missing.

Midnight dropped them in a clearing like a giant womb. They had Wolfitz spread open over a rotting tree stump. He was silently crying. Cal kept thinking that if Wolfitz would just scream, it would all be over. Not that he wanted it to be over.

A giant mosquito landed gently on the fused sack of Wolfitz's scrotum. Finally, Wolfitz moaned. The boys dropped him. Naked on the rustling forest floor. Kids can be so cruel. Toby caught up to Cal, waddle-running the way only fat boys do. Toby's rabbinical nose in the midnight sun. He looked sad. A scholar in sweatpants.

Did you see his balls? he panted.

Saturday morning. The water-ski boat tugged the Mad Zionist out over the glossy lake. He was singing, his voice overwhelming even the swell of the boat's engine. The song, proud despairing litany, seemed to inch its way across the camp, covering everything with a thick pine-cone sap.

Yerushalayim shel zahav, ve shel choshech . . .

Saturdays were free days.

Cal woke up Toby. Together they slipped out of the dark cabin. Dappled sunshine through the trees. The Mad Zionist's song catching in the corners, spreading like a rash.

They ambled down the wide dirt road into the centre of camp. They kept looking behind them. They weren't doing anything wrong. But free time seemed so . . . free. Why give them this present, these hot dry dusty afternoons empty of violent games of murder-ball, embarrassing lessons in the art of that insufferable two-step dance the hora, droningly inscrutable lectures on the economic philosophies behind kibbutz life? The sun and the air and the sound of the boat as

27

it cut its own wake. It was almost too much for Cal. This freedom. This wide open day.

Behind the flagpole they snuck on to a smaller path through the woods. They passed the tree house, steps dangling in the air supported by fraying rope. At Camp Gesher, everything was made with rope and wood. No nails. The Mad Zionist explained that Uri Gershotits, the camp founder, had been an expert in *tsoviiout*—the pioneer skill of rope tying. Toby's fat fingers working twine: this was the legacy of the camp forefather.

They crossed the bridge, the logs rolling in their rotting rope moorings. Dark water swelling below them. Snake Island. There was nothing expressly forbidden at Camp Gesher. Certain things seemed to be against the rules, but nothing was forbidden. They crossed, heads down, trying to distinguish the loose rotten logs from the equally submerged but still intact timbers that would offer them safe passage. They crossed in half-steps, in a tiptoe shuffle. Cal held his breath, watching Toby's heavy feet, the wood bending, Toby's ample buttocks jiggling.

On the island, between the fissures and iceberg boulder chasms, there were snakes. Garden snakes, light green like spring conifers. Water snakes, rumoured to be poisonous, long and tubular, black and sinuous. They saw one floating in the brackish water lapping at their feet. Jumped back, laughing and pulling at each other. Cal was young. He didn't miss home. He wanted to see a snake. Didn't he see one, just barely submerged? Didn't he see its shrivelled wet face, wizened knowledge and hooded eyes, memories in half-shadows? A family of russets or rock snakes, olive tan bodies, pink kissing tongues.

They took off their shirts, Toby white and distended, Cal slim and weedy. But they were both pale and smooth and hairless; new. They leaned in close and talked about girls. Time in sly inevitabilities. They had heard the other kids talk this way. The wind blew bog weeds against the craggy rocks. They talked about girls. The Chaverot and the Bonot. Budding breasts, tight bodies under baggy sweatshirts, big hair, heavy lipstick.

Their conversation slipped through the wind as if, for once, talk was going to make fantasy possible.

Cal's hand grazed Toby's sweaty thigh.

A cloud drifted over. Trees and the clinging veil of the lake's mist. You could touch things. He tasted hot flesh on his tongue.

Bonot Barbara's tits were real. As real as anything would ever be real.

They used the word *tits*. Cal's shorts tented up. He sat with his legs crossed, Toby next to him. Toby pulled an illicit chocolate bar out of his pocket, hot and slick and delicious. Cal leaned close into Toby's chocolate breath and said: Were you there? Were you there when your mother died?

In the middle of the night, Cal woke up. The air dense with mosquito-repelling smoke. He peered through the gloom. A rustling. Mouse in the junk-food box? The Bonim staging a raid? Something kept him from yelling. A lot at stake: chips—sour cream and onion, salt and vinegar, ketchup, barbecue, ruffled, ridged, regular—red and black licorice, bars of sticky chocolate fluffed with rice and wafer and marshmallow.

The communal junk-food box was the result of the Mad Zionist's proscription against candy ownership. He had told them about it on the first day, rooted through their duffles for contraband sweets. Toby had a convenience store under the false bottom of a suitcase. The Mad Zionist dumped T-shirts, underpants. Knew all along. Toby's face like a melting chocolate bunny. I believe in the communal, the Mad Zionist had told them. Everything goes in the box. Share and share alike. Best friends forever as we build a new nation based on equality, hard work and the resolve that runs through our collective blood. The Mad Zionist kicked a cardboard box to the centre of the bunk. This is called kupa, he explained. Cookies hitting bottom with a thud.

Cal heard the rustling get louder then abruptly stop. He rubbed his eyes. Made out a skinny tall figure—the Mad Zionist—digging through the junk-food box, pulling out a big bag of chips. He watched as the Mad Zionist returned the kupa to a high top shelf inaccessible to his short charges.

In arts and crafts Cal painted a rock black, gave it to Toby without a word.

Toby might have once touched his lips with a squat finger under the pretence of wiping off a glob of smeared marshmallow, bonfire darkness, bunk cookout, weenie roast.

Moira had long black hair. The lumps on her chest were like predestination. After that night in the woods with her, he got a rash.

Cal still wakes up in the middle of the night, itchy and sweaty, and sees himself back in that living dream. Moira is with him. The clasps of her bra, her mosquito bite lumps. The Mad Zionist stealing their snacks.

Institutional settings remind him of certain aspects of camp life. Make him horny. Make him mad.

Camp Director Moishe initiated a new tradition that summer, a game to be played out between the hours of one and six a.m. Night game.

Cal lay in his sleeping bag, not daring to open his eyes. He could hear the shuffling of the Mad Zionist's sneakers as the counsellor ambled around the Condemned Cabin, pulled back sleeping bags here and there to inspect cherubic faces for signs of misdeed, of panty raids and nocturnal emissions sweet with the sour optimism that is growing up. The Mad Zionist's steps getting louder and closer. Cal could smell something decaying, at once rotten and intoxicating. The smell reminded him of his mother.

Happalah! the Mad Zionist suddenly yelled, ripping sleeping bags out from under his startled charges. It's *Happalah!*

They painted their faces black and coated themselves in bug repellent. The Mad Zionist herded them
out and over to the Beit Tarbut, the meeting hall. They
were counted and accounted for, divided into groups
of boys and girls from different bunks. He was put in
with Moira—a Chaverot. He stood next to her.
Looked down. Mosquitoes buzzing ankles. They were
all shaking. The night seemed cold, enormous. The
once friendly counsellors wore outlandish military
outfits, prodding the campers, telling them that their
lives depended on absolute silence. He could see
Wolfitz and Toby, in another group. Wolfitz sniffling
back tears. Terror in weak brown eyes. And his older
brother Maury, dressed as a soldier, sporting a red
beret, standing with other counsellors-in-training,
looking confident and aloof, as if he alone already
knew what would transpire at night out there in the
open spaces between trees and marshes and country
roads. The Mad Zionist patted Wolfitz's head toler-
antly, reminded him in a loud lecturing voice that
tonight they were the pilgrims to Palestine, the dispos-
sessed, the unwanted, the dreamers of future conflict
who stood in brave glory on the precipice of history.
Wolfitz sniffled.

The Mad Zionist joined his group and led them out.
They trudged down the dark road leading away from
the camp. Cal squinted at the stars, watched them
blur. Nobody spoke, fearing that a question—an
inquiry into the nature of these timeless pioneers
whose actions they were somehow to imitate—might

drive the Mad Zionist into an impromptu bout of folk dancing.

You don't know how dark it can get until you're in the woods at night, winding down a rutted track through the trees. Cal doesn't look above, because the sky is low, a tent canopy falling, crushing him. His heart skips a beat, then thumps twice to make up for it. They march and Cal holds the hands of the campers in front and behind.

In front is a little girl named Rachel from the youngest kvutza in the camp, the Amelim. Rachel is luminous, you can see where you are stepping on account of her terrified innocent shine. Her hand disappears in his. Behind, his hand rests in the palm of Chaverot Moira, a shy quiet girl with protruding front teeth and black hair. She smiles as they move along the road, urged on by the Mad Zionist's frantic whisper:

There's only one way into Palestine. Do exactly as I say. I'm a member of the Haganah—the secret underground Zionist army. I was sent to sneak you in. You have to do exactly what I say. When I give my command, you run like hell. Otherwise, the Brits will grab you, take you to Cyprus and torture you.

Rachel squeezes his fingers.

The Mad Zionist whispers, I go *psst* once and we stop in our tracks. I go *psst psst* and we jump off the road and hide in the bushes. You don't move till you hear me give the signal again—*psst psst*.

Rachel cries. Glows. She's afraid to jump in the bushes, doesn't want the Brits to torture her, doesn't want to go to Cyprus, wherever that is.

Be strong, the Mad Zionist says. Do what I say. No crying. You're on your way to Palestine.

They march.

Psst.

They stop.

Okay, the Mad Zionist says. We're ready.

Cal holds Rachel's little hand and Moira's big one. They walk in a line. He doesn't have to think about making his legs move, they step out on their own, awkward angles, stiff limbs. His hand in Moira's, his dark crotch straining under zipper jeans. He thinks: I'm holding her hand.

Psst psst.

They jump into the bushes.

A pickup rattles to a stop. Tires and crushed dust.

Well well. A fake Brit accent.

Cal holds on to Moira. Together they take maybe one breath.

A cute little Yew!

A sacrificial yitlle yamb!

Rachel cries. Her glow lost in the headlights.

Two counsellors jump out of the pickup. Pressed uniforms. Their hair shined and combed to one side. Red berets gleaming. One of them tucks Rachel under his arm. The other one waves his fist at the whistling branches.

We'll be back for the rest of you Yids, he says.

Rachel kicks. Pisses herself.

Oie! Would'ya look at 'er! A little Yid!

Cal feels Moira against him. He lets himself breathe. The smell is birch trees. Insect repellent. Sweat. Perfume.

He's so hard.

Psst psst, the Mad Zionist hisses, clambering up the embankment like a wild animal.

He knows her name is Moira. He doesn't dare say her name. They could be walking circles. He doesn't care. They could be locked in dungeons. In Cyprus. Blackflies dive-bomb. Their buzzing descent sounding her name. *Moira.*

Pickups pass. Patrols. Nothing looks familiar. The path narrows. Spills into a wide avenue, bog bordering both sides of the road, a rank urgent odour lapping pressed dirt. The Mad Zionist has them sprint, warns them not to jump into the swamp. They are better off in Cyprus, he says, than floating dead under lily pads. Which are edible in a pinch, he adds. They run as fast as they can without letting go of each other and then dive into the moist brush just in time to avoid the patrol.

The truck slows.

Yids!

Yews!

Yiddle Yid Yews!

I smell Yews!

Stinks here, doesn't it.

Quite.

They laugh. Drive on. The British are increasingly vulgar, if he knew to know he might think they were drunk. Spot of sherry. Touch of port to warm the bones on a cold northern summer night.

The Mad Zionist says: *Psst.* He has them gather around him in a semicircle. He points to where the road disappears into the night. Campers peer, think they might see something. Maybe the first blush of dawn, though no one can imagine it, it's as if they've lived in the dark all their short lives. The Mad Zionist says: Okay we've got to split up. Everyone listen. Just over that hill is the *machane*—in other words, Palestine. You've got to get to the flagpole, where you'll be given a forged passport and then you're safe. We're coming in from the side. Go west—that's a right turn, this way—you'll cross the path. Head for the back of the cheder ochel. Everyone pick a buddy. Be careful. May we all reach the promised land. May our days be filled with milk and honey and collectivism. Death to the Brits.

Death to the Brits.

Death to Palestine.

Death to Palestine.

Long live the Eretz.

Long live.

Cal holds Moira's hand, closes his eyes, opens them. Stars everywhere. Very bright. They crest the hill and it's like they've fallen off the planet. He kisses her, feels her buck teeth press against his lower lip. Feels the swell of her tits against his heart-pounding chest. They run. Through woods, into woods. The night clearer than any day. The mosquitoes buzzing, chanting: *Moira*.

They fall into a cocoon of weeds and leaves and old pine needles gone soft. She takes his head in her arms, brushes his lips.

She sticks her tongue in. He makes a noise in his throat. He's never done this before. Didn't know people did this.

He'll say to Toby: It's not something I want to talk about.

He'll say: I don't want to talk about it.

He'll keep it inside. One day when he's much much older he'll wake up in a room with no window and think about little Rachel who glowed like a firefly and spent the night in the cheder ochel helping the Brits slap the camper captives with jam.

He kisses with spit and passion. In the distance, kids scream, slip past the drunken Brits like mice between the hairy legs of the camp cook.

Moira pushes, slips to her knees, pulls off her sweater. Her bra the colour of wet stars. Her nipples in fat pebbles. He feels them swelling. She puts her hand down his pants.

A light rain at dawn. Then the morning sun. Steaming over wet logs. The bridge to Snake Island. The teetering tree house. The ripped-open walls of the Condemned Cabin. The *machane* flagpole, camp colours beseeching the heavens.

She touches his dick. Pants trapped at the knees. He fumbles. Gets her bra off. White shoulders. A light rain at dawn.

He whispers: Which way to Palestine? She smiles. Strokes him.

He takes a breath, rubs against Moira. She grunts and over-bites her lip.

Yids are marched down a forest path, their hands in the air, their faces smeared with peanut butter and jelly. Wolfitz sniffles. Rachel licks a red glob off her cheek, tastes strawberry and something she doesn't recognize, some other taste.

Cal grinds against Moira.

Flashlight like a target, beaming where their bodies meet.

Well well! a jubilant Brit proclaims. What do we have here? Ywo fornicating Yews!

A cold hand closing around the back of his neck.

Cal twists frantically, trying to see behind him.

Catches a glimpse:

His brother Maury, counsellor-in-training, wide insane grin obliterating dawn.

SHE THOUGHT SHE WOULD TREAT HERSELF.

That was her thinking, a week ago.

They left with great fanfare. Becky waved and threw confetti—

not really. I didn't—

She stood at the top of the driveway and flapped her hand. It was morning. She was wearing her robe. After their old car rounded the first curve and her men—Danny and Maury—disappeared, she felt a cold chill whisper under the lip of her housecoat. She shivered, bit the fat of her cheek.

She loves her boy.

She pulls into the strip mall, eyes the lineup at the dry cleaners. It's a little—completely—out of the way, but it's the cheapest cleaners in the area. Always crowded. Always a lineup. So what if you have to line up to save a few bucks—that's what Maury says.

She smooths the sides of her skirt. Habit. Who cares what I look like?

In line she takes the claim stubs out of her purse, holds them between her fingers, ready. The little slips remind her of a horse race they went to once, before Danny. They bet at random, Maury paid, flashing his cash, she knew it hurt him, throwing all that money away on nothing, but he was willing at the time. Everyone else left after the big race, but Maury insisted they stay, get their money's worth. So they stayed to watch the last three races. Sun in their faces, glinting off the crushed beer cans littering the inner track. Becky looked around the empty bleachers, held a fist-ful of worthless tickets in her hand.

She gives the claim stub to the Chinese lady.

Mom-and-pop operation, Maury calls it. Sometimes a daughter works weekends. To help get the lines down. The lines are all the way into the parking lot on a Saturday. Or so Maury claims.

A skirt and a blouse. Really she doesn't even know why she brought them in for cleaning. I don't wear them any more. They're not right for work. They're for going out. I don't go out. Anyway, even for out, she thinks, they're inappropriate. Or something else. Bold. *Slutty.*

She found them hanging in the back of the closet and thought: Why not just try them on, see what I look like?—treat myself. Treat yourself.

The old woman comes back with the skirt but not the blouse. She looks down at the ticket, looks back up at Becky. Becky thinks that the old woman might not be all that old.

You bring in Monday?

Monday, Becky agrees. The door opens, the bell dings. Another customer.

Dry-cleaning woman hangs the skirt on a hook above the counter, moves down the aisle again, wending her way through dresses, pantsuits, sports jackets.

Danny's sombre smile as he waved goodbye to her, to everything.

Treat yourself, she thinks.

The door jangles. Gets on her nerves. The store is small, shaped like a coffin.

The dry-cleaning lady returns, shakes her head. No, she says.

Becky feels herself blushing. The woman behind her inhales a short clapped breath. The dry-cleaning lady mutters something in another language.

No? Becky says again. But I brought it with the skirt. She says, louder, I brought it in on the same day as the skirt.

The dry-cleaning lady looks at her.

How can they have one and not the other? Becky feels late for something. Grab the skirt and run, she thinks. Whatever happens next, it won't be about dry cleaning. Close your eyes. Rows of abandoned outfits in the corridor behind the counter. She misses her men. Or else, she thinks, I don't miss them.

Behind her, people jostle for position.

Very sorry, dry-cleaning lady says. She disappears again. The others groan. It's not my fault. I hate the dry cleaner. It's Maury's job. He *likes* the dry cleaner.

How could that be? But it's true. There must have been something she didn't do right, some form she should have filled out, some fine print she should have read or—

The dry-cleaning lady comes back with her husband.

Very sorry, the husband dry cleaner says.

Yes, Becky agrees. She'll have to handle this.

The door opening and closing. That bell, ding, ding-a-ling. Dinging.

Take it or leave it! a man proclaims from the back of the line.

Danny didn't so much wave goodbye as prop his hand up in the air and hang it there.

Never happen before, the husband says.

Very sorry, his wife says.

Becky thinks: Did he have his seat belt done up? Could he be sitting like that and still have his seat belt done up?

Never. In all life. Twenty years, the man says.

So you've lost the blouse? Becky says.

For god's sake, someone mutters.

The dry-cleaning couple stand there, seemingly oblivious to the after-work lineup.

Take it or leave it, Becky thinks. She doesn't care about the blouse. It's the principle of the thing, Maury would say.

Well look, Becky says, we can be reasonable about this.

The laundry couple nod.

I'm a very reasonable woman, Becky says.

Something rustles behind the laundry people. A sweater, maybe, or a tangled vine of unclaimed ties.

I didn't send the blouse to a company, Becky says. Not to some company. I gave that blouse to you. The laundry people nod again. There's a pause. Twenty people wait. They're waiting on the sidewalk. They're waiting in their cars. Why should I care? Becky thinks. She fans her face. The laundry couple watch her.

I didn't give the blouse to the company, Becky says. This seems important. Reasonable.

Maury's not here.

Just give me the skirt, Becky snaps.

She lies on her stomach. She's wearing the skirt. Sleek nylons she just bought. A bra.

She talks on the cordless, describes what she's wearing to Suze.

Your legs are so skinny, coos her friend.

I don't think so. They look bulgy.

So why are you all dressed up? Suze says.

Becky flexes her butt.

Felt like trying something on.

New nylons? Makeup?

A little makeup.

Suze giggles. Heard from Maury?

What about you? Becky asks. Big plans tonight?

No plans, Suze says expectantly.

Well, Becky says, I'm feeling a little . . . sleepy . . .

It's seven-thirty, Suze snaps.

Lately, Becky says, I don't know. Maybe because it's almost fall.

You're depressed. That's a symptom.

They lost my blouse at the cleaners.

Oh my god.

It's not that big a deal.

No no, tell me about it.

There's nothing to tell. It was that dingy little place where Maury goes, Lakeview Cleaners—

They're the cheapest—

Free if they lose half your cleaning.

Suze laughs. What are you going to do?

Becky shrugs.

You should sue.

Talk to you later, Becky says.

She wakes up.

The phone under her.

She digs it out of the covers. The bedroom is dark.

They might have tried to call.

It's either too late or too early. Maury's digital clock glows. It's huge, like a seventies prototype. Becky is ten years younger than Maury. They had Danny when she was thirty and he was forty. The numbers change with agonizing slowness, fill the bedroom with clumsy red shadow.

She puts the cordless to her ear, hears the bleeping of the dial tone announce a message on the line. Someone called while she was asleep.

Becky's sure it'll be Maury. But then Maury's mother comes on the line.

Bubby Stern is crying—for once, Becky thinks. Nothing new there. But Becky is struck by the sobs emitting between disconnected words. This isn't like Bubby at all. The old woman generally has a very clear message to leave, and if she doesn't feel she's got it quite right, she'll call back and do it again, complete with sniffles.

Goddammit, Becky thinks.

The message starts again. She presses the phone hard against her ear, picks out words: Maury. What have I. Your. After all these. Brother! A dream. It's. Maury. Horrible. I saw—I can't—he's—Maury. *Maury.*

Wonderful, Becky thinks. Terrific. A *dream*.

She saves the message. The messages are saved for seven days.

Bubby Stern lives in another city three and a half hours away. She's been known to take the bus, show up unannounced. What if she— He'll be back by then, Becky thinks. He'll be back early. He'll probably be back tomorrow. Becky drops the phone into the crease in the covers where her body was.

She walks into the bathroom. She takes a lipstick out, forces the red tip up.

She smears it on heavy, pouts her lips out, gives the mirror a kiss.

Hotel rooftop. Becky would giggle, but she's not like that. Suze giggles. I don't giggle. The elevator goes up.

She checks herself, stands back, fingers the button of her blouse. Mirrors everywhere these days, Becky thinks. She looks good, slim. She looks good.

The other blouse was the blouse she wanted. It was perfect.

She hates me, of course. I took her son away and what did I ever give back? She wants me to call her, to comfort her? No, I don't think so. She doesn't ask for me. It's always Maury, Maury, Maury. I'm like: I live here too. Hello? Remember me? The mother of your grandchild?

If Bubby was dying in a coma, she'd rouse herself to give Maury the what's-she-doing-here? look.

There's another mirror over the bar. Catches herself, can't escape herself. She's got the wrong blouse on. Becky orders a martini.

Oh well. It's too late. Or it's too early. Lipstick smears the brim of a glass. Another? the bartender asks. Older gentleman with not much in the way of hair.

Bottoms up, she says.

She can't imagine what he's feeding the boy.

The bartender brings her another martini, looks at her outfit. Keeps looking.

She takes her drink, walks carefully up two steps and occupies a table by the window. The lights of the city flicker. Becky looks out and down, imagines that one of the orange blurs is their house on fire. She'd be glad for it, or else she'd fall on her knees and cry. She has on the wrong outfit altogether for a cataclysm.

May I? He's also a bit on the balding side, but younger and tall.

That didn't take long, Becky laughs.

If I'm interrupting—

No, no, sit down. I mean, yes, but, you know, sometimes we need, interruption.

Jack Hodgins, he says. He sits down. She's never been with a tall man, thinks his chest would be smooth, shiny like armour, but mysterious like the black velvet curtain of night draped over the city reminding her how late it is.

—too late, she thinks.

She sticks a hand out, shakes.

Becky Smart, she says.

—anyway why not? I should never have—should've kept my maiden name in the first place. One adjective for another. Is it better to be stern or smart?

So, Jack Hodgins says. It isn't his real name. She won't believe it's his real name.

Let's just—Becky says. She stops, takes a hefty sip.

Yes?

Let's just avoid the obvious stuff.

You mean—

Where you're from. What you do. What your ex-wife would tell me if I sat next to her by accident on a flight to—

My ex-wife?

You all have one.

Becky wants another drink. You have these preconceived notions, going to the bar, meeting a handsome stranger, tall and groomed like an Arabian racehorse, you chit-chat, he pays for everything, and the next thing you know you're riding him into the sunset. Becky wants her boy, her blouse, her husband. She wants the night to be over.

Treat yourself.

I'll get you another. Jack signals the bartender.

I'm sorry, Becky says. I'm not very good at—this kind of thing. Let's start over. So, where are you from? This your first visit? What kind of business did you say you do?

If it doesn't matter, Jack says, it doesn't matter.

You're right, Becky says. You're absolutely . . . right.

She pulls the swizzle out of her martini, sucks on the olive.

Looks away, out the window.

Excuse me, she says. She stands up. Pushes her chair back. I'm just going to—she makes a sound like a hic-cup—freshen up. She moves down the stairs, looks back at him. Be right—

Jack smiles. Nods.

Becky pees, comes back to the row of mirrors. Measures out a shot of mouthwash, knocks it back, spits into a sink. The last time she threw up was the night before the wedding, family dinner, she had just met Cal. His eyes looking through her, at her, looking everywhere. His eyes—even then. After the dinner, as soon as they got back to the apartment, she ran in and locked the bathroom door. Spewed.

———

She catches Jack Hodgins paying the bill, slips her arm in his, says: Are we going?

I was—he says. Let's get out of here.

She raises her eyebrows.

No, he says, I didn't mean—

At the next bar Becky says: I'm more myself on the ground.

He's drinking gold on ice. She takes a sip, says: Tastes like jazz.

You like jazz?

She nods, thinks, Maury hates jazz. Becky looks at Jack Hodgins's square jaw, turns away.

He orders a plate of something, oysters in the half shell, lobster-stuffed ravioli with a wasabi-horseradish dipping sauce. She doesn't touch them.

He's nice. Typical without being typical. Perfect for Suze. Suppose I call her? Tell her everything.

Becky wants to know what she looks like. Jack taps his fingers on the table. It's enough to enjoy yourself, he doesn't expect anything.

She takes the rest of her drink and swigs it. Her lips feel soft, bruised like marinated meat smashed flat.

Care to dance? Jack Hodgins touches her hand.

Later, Becky says: So you staying in that hotel?

A night that doesn't know how to end. A phone keeps ringing. A head on a marble chest.

Do you mind if we don't—? She lies on top, wears all her clothes except the blouse, goes cold.

He sighs, tired, half asleep.

She'd feel better if she threw up.

The next morning.

The house hasn't burned down. But the door is wide open. A dusty duffle bag in the living room. One of the bags Maury and Danny took camping.

Hello, Becky calls. Anybody home?

Her heart beating. He came home early. She wasn't there. But why would he—? Maury would never leave the door open. She keeps her voice cheery. She can explain. Sleepover at Suze's. Girls' night out.

Hello? Where is everybody?

She walks upstairs, her heels digging into the carpet. The boy's room. Empty.

Back downstairs. In the kitchen. Becky is cold in her sheer blouse. The light on the phone, blinking fiercely. Messages. Becky shivers.

In the hall outside the hospital waiting room, Becky sees Maury pacing. She stops halfway, keeps her distance.

Becks, Maury says. He opens his arms. Approaches. Becky knows what comes next. Comforting hug, the dance of shared pain—reconciliation leading to reciprocation.

Becks, I'm—it was . . .

She's worried he might cry.

Where's Danny? she snaps.

He was . . . fine. He took a tumble . . . down a hill.

But he was fine. And then, on the way home, he . . .
fell asleep.

He fell asleep?

I thought he was fine.

You thought he was fine?

Maury cringes. The Ranger said he was fine.

The Ranger?

Everyone thought he was fine.

Everyone?

Becky doesn't know what to do with her hands. She
has them in fists. She wants to hit him. Why shouldn't
she hit him?

Maury advances, slowly closing the distance, the
brightly lit hallway painted in pink and green.

Stay away from me! She's yelling. She doesn't want—

I—Maury burbles.

She doesn't want to see him cry.

A nurse comes out.

Is everything okay here?

I'm Becky Stern. I'd like to know the condition of
my son Daniel.

Mrs. Stern. The nurse takes Becky's arm. Let's just
go sit down.

Becky doesn't move. Tell me now.

If you'll have a seat, I'll go and get the doctor.

Just tell me.

Mrs. Stern . . .

Just tell me!

Becks . . .

She gives Maury a warning look.

Tell me.

Daniel's in a coma, the nurse reluctantly announces.

Becky folds her arms, hugs her body. She's changed into jeans and a sweatshirt. No mirrors in the hospital foyer. She sees herself anyway. The gleam of the hall-way. Light revealing everything.

Becks, Maury says, finally managing to bridge the gap between them. He embraces her limply. I have to—I have to tell you something.

She leans into him. Can't help herself.

It's my . . . brother. He was . . . I think he was—there. There?

Under the fluorescent lights, Becky can see every-thing. The slivers of grey in his hair, the wide pores of his broad nose, the nervous titter of his Adam's apple.

I'm going to find him. I mean, he wasn't there, but he was . . . somehow . . . *there.* I know it sounds—he—I'm going to find him. I have to know. What he did. If he . . .—to Danny.

Becky jerks away from him.

I need my son, she says to the nurse. Where is my son?

WAKE UP, BECKY SAYS. She whispers it, then tries it in her normal voice.

Wake up, Danny.

Wake up.

Danny's breathing is soft, gentle. The methodical rise and fall of the blanket over his chest. He's always been a jittery sleeper, tossing and jerking his arms. When he sleeps, his smallest gesture spreads, his fingers wave, a gentle ripple through his chest, his spine. His leg thudding against the soft mattress, three, four, fives times. She never gets used to it, the perpetual rustle, the sound of her son's head heaving against his pillow.

Now Danny's face is placid. Becky can't think about it, can't imagine how he looked, last month, the month before that.

Is he—

Will he—

Try and get back to normal, the doctor says, go on with life, do the best you can.

A machine helps him breathe. Breathes for him.

He's so still.

The doctor crosses his arms in a fold, sticks his jaw out. Becky stares at a point just above Danny's head. The doctor leaves.

The walls in his room are painted yellow. There are cartoon animals on his walls.

Danny's room is not the way he left it. He hasn't seen his room in a long time.

He knows how it looks. It's not the way he left it.

This isn't his room.

He was camping with his dad. Then—after that?

There's a machine, making noises. Like breathing. And there's another machine, showing jagged moving mountains. Also a jar. Liquid. Dripping.

Danny sits up. The machines respond. The mountain spikes. The breathing gets louder.

Whose room is it? He's in a hospital. He's seen these kinds of machines on TV. Danny moves to swing himself off the tall bed. Machines tugging at him. He's attached to them. He rips and pulls. The machines get louder, then go silent. Mountain to hill to flat valley. He slides off the bed. He's in his Dinobot pyjamas. The Dinobots are robot dinosaurs who roam the blighted earth forever in search of justice. His friend Brock explained to him what it meant, *blighted*.

There is a TV on a dresser. He goes over to it. He doesn't like it. He puts his arms around it. It smells of new. His arms slip, he can't lift it. It's big. He doesn't want it. He isn't allowed to have TV in his room.

—this isn't my—

He's not allowed, but he turns it on anyway. Presses the power button. Why does he turn it on?

Onscreen: A cold wind blows. Animals growl. A man walks out from the woods.

Is it a game? If it's a game, what is he supposed to do?

The image is pixilated, jerky. Animals creep up behind the man. They are wolves. Their eyes are yellow.

Danny doesn't like this game.

The man doesn't see them. The wolves jump. The man falls. The TV screams, canned digitalized agony tinny through internal speaker. It's too loud, Danny thinks. I'll get in trouble.

Danny pulls the plug.

But the image sharpens. Grows. Spreads. Danny retreats. Backs into the hospital bed. Still staring. Around him, the animals on the walls twitch. They are expanding. Morphing. The light green walls shift inward, as if attracted to the magnetic compulsion of the TV screen. Danny looks for the door. The walls are underbrush, leaves swaying. Underneath his bare feet he feels the ground sharp and cold. He smells pine needles. Hears breathing. Not his breathing. He closes his eyes.

Wolves.

Danny runs.

———

Stumbles out of the woods. Onto a road. He follows the road into a town. He's never seen this town before. He goes into the store. Empty.

Hello? Anyone here? He-*lllooooo?*

He takes a can of Dr. Pepper. The can is warm. He opens it. Drinks. It hurts. Someone is watching him. He looks around. No one. Brock calls it a brain freeze. When you drink Dr. Pepper or Crush or Coke too fast. He crawls under the counter. Stands behind the cash register. He imagines he's the owner. His dad says they make Dr. Pepper with prunes. Bubby makes cookies with prune filling. He only pretends to like them, because really he hates prune. Dr. Pepper should be cold. Dr. Pepper doesn't taste like prune. Dad lies because he doesn't want me to drink Dr. Pepper. Dad thinks I'm stupid.

Danny has to pee.

He opens some chips. Cracks them under his teeth. It's so quiet. Someone else should have come in, but nobody else came in.

Everyone else is dead, Danny thinks. It's true. It's true. It's true. Three times true, means he knows it.

Danny eats chips. Tries to swallow. His tongue tastes bad. After I'll be dead. He leans on the counter, suddenly dizzy.

He really has to go. Can't hold it.

Chip bits falling from his mouth.

Danny wakes up in the middle of a road. Hot sun, the asphalt burning his stomach, his thighs. He stands.

Sways, almost collapsing. On either side of him, the forest. Where is the town? Where is the hospital? The road stretches. He takes a step. Feels his hips.

Walks until the forest falls away. Fields now, though nothing grows but grass and weeds. Danny sees barns, their doors swinging in the breeze. Tractors rust in fields. Nobody needs them any more, Danny thinks. His skin bubbles where the burns are. The road slaps his feet.

It gets dark. He sleeps in a field next to the road. The grass irritates his sores. He sleeps anyway, without moving, without dreams.

In the morning, he's hungry. He walks through the grass to a farmhouse. Opens the door. Dust everywhere. Dust and mothballs. Bubby smells. He steps in, sees his shadow stretching in front of him. The sun pours into the hall. He runs through, legs shaking. Finds the kitchen, opens all the cupboards and drawers. There are rows of cans, their wrappers bright and strange. His fingers shake. He drops the can opener. Picks it up. The point is rusty. He can't get it into the top.

He throws the can at the wall. It hits. Leaves a dent. He picks up the can again. Puts it on the counter. Presses the opener, harder this time. Slowly the point goes in. Inside, there are peaches. He grabs with his fingers. Sweet. When he swallows, his whole body goes slippery. He eats, scraping his knuckles against the sharp edges. The thick clear juice runs out of his mouth, down his chin.

He finishes the can.

The road gets narrow and goes up long hills, then comes down fast into a sharp curve. The fields are grey and yellow and a little green. The nights are cold. Tonight is Halloween, Danny thinks.

He goes into any house. Eats whatever he finds. At night the wind is cold and the ground is hard. The empty houses are full of dust. He sleeps outside.

Wakes up with a hard-on. That's what Brock calls it. The most beautiful girl in his class is Debbie Saunders. She doesn't talk to Danny.

But there's nobody here. They're all dead now.

The road gets flat and wide. Highway. Danny counts eight lanes. There are no farms. Just the big road and fences lining the road and over the fences you can sometimes see houses. Danny comes to a rest stop with a McDonald's and a gas station. There's also a gift shop and a donut place. Danny likes chocolate donuts. Bubby loves McDonald's. When Danny visits her she takes him there. She eats a Big Mac really slowly. Chews each bite like a cow.

There aren't any Big Macs or fries or anything. There's no one working. The rest stop smells like the locker room after gym. The gift shop is locked. On its door is a big poster for Fantasy Kingdom. There's a picture of the castle with Willy Wolf waving from the castle tower. Danny goes back outside. Stands in front of machines that sell drinks and candy bars and sandwiches. He puts his hand in the slot of the candy machine. Feels around for a Skor or a Mars bar. Pulls out his arm and the slot snaps shut on his fingers. Danny hits it with his fist. It shakes. He leans against the side, pushes. It rocks. He pushes harder. Rocks it back and forth. Jumps out of the way. It falls over. Candy spills. Eight different kinds.

Danny walks down the giant empty highway. His soles are black, cracked. The wind blows cold and full of grit. The wind blows down the road and through him. At the rest stations, he tips over machines. They crack and spill. There are more posters and signs for Fantasy Kingdom now. On the highway, there are billboards showing the rides and the games and the water park. They show the castle and Willy Wolf. The billboards are bright. They shine in the grey cold air. Fantasy Kingdom, Fantasy Kingdom, Fantasy Kingdom. If you speak something three times, it's probably going to come true. Brock says. Or is it the other way around? Danny closes his eyes. Smells the gritty wind.

At the exit, he sits under a Fantasy Kingdom billboard. He can see the Ferris wheel, Magic Castle, the pirate ride with its swinging boat.

The lights of the Ferris wheel. Spinning. Blurring.

Danny crosses the parking lot. It's the biggest parking lot he has ever seen. It's the biggest parking lot in the world. In the distance, the castle shimmers. All lit up. There are no cars. Just the huge asphalt square and the white lines where the cars would park if there were any cars. By the time Danny reaches the main gates, it's getting dark.

Danny's Dinobot pyjamas are ripped and stained and don't cover anything. The wind blows. Danny shivers.

The ticket booths are empty. Rows and rows of them. It costs a lot of money to go into Fantasy Kingdom.

All the booths are empty. For me it's free. Ha ha.

Past the gates is where you get your map and decide which way to go. There's Magic Castle Pavilion, Adventure Palace, Kids' Fun Centre, Safari Circle and Tiny Village World.

It's dark inside Fantasy Kingdom. Where are the lights he saw, the Ferris wheel, the pirate boat ride? Fantasy Kingdom is gloomy and abandoned, just like everywhere else.

Behind him, the gates lock shut. There's a loud click, then nothing.

It smells like popcorn. Danny can eat a whole bowl himself. He walks past all the food stands, but they're empty and there's no food. He goes into a dark gift shop, plays with wind-up Baby Ducks. They have their own cartoon. It isn't so cool. He used to like it. He was little then—a baby. Brock says they never do anything cool. Danny grabs a duck from a display. Throws it. Goes back outside. It's night now. Everything in shadow.

The castle lights turn on. The whole sky lit up. Pink, orange, red, yellow, blue. Danny rubs his eyes.

Once, he went camping with his dad. He remembers waking up in the tent in the morning. The sun streaming through. Tinted.

He walks toward the castle. The castle is where Willy Wolf lives. Everyone knows that. Willy Wolf is his favourite. Brock says he's stupid. The rides light up, the games beckon. Music plays from the loudspeakers. The Baby Duck song. Everybody knows the Baby Duck song.

Danny stops at a booth where you shoot robbers with a rifle. Picks up the gun. The lights at the booth go on, the robbers pop up, then disappear. When you hit a robber he makes a noise like screaming. They go fast. He can only hit three. If he wanted he could take the biggest prize, he could take the giant-sized stuffed Boo-Boo Bear that's even bigger than he is. He throws the rifle at the prizes. A row of stuffed Baby Ducks falls over. Up ahead is Magic Castle where Willy Wolf lives when he's not out in the forest tricking hunters and playing with his best friend Christopher Parrot. Christopher Parrot isn't allowed to go out into the woods alone. When he gets caught at the end of every episode he always says, Oh, Ma, don't worry, I *wasn't* alone. Then he winks.

Next to the Scary House ride is Space Cavern. Space Cavern is the fastest roller-coaster ride in the world. It's in a huge building that looks like a mountain. Danny goes past all the ropes where the people line up. There is no line. The train pulls up and the door swings open. Danny gets in. The safety bar snaps down. The seat is cold. Fake stars overhead, muted, flickering. The train rattles up the track. Danny squirms in his seat. The bar digs into his stomach. He looks over the side, all he sees is black. Why did he get on the train? He hates Space

61

Cavern. If there was a space battle it would be in space, not inside a fake cavern.

He goes over the top.

At first he thinks he's falling.

He doesn't scream.

He screams.

The train moves sideways into a wall. Danny grips the bar, prepares for impact. The train veers at the last second, runs through the remains of a spaceship. Lights flash and clouds of smoke billow everywhere. Explosion. The train plummets. His head snaps back. Then into a loop, he's upside down.

I want to get off. I want to get off. I want to get off.

When it's over, the safety bar pops up and the seat belt clicks open. He runs out, past the long empty lines of rope.

Down the path into Tiny Village World. The road is narrow here, made of stones. Danny's bare feet slapping. He turns back to the exit, but the path winds around, points him to Magic Castle. Lights switch on in front of him, go dark behind him.

He's on Magic Castle Row, where all the animals live. The Baby Ducks, Boo-Boo Bear, Mrs. Funny Lamb. They stand outside of their houses, and wave. Danny runs. They look just like on TV. Except here they are all wearing dark glasses with wires running down the sides. The wires are attached to tiny microphones perched an inch from their soft furry mouths. They wave and call out to Danny in booming amplified voices. Hello there! Well, *hi!* Hi Danny! Hi Danny! Well, *hi!* Danny!

The cobblestone road veers, twists back. He runs faster, away from Fantasy Kingdom. But he ends up facing Magic Castle. The drawbridge. The drawbridge going over the moat. A wolf would never live in this stupid castle. Willy Wolf isn't even cool. That's what Brock says.

Behind him, Boo-Boo Bear, the five Baby Ducks, Mrs. Funny Lamb. They walk down the street toward Magic Castle, waving and smiling. Hello there! Hi Danny! Hi Danny! Louder and louder as they get closer. He looks behind him. Fabric fingers flapping. DANNY! HELLO THERE! Now their arms switch from waving to hugging. Paws methodically bounce against each other in anticipation of holding him. Strings of coloured paper fall out of the sky. Fireworks go off above Magic Castle, red silver purple green. The Fantasy Kingdom song: *It's a fab-u-lous pl-aa-ce, It's a won-der-ful tyy-me, If you want to, come visit, If you can, stay a wh-yyy-le . . .*

In the turret of Magic Castle, he sees Willy Wolf. Looking down at him. Willy Wolf, wearing dark sunglasses, waving claws, big red grin threatening to consume the tiny microphone poised in front of his cartoon lips.

Brings a paw to his snout. Blows Danny a loud wet kiss.

Becky starts from her reverie. Night now, the hospital room gloom punctuated by the red and green displays of the monitors.

She gets up, leans over her son's prone form.
Did he twitch? Move? Moan?
Something. He did something.
Relief stirs through her.
She takes the boy's limp sweaty hand.

part 2: **history**

ON THE COMPUTER, AT WORK, Cal typed things, then erased them. The cursor moved backwards, ate up the words.

He went crazy slowly.

He went crazy sl

He went craz

He went

He

called her.

Patricia was at home studying. She was a student at the university, taking a doctoral degree in social work.

Hello wookums, he said.

Hi, she said. Her voice was shy. She was probably smiling. He imagined her smiling.

So . . . he said. What are you wearing?

What?

What are you wearing?

Stop it.

Why? Are you naked?

No, Patricia giggled.

Tell me, he said. I need to know.

She sighed, preferring to be exasperated.

If I'm bothering you so much, he said, why are you smiling?

I'm not smiling. She laughed.

They didn't speak.

So? he finally said.

You . . . she said.

Just tell me, he said.

The blue sweater.

The tight blue sweater?

She could hear the pleasure in his voice.

No.

The ugly blue cardigan, then?

What's wrong with it?

The really old one with the buttons?

I've had it since I was twelve.

Twelve, huh?

It's comfortable.

Oh, he said. *Comfortable.*

It's not like I'm going anywhere. You know what I'm doing?

What are you doing?

I'm sitting at my desk reading the boring journal articles assigned by the instructor of Multicultural Approaches to Systemic Individual and Social Change.

What else are you wearing?

Did you know, she said, reading, a child who is not motivated to have success with a second language will engender less success in that course of study than a child with motivations to pursue a second language?

What else are you wearing?

I stole this sweater.

When you were twelve?

I stole this sweater when I was twelve years old.

Twelve. What a precocious, budding, gorgeous little criminal young thing you must have been.

I wasn't—

I wish I had known you then. Back when you were devious. Perverse, even, maybe?

Stop it.

What an evil little girly thing you must have been.

Enough.

In your stolen sweater.

I shouldn't have told you.

Why?

I have to go.

I'm just kidding around.

I'm hanging up.

C'mon.

I have work to do.

All right. Fine. But first, tell me how much you love me, you little thief you.

I love you.

How much?

Cal had never stolen anything. No time like the present, he typed on the screen of his computer. He printed the words on the screen. Erased the words.

I'm just going out. Have to get some copies made, he told the department secretary.

That's my job, she said.

It's a . . . personal thing.

Sounds mysterious. She smiled at him. Her lips painted pink. I won't read it. Don't worry. No one has to know. Chicken Neck will never know. Besides, Bob had me make two hundred copies last week. A flyer for his garage sale. I suppose that's company business?

Ha ha. I suppose. Maybe he's hawking our staplers? Ha ha. Anyway, thanks, but it's fine, need a little air, you know?

Suit yourself, she said. Her phone rang. She smiled at him again. Rolled her eyes.

Davis and Bookburger Marketing, she said.

In the copy shop, there were ten machines for self-service. You got a little box, a counter, and it counted the copies you made. A machine wouldn't work until you put a counter in the slot. After you made your copies, you brought your little counter back to the register, where you paid per copy.

He picked a copier between two other copiers being used by other people.

What do people copy? he wondered.

He had the pages he printed at work. Many of the pages held only a single word. He had done these pages on the computer in his office, printed them out on that printer. Then he had erased the word or words from the screen. The pages were all that was left.

He copied slowly, randomly selecting pages, discarding others, shuffling through the thick stack. He had not been in this copy shop before. But he liked the smell of it, toner and electricity. He liked the industrious look of the patrons. The young man next to him copying as if his life depended on it. It made him feel that he too was engaged in a life-changing enterprise—putting together a slick portfolio, an application for a school or job that he absolutely had to have. He stopped photocopying. Considered a page from his stack of material. He liked the way the words were arranged on the page, the white and the black letters. Capital letters.

He copied for maybe ten or fifteen minutes. Then he gathered his papers together and walked out of the copy shop.

Nobody tried to stop him.

Cal gave her flowers. He brought her chocolates. He gave her a stuffed moose. Remember, he said, when I asked you to marry me—across the lake from the campsite there was a baby and a mother moose?

What's all this? Patricia asked.

I just—love you, Cal said.

All the lights were off. They sat together on the loveseat. His arms wrapped around her. Rain came in sheets, blurring the street lights, soaking the sound of passing traffic.

The window was open halfway. Tiny splatters of wet on the inside windowsill. They did not close the window. They did not move. Her hair. Light brown with flickers of grey. She was a young woman, already going grey. A car passed. Made a wet noise. Part of the rain. They too were part of the rain.

The bad times are over, he explained. The good times are here.

He buried his face in her sweet hair. Her hair, also a kind of perpetual rain.

They did not talk about what had happened before, at his old job. They did not talk about his new job.

Her small body, wrapped in his bigger body.

Now they would be happy. Everything that had happened was already fading.

Her smooth neck. Her ankles. Her wrists. Her tiny wrists. Her big hands, opening, flowering.

The rain was one thing, not a million drops of moisture. He kissed her so gently, it was like he was not kissing her at all.

It's all over, he said, stroking her hair. All the bad times are over. He stroked her cheeks. Trailed his fingers down her nose, down her upper lip.

He pulled away slowly.

Got down on his knees. Took her feet. Kissed her feet. Small fervent kisses. The toes. Nails cracked and crooked. The soles. Callused and blistered. Her feet gorgeously ravaged. His kisses on them.

He slipped off her orange track pants, guiding them down her hips. Stroked her thighs. Pale in the darkest night. His hands on her knees. He kissed below her belly. Her soft parts there. And below that. Her wet parts there. He kissed the rain there. She touched his head. She pulled him up. She pulled him into her.

It was raining.

Cal counted the pages of the report. A report had to be at least fifteen pages. He scrolled down, through the file. When it's printed out, he thought, it's pages. He counted the thin blue lines between hypothetical pages as shown on the computer screen. There were at least two faster ways to find out how many pages his document might be. Instead, he counted, scrolling down slowly. Page nine. Page ten. Page eleven. His report ended at page eleven. You couldn't even really call it eleven pages. You would have to say ten and a quarter pages. Because page eleven was such a slim wedge on the screen, barely any words on page eleven at all.

He scrolled back up to the beginning. Read the first sentence again.

Jim Franklin's Traditional Bourbon stands at a crossroads.

It was a sentence that could be expanded on. It could be made to sound longer. Longer was often confused with more important. The clients, Bookburger often told him, want to get their money's worth. They want a report that seems to be worth something. Bookburger said: We are in the business of finding out what clients want and giving it to them.

Jim Franklin's Traditional Bourbon is like a man standing at the proverbial crossroads.

He paused to read the longer version. Nodded to himself. Continued.

At this moment of historical fluctuation, many brands are finding themselves uncertain of how best to capitalize on past success while still taking advantage of the looming 21st-century zeitgeist. Jim Franklin's Traditional Bourbon is a product standing at the proverbial crossroads, not unlike a well-off man who, sensing opportunity, must proceed cautiously but boldly, both to protect what he already has and to ensure his wealth will continue to grow in an era of change and uncertainty.

He checked the word count, watched as the computer ticked off the nouns, prepositions, verbs.

2,311 words.

He scrolled down to the end of the document. Page eleven was now more half-page than quarter-, more a block than a wedge.

Word count doesn't matter, he told himself. Nobody does word count.

He shortened the margins and added slightly more space between individual characters and their words. Kerning. Leading.

Back to the bottom. Page eleven filled with a solid block of text. Page twelve, three-quarters filled. You could call page twelve almost filled.

Back to the top.

He typed, ignoring the ringing phone.

Things change, but also stay the same. At this precarious moment of flux in history and society, brands provide both comfort and excitement for the anxious consumer-citizen. A well-regarded brand is uniquely positioned to take advantage of the looming synergistic zeitgeist of the 21st century by providing both stimulation and stability. Picture Jim Franklin's Traditional Bourbon as a man standing at the proverbial crossroads. This is a well-off man, a leader in his field, unparalleled, in fact, and yet better known by his peers than by the young upstarts who owe so much of their success to him. This man wishes to make an impression on the younger colleagues, but he cannot afford to alienate his followers by appearing to kowtow to the ungrateful upstarts. All the same, the world is changing and he must change with it; he is a survivor, and a survivor is somehow able to mutate and change without perverting the core that shapes the survivor's enduring legacy.

He scrolled down. Thirteen pages. He highlighted the text. Increased the size of the words. 12.4 point. He scrolled down. Sixteen pages. Fifteen and a bit pages. He looked at his watch. Some time had passed. He could leave. If he didn't mind being one of the first to leave, he would be within his rights as a worker to leave. Better to wait. Better not to be the first person leaving. The first to leave would be Enchin. Enchin was a slightly overweight woman who had slept with Bookburger twice shortly after coming to the company. She could leave. She could turn in twelve-page reports. She could get away with wearing metallic silver blouses just a bit too tight.

He called the boss.

Calling to report on the Jim Franklin's Traditional Bourbon account, sir, he said.

Great. Hey. Great. You read my freaking mind.

Did I, sir?

Will you quit calling me sir? Who calls me sir?

Yes, boss.

Boss. Ha ha. *That* I like.

I'll have something for you tomorrow. I'm in a groove. Just need to cut it down some. As it stands now, too many ideas, too much there. Want to simplify. You said it best yourself once, boss. Always give the client just what they want, that's the way they like it.

Ha ha. I said that? Didn't know I was that smart!

I'm exploring a crossroads approach, sir. Tradition versus modernization, the rugged individualist who is, nevertheless, attracted to certain rituals, the manifest destiny perched on the crossroads of global expansion—

That's fine, son. You're on to something there. Keep me posted, all right? I like what I'm hearing. Yes I do.

Thank you, sir.

He could hear people saying goodbye to each other in the hall. He could leave now, go home to his wife. He could be passionate about products. He owed it to his brother. Maury had gotten him the job. A connection. Don't screw it up this time, Maury said. He blushed and jammed his hands in his pockets. He won't blush any more. He's a grown-up now. He can go home to his young bride. He can call his boss

Boss or Sir or Mr. Bookburger or Chicken Neck. He can make a living.

He saved the file. Fifteen and a smidge pages. Sixteen pages, he said out loud.

He changed out of his work clothes. He hung them up in the closet.

He pulled on a pair of sweatpants and a T-shirt and went into the kitchen. Patricia was stirring sauce.

Pasta, she said, and smiled at him.

He put his arms around her from behind. Kissed her neck.

How come you're so fucking beautiful? he asked.

Stop it, she said. She was smiling.

He ate pasta.

How was your class today?

She shrugged. We talked about Freud, she said.

He chewed and swallowed.

He discovered the subconscious, she said.

A lot of good that did us, Cal said.

You know what was weird? For such a smart man he seemed very self-destructive. I mean, he was very set in his ways. He wanted to do the same things in the same ways at the same times. He couldn't stand any criticism. You could be his best friend for twenty years, but you say one word about his work that he didn't like, he would never talk to you again. You would be practically his brother, but one wrong word and he'd never talk to you again. Which reminds me, your brother called.

He speared a piece of pasta, frowning. The kitchen was maybe a little warm. He felt hot. He could feel his legs sweating.

Did you close the window?

I was cold.

Is it cold?

Your brother wants to know if you're ever going to come up and see him. Says he has a little boy who misses his uncle.

He said that?

That's what he said.

Asshole.

She took a sip from her glass of milk. He watched her do it. Frowned. She drank milk during dinner, like a little girl.

It was a Tuesday night. The cop show was on later. They watched two shows every week. The cop show and the gangster show. Tuesday night and Thursday night. Other nights, they might watch TV, but not necessarily. There was no particular rule one way or the other. They almost always watched TV on Tuesday and Thursday nights. Cop show. Gangster show.

So?

So what?

You should call him, that's all.

She cleared the plates.

I'll do those, he said.

The cops investigated a series of heinous and brutal rape murders. They found the perpetrator, a pale white man with a stutter, and brought him to justice. One cop had a developing relationship with another cop. Another cop had a drinking problem. He drank something that looked suspiciously like Jim Franklin's's Traditional Bourbon. Another cop might have been gay. But they got their man, their evildoer.

When it was over, he quickly stabbed at the power button on the remote.

Cop, cop-out, copy, he said.

She plucked the remote out of his hand and turned the TV back on.

Do you mind? she said. I want to watch the news.

The news? he groaned. He hated the news. Let's go to bed.

Just for a minute, she said.

Fuck, he said.

He had wanted to tell her, as they were brushing their teeth and washing their faces and otherwise getting ready for bed, that the cop with the drinking problem illustrated exactly the kind of complex identification with product that the Jim Franklin's Traditional Bourbon brand had to grapple with. He wanted to tell her that.

The news came on. He got up. He went to the fridge. He opened the refrigerator door. He peered inside, the light from the refrigerator door leaking out. Cold air. He slammed the door shut. He stood there. He could hear the newscast. There was bombing in central Asia. There was bio-terror in the Prairies. There was the potential for economic downturn.

Great, he said. He said it out loud to himself. He didn't want to hear the news.

Then she was there, behind him.

Hey, she said, squeezing his shoulders. Bad day at work?

His brother called him the next day at the office. He was still struggling with the Jim Franklin's Traditional Bourbon report. He felt upset, unbalanced. Yesterday he was smooth, skating across clear ice. Today his mind, full of bumps. His phone, ringing, ringing.

Cal Stern here.

Hey, his brother Maury said.

Hey yourself.

So, what? You don't call me back?

I do so call you back, Cal said.

But not any time after I call you, which would be the definition of calling me back.

We're talking now. Aren't we talking now?

Yeah, okay, his brother agreed. We're talking.

Cal fondled the keys of his keyboard, grazed them with the pads of his fingers. He didn't type.

What's the matter? Maury said. You busy?

Yeah, listen, what do you think of this? The Jim Franklin's Traditional Bourbon man is today's post-colonial warrior, fighting not just against the very dissolution of his character, but also against the fragmentation of core values like trust and humanity and a deal done with a handshake. He seeks a path for global harmony, for the coming together so important in an age when so many things seem to be coming apart. At the same time, he seeks a truth, a rebellion that allows him to be more fully himself than ever before . . . It goes on like that. That's part of the conclusion.

Baby brother, your talents are wasted.

What's that supposed to mean?

Exactly what I said.

No, I think it means something else.

Well, it is a little . . . over the top. Don't you think? I should have gotten you a job writing for the movies.

C'mon.

You don't think so? It's a little much for bourbon. You think they'll know what you're trying to say?

It's a very sophisticated team.

The Jim Franklin's Traditional Bourbon *team?*

Yeah.

Well, you know better than I do.

That's a change, Mr. Famous Author.

Talked to Mom?

Why?

Just asking.

Mom mom mom mom. Cal said it like it was a little song. Mommy momster mummy monster.

Do you have to be an asshole?

What? What did I do?

I need you guys to do me a favour.

You call me an asshole then ask for a favour?

Can you babysit?

For Danny?

No, for my other ten offspring.

Ha!

Well, can you? On Saturday night? Have him sleep over?

I guess.

Don't sound so excited.

No, sure, it's cool. We'll have fun.

I think it'll be good for him.

Why's that?

He's been a terror lately.

Really?

Yeah, like all of a sudden he just doesn't want to listen. His mother is saying *stop that* and he just looks at her and goes ahead and throws a handful of peas on the floor.

He's just five . . .

He's a menace. A four-year-old danger to society.

So punish him.

How?

What do you mean—how?

How am I supposed to punish him? You can't hit them any more. So what are you supposed to do exactly? I tell him he's Earned Himself A Time Out. You should hear me, I sound like a jerk. I pick him up. He's freaking. He's kicking and screaming, No time out, Daddy, no time out. So I put him in his room. I close the door. He opens the door. He sticks his tongue out at me. I put him back in his room. This time I lean against the door so he can't open it. He starts sticking his fingers under the crack. He's laughing. He thinks we're playing a game.

You could lock him in the basement.

Yeah. His mother would love that.

He'll get over it. Just a phase.

How would you know?

How would I know?

Maybe a weekend with his uncle and auntie will show him how good he has it at home.

Ha. Yeah. Maybe. Hey, a weekend? Since when did we start talking about a weekend?

One night. That's what I meant. One night. It won't kill you.

I'll ask Patricia.

Get back to me.

Yeah.

Good luck with the report.

Yeah.

After Cal hung up the phone, he opened a new file. Blank screen. Suddenly his head hurt. Headache, he thought. Heartache, earthquake, crab-cake. He typed: weekend with my brother's baby. He printed, plucked the page out of the printer, folded the paper, put it in a pocket. Deleted the words on the screen.

He sat back in his chair.

His brother was right. The report was shit.

He went for a coffee in the coffee room. Bob was in there, idly stirring a beige concoction. The sound of the spoon clanging against the side of the porcelain mug.

How's it going? Cal said.

Fine. Yourself?

Not bad. Hey, heard you had some kind of garage sale.

Yup.

How'd that work out?

Pretty good, you know. People will buy any old thing, so long as it's, you know, thirty cents. Bob laughed, showing a brown tongue.

Why do you think that is?

Bob shrugged. Finally stopped stirring. I dunno. We're just suckers I guess. He lowered his voice. Hey, he said. Did you hear the news?

What news?

You haven't heard?

Haven't heard what? Cal whispered.

Big downturn this quarter. They're laying off. Maybe as many as twenty of us.

You're kidding. Layoffs? I haven't heard anything.

You didn't hear anything? Bob was shaking his head in amazement.

I swear, Cal said. I haven't heard anything.

It's true. Enchin told me. Heard it straight from Bookburger. Not that she's in danger of getting the axe.

Any word, though, on who—

They're going by seniority.

Really? That's how they're doing it? By seniority?

That's what I heard. Hey, my man, how long have you been here? Not that long, huh?

Cal didn't answer. Sweat on his brow.

Bob laughed, his brown tongue rolling.

The kind of thing Cal could see himself doing very clearly. Ripping out that tongue. Bob with a bloody stump in his mouth. Flapping.

Bob laughing.

What's so funny?

I was just kidding, man. Ha ha. You should have seen your frigging face.

They borrowed a car from a friend of Patricia's. They drove out of the city.

He drove with one hand on the steering wheel. With his other hand he caressed her big palm, circled its rough circumference. She had hands like a construction worker. He wanted to hold them. Squeeze them. Shrink them.

Wakey wakey. Don't fall asleep on me now. Wakey wakey wakey. He poked her with sharp fingers. He did that thing he did where he pretended his fingers were little men walking over her.

Patricia laughed, wiggled away.

Quit it, she said. No, she said, c'mon. It's not funny. She took his hand and put it on the steering wheel. Watch the road, she said. She looked out the window, her forehead tightening.

What are you thinking? he finally said. Why so quiet?

It was a two-lane highway. Sweet afternoon. He liked driving, the motor of it.

Nothing, she said.

Nothing, he said, imitating. He resisted the urge to poke her again.

I'm just thinking about this little kid I saw. I was trying to arrange a support group for him and his mother. There was a group, but they couldn't get in. No room. They really need some help. Nobody seems to care, you know? It's fucked.

He had both hands on the wheel. Gripping. Accelerating.

He didn't say anything.

What? she said. What's wrong?

Nothing.

C'mon, she said. Don't be like that.

Why can't you just forget about it. For once.

Forget about what?

You know. *Work*.

She turned away from him. Fields and sunshine. The brown trickle of a drying river.

How about you stop yelling at me for a change, she said quietly.

Who's yelling at you?

It isn't a joke, you know, she said. Not everything is a joke.

All right, he said. He patted her hand.

They hiked through the park. Birds and a gentle breeze. The part of the park that used to be an orchard, now covered with scrub grass and stunted trees dangling wild fruit. The occasional remains of some old stone building. Then the part of the park in the process of becoming forest, patches of meadow threatened by clusters of immature birches swaying.

Here, he said.

They slipped through a space between trees and bush. A sunny grassy patch, line of firs at their back, grove of birches and brush hiding them from the path.

Smells like my old summer camp, he said.

She spread the blanket. A sheen of perspiration on her elfin face.

The gentle breeze. Something sweet in the air. White trilliums spreading.

Listen, he said.

I know, she said.

She fussed with the blanket. Didn't look at him. He wanted to hold her.

Will we always be together? he said.

We will, she said.

He kissed her. Her smell, fresh, sweaty.

She pulled away. I'm hungry, she said.

So am I. He felt her.

No, she said, slapping at him. For lunch, I mean. She laughed.

He clapped his hands together. The sound disappearing like an echo.

Picnic, she said.

They spread the food on the blanket on the grass in the sun.

There was cheese and bread and dips and a potato salad made fancy with olives that he did following a recipe.

That's really good, she said with her mouth full.

He watched her eat. He was hard. A fullness down there. She scooped dip onto pita bread. Really loaded it up. Then engulfed it, her mouth suddenly big.

As soon as she stopped chewing, he kissed down her neck.

Hey, she said. I'm still eating.

After, then, he said.

After, I have to digest. She popped an olive in her mouth. Sucked at it. Smiled at him.

His hands in fists. Smashing her.

He flew to another city. He was to preside over a Jim Franklin's Traditional Bourbon focus group. The Jim Franklin's Traditional Bourbon in-house sales and marketing team had been impressed with his report. Wanted to talk to him in person, watch him in action. An opportunity, crowed Bookburger. Give them what they want. Make us proud.

He said to her: I'll call. She pecked him on the cheek and left for the library. He watched her go. He waited for the cab to pick him up and take him away.

It seemed much colder in the Western city. Perhaps it was the wider roads, the flatness flowing to the folded river. Driving by the river on his way to the focus group, Cal closed his eyes, leaned into the back seat of the taxi. He could be happy in a city like this one. Big and empty. He could bring her here, and they could be happy here. It would be like starting over, he thought, without having to start over.

The good times are here, he said out loud.

The past is the past, he said.

He closed his eyes. Saw himself. Doing things. Suddenly, he was having trouble breathing. He snapped open his eyes.

The focus group was in a suburban office building surrounded by hotels with names like Best Western and Prairie Palisade. Steak restaurants sat kitty-corner on each block.

Behind the glass, the Jim Franklin's Traditional Bourbon senior marketing team watched expectantly.

You work your magic and forget all about us, they told him.

He imagined a magician. Magic man wearing only a cloak. Waving a long thick wand.

The head of the team was Frank Apollo, VP, Sales and Marketing. Love your chops, Apollo told him. Raises it to a whole new level. Old versus new. Ya. I get it. Everything's changing, sure, like Communism, remember that? Ha ha. Apollo slapped him on the back. Cal felt the sting through the tan of his sports jacket.

He went to the bathroom. Took a deep breath of the urinal air. He looked at himself in the mirror. He felt pale, but his reflection was ruddy and confident. Tan jacket, blue slacks, yellow tie. She had picked the tie out. The tie didn't go. He wore it anyway. It was a birthday present. When was her birthday? It occurred to him that tomorrow was her birthday. Was that possible? Tomorrow *was* her birthday. Take deep breaths, he told himself. He took deep breaths. His neck swelled around the tie. He squinted at the mirror. The bathroom was bright.

I'm not sweating, he said.

Apollo appalling apathy appendectomy access abscess anarchist anxious Antichrist, he said.

He turned the tap off.

Happy birthday, he said.

The room was typical. The dark window where Apollo and the in-house team watched. The boardroom table. The bottles of Jim Franklin's Traditional. The lectern with the pointer. The screen for slides. The video camera in the corner unobtrusively recording the seven participants. The seven nameplates sitting on the boardroom table in front of the seven participants. The seven participants, all employed males aged twenty-two to fifty-two. They were guys' guys, solid average workers with real jobs as foremen, repairmen and salesmen.

When he spoke, he didn't recognize his voice.

Thank you all for being here. I'm your facilitator for this evening, and I'm sure we're all going to have a great time. Right answers, you get a shot of Jim Franklin's Traditional Bourbon. Wrong answers, you have to jog around the boardroom fifty times.

The group of men chuckled. Looked longingly at the bottles of Jim Franklin's clustered in the middle of the table. Seven bottles.

No, seriously, though. We do appreciate you taking the time out of your busy lives to help us out tonight and I want you to keep in mind that the important thing to remember is that there are *no wrong answers*. The only wrong thing you can do tonight is not speak your mind. So let's get started. I'm going to show you a series of pictures put together as a potential basis for future Jim Franklin's Trad campaigns. I want you to look at the pictures and then give me your gut reaction. The first thing that pops into your mind, anything at all, we're talking gut reaction here.

A portly type in his fifties loudly slapped his protruding belly. Plenty of gut reaction here, he bellowed.

Ha ha. The men laughed.

First image, he said, dimming the lights.

An astronaut on the moon, helmet cracked open, swigging from a bottle of Traditional Bourbon.

Nobody spoke. The fan on the projector. The hum of the office-building air being circulated.

C'mon you guys. You're killing me here. I'm dying here. Cal grasped his chest in mock death, made a choking face.

The men chuckled.

I don't like it, a guy in his forties said. He had sideburns and a leather vest.

Why not?

Well, it's, uh, stupid I guess. I mean it's supposed to be funny. But the expression on the guy's face, like he's surprised, it makes it seem too . . . ah, what's the word . . . like stupid, you know?

Obvious?

Yeah, obvious.

But that's the whole point, piped in a lanky blond in a blue flannel shirt. It's not what you expect, right, that's the whole point.

Why isn't it what you expect? Cal asked.

A red-bearded man in shorts: Because, like, we think of the types who drink bourbon and we don't think of astronauts.

Who do we think of?

Oh, I dunno. Tough guys, I guess.

Cowboy types, sideburns said.

Astronauts aren't tough guys?

Red beard: I guess they are. But it's . . . different.

Different how?

Red beard: I mean, yeah, Jim's more for the rebel types, you know? Tough guy rebel types . . . uh, you know? Help me out here guys.

Sideburns: Who ever heard of an astronaut *kicking ass?*

Cal pressed the button. The machine's carriage clicked over one.

New slide. An attractive young woman in a bikini top and a tartan skirt. She sported a green mohawk. She stood in the middle of the busy sidewalk and seemed to be challenging suited passersby as she swigged from a bottle of Jim Franklin's Traditional Bourbon.

Oh baby, moaned a salt-and-pepper business type sporting a golf shirt. I'd drink to her!

Ha ha.

Portly: My gut's giving me a good reaction here.

Ha ha.

Portly: Getting serious now. This is something you notice. Really stands out. I mean she's stacked and everything—

Ha ha.

—but also it takes things in a different direction. You know what I mean?

Flannel shirt: I love the punk hairdo. I mean, you wouldn't expect a girl, like that, to drink bourbon. But then you think, why not? She's a rebel, right. What else is she gonna drink? So it takes you by surprise. But it's also that she's nice, built, hot, green hair or no green hair.

Sideburns: If it was my daughter, I'd lock her up and throw away the key.

Ha ha.

A guy in his thirties, nondescript in khaki pants and a polo tee: My son's got a friend with that kind of hair. She's the nicest of all his friends. Comes over to the house and it's all yes sir, thank you sir.

What about you? Cal turned to the only person in the group who hadn't spoken yet, a kid in his twenties with a tattoo encircling his right wrist.

I'm just here for the forty bucks and the bottle, he said.

Ha ha.

Cal waited for tattoo to say something else.

Well, Cal finally said, frowning and smiling at the same time, you have to earn your cash here with an opinion.

The kid thinned his thin lips.

I hate it, he said softly. I hate all this crap. I know what this is about. You want to be cool. You think everyone will drink it if it's cool. But this isn't cool. This is—uncool.

He had not yet tasted Jim Franklin's Traditional Bourbon. He wasn't much of a drinker. Wine some-times, the occasional beer. He brought a bottle with him back to the hotel. He took off all his clothes. My brother never drinks, he thought.

After the focus group, Apollo and the team took him to one of the steak restaurants. They drank taste-less bottles of beer and picked at the remains of a foot-ball game.

Apollo slapped him on the back.

I like you, he said. You take the product seriously. That's the thing about you. He waved at his team, watching football, drinking beer, gnawing chicken wings. They don't take things seriously. Apollo leaned in. A tan face, smooth and leathery. They don't take the product seriously.

Cal lay back on the plump hotel bed. It was just past midnight. He had the bottle of Jim Franklin's Traditional Bourbon. He had the hotel water glass. He wanted to taste it. He tasted it. Swirled it around his mouth. Swallowed. Swallowed again. His tongue per-spired. Rotten fruit.

He finished the glass. Forced himself.

Poured another.

As he drank it down, he thought of that angry

young man from the focus group, his muscles, his
T-shirt, the tattoo manacle around his wrist. When he
smiled, his white teeth flashed. Smile, Cal said. He felt
himself getting strange, drunk. He wondered if he
could get hard. He got hard. He was naked on the bed,
propped up on the pillows. He poured himself another
glass. Spilled on his hand and his chest and the bed-
spread. He felt hot inside. He looked down at his hand
and realized it was fondling. It was like a different
hand, a different dick. He wanted to call her, but he
couldn't call her. He pulled at himself. He spilled
more, pouring and drinking. He said: You've got to
take the product seriously. Tomorrow and the day
after tomorrow and the day after the day after tomorrow. Apollo appalling accident assent affect asshole.
Tomorrow is another day. Tomorrow is her birthday.
Today is her birthday. He wanted to hold her. He
wanted to whisper in her ear: the bad times are over.
The phone rang. He noticed that the phone was ringing. He was asleep.

He woke up, face in a puddle of puke.

The phone still ringing.

Hello, he managed.

For a moment, he pictured Apollo in a white cowboy hat smiling over him.

Hello? she said.

Patti? he said.

Who else were you expecting? He thought she
sounded cheerful. He thought maybe it wasn't her

birthday. What time was it? The clock on the night table. 8:02 a.m.

How are you? she said.

She waited for him to answer.

He noticed his hand was shaking. He was gripping the phone tightly.

How did it go last night? she asked.

Hello? she said.

Is there something wrong? she said.

Why are you being like this? she said. I called you like ten times last night. I called you at three in the morning.

He wanted to say something. He couldn't say anything.

I was worried.

———

You know what? Fuck this.

———

Fuck, she said.

He could hear her breathing. He pictured her wearing the blue cardigan she stole when she was twelve. He pictured her with Apollo and tattoo boy in a wide Western city. He pictured himself doing—

Whatever, she said. I'm hanging up now.

Dial tone.

Happy birthday, he said.

Back home, back at the office. Cal felt like something had happened, something had changed. He wasn't sure what had happened. He was closer to something—some realization like an action, some unveiling of his essential nature. Everybody has a destiny, he thought, sitting at his desk. He was playing with the two glass balls Patricia had given him. They were supposed to relieve worry. You were supposed to roll them around in your hands, listen to them click. Close your eyes when you do it, Patricia had told him.

Cal closed his eyes.

The balls slipped out of his hand. Rolled around on his desk like spilled mercury.

His phone rang.

Yes? Hello? Cal here.

So you're taking him, right? This weekend, right?

It was his brother.

Yeah. Yeah. I said, didn't I? We're taking him.

Did you tell Patricia?

Didn't I say already? We're taking him. Stop asking about it.

All right, don't get overexcited. Becky will probably want to call Patti.

Why?

Because that's the way women are.

Why?

Maury sighed heavily into the phone. Becky would feel better, he said, if Patricia were there.

Just drop him off, professor man.

Cal hung up the phone. He typed on his computer screen:

My brother does this to me. Does everything to me.

He printed it.

―――――

It was dark in his office. Cal read several memos. He faxed. He dispatched phone calls. He touched his tie. Blue. Dull metallic blue. It was one he picked out himself. He had several reports due. He liked having reports due. Outside, it was raining or snowing. He had several options to choose from. Calls to place, faxes and memos to compose, filing to do, reports to write. Later in the day, after lunch, there was a meeting. The meeting had been rescheduled from a day when he was away conducting focus groups for the Jim Franklin's team. For Apollo. Rather than hold the meeting without him, they rescheduled. He often had good ideas at the meetings, ideas he shared with his colleagues, he did not hold back his ideas simply because they would be applied to accounts that were not his own. Perhaps he should hold back some of his ideas. Perhaps he was too generous in that way. He arranged the things he needed to do in piles. He had an In box and an Out box, but things tended to spill over, mix up. A little disorganization was normal, inevitable, but you wouldn't want it to get out of hand. He looked at his watch. She would be leaving for the university soon. Her Thursday afternoon class. Perhaps she would call him? Or he could call. Talking to your wife on the phone from your office at work, what could be more natural? There was a bad moment. A few weeks back. He missed her birthday. He— That's all over now. All in the past. The recent past. The past past. All is forgiven. Sure. Why not? He was free to call or not call. He held the phone in his hand. He selected a line. The dial tone. He did not dial the numbers. What were the numbers? In twenty minutes she would be off to class. He knew her schedule. She had class. She had meetings, she had supervised sessions with troubled families. He kept track of things. He kept an eye on things. He had an affinity for product. He admitted that to her, to himself. At other jobs, there had been difficulties in that regard. He had believed himself to be not the kind of guy who could have an affinity for product. Here, his office was smaller but well within his expectations. His desk was organized. He had his own printer, did not have to share with his colleagues. Not that he objected to sharing or colleagues. But one values the little privileges. The tiny symbols of status. He would buy her something. What would he buy her?

Outside, it was not raining. Cal walked over to the copy shop. It was a walk of four blocks. He walked slowly, resolutely, clutching a leather folder. He felt his tie bob against his dampening shirt.

In the copy shop, he requested a counter to put into a copy machine. The girl looked at him, then looked at him again. He smiled at her. She hesitated. It was not as busy as last time. Perhaps the copy shop was not doing so well. She gave him a counter, indicated he should use a particular machine directly in front of her station. He went to the machine. Put in his counter. He selected a sheet from his satchel. Opened the copier. Adjusted the sheet. Copied. He wanted to make enlargements. He could feel her staring at him. He looked down at the control pad. He knew there was a way to do enlargements. He could not concentrate on his copying needs with her staring at him. He pretended to focus on the control panel, then quickly turned his head. He was right: the copy shop girl was staring at him. He stuck his tongue out. Wiggled it. Turned back to his copier. Found *Enlarge*. Made several copies. Pondered the results. Put the original back in the satchel and picked out a new sheet to copy. He liked it in the copy shop. He recalled his first visit, how he had felt the atmosphere was serious and aspiring.

He fumbled at the copier controls. He stared down at them, they should be simple, but they were not simple. With the attendant staring at him, he could not copy. She was ruining it.

A tap on his shoulder.

He turned. A nervous fellow, wearing a moustache and a name tag. The manager.

Excuse me, sir, said the manager. Is there a problem here, sir?

Well, he said, frowning. I am having some difficulty creating enlargements. How much bigger can I make this?

He could feel her, hovering.

Sir, um, said the manager, I think it's best if you, uh, finish this copy and, um, leave the premises.

Leave? But I've got quite a few copies to make. Why would I leave? Listen, do you know how to work these things? I'm trying to enlarge, you know, make something bigger than the original. Are you familiar with the process of enlargement?

Sir, um, I'm happy to help you with your reproductive needs, sir, it's just that we have a report of you, um, in the past, not paying for services, and um, harassing the employees.

What do you mean? Reports? From who? He stared past the manager at the girl sitting in her raised station.

Perhaps, sir, some misunderstanding . . .

What kind of misunderstanding? This is ridiculous.

Cal smoothed his tie, soft and slick.

Well, sir, we do have, from the staff, you see, sir, an allegation of nonpayment—but perhaps, as I said, sir, perhaps a misunderstanding regarding our payment policies and procedures, an oversight—

You're calling me a thief. Outrageous. I work for a living just like everybody else! You there? He pointed to the girl at her station. Come down here.

The girl hesitated, then slipped around the counter. She was short, stout, brown skin with some acne. The name tag hanging on to the swell of her breast said *Maria*.

Maria, the manager barked. He reddened saying her name. Go back to your station.

No, Cal said. Maria. Come here. You've clearly got something against me. Let's hear it. I have a right to face my accuser. This is a free country, after all.

Maria! Please take your break right now.

Stay right here, Maria.

She was close enough for him to put his hand on her doughy bicep. Cal wrapped his fingers around, sinking in. She made no move to free herself.

Now then, what are your accusations?

Sir, said the manager, if you would please—there is no—no one is accusing you, it's simply a matter of—a misunderstanding.

Thievery and harassment, doesn't sound like a mis-understanding to me, does it, Maria?

Maria just stood there. He could feel the soft give of her muscle in his grip, the arm bare under the rough fabric of the purple copy shop shirt.

Sir, if you'll just—it really is—

I think you owe me an apology, don't you think you owe me an apology, Maria? I think you and this store owe me an apology. His voice was loud and firm like a grip.

He squeezed her arm. Hard. Harder.

You crazy man, she said, gasping.

He gathered his papers and left.

Later, in bed, he wanted to suck her. He wanted to put it in her.

Patricia turned away. Yawned.

I'm getting up early tomorrow, she said.

Saturday evening. Patricia read from a thick sheaf of case studies. Cal idly flipped through the pages of the newspaper. She took notes. He kept looking up, looking around.

The buzzer rang. He raised his head from the newspaper.

He didn't move.

She called from the bedroom. Are you expecting someone?

No.

Well, will you get it?

The buzzer. Buzzing.

I'm reading, he said. He sighed. He got up. He pressed the button and leaned into the intercom. Yeah?

It's us.

He buzzed them up. Opened the door.

Jesus, Maury said. It took you long enough. The little boy, bright-eyed, eager. Small tongue darting out of wet mouth.

Cal stood there, staring past them, peering down the apartment building hall.

Patricia came out of the bedroom.

Hello, she said. What a nice surprise. She pushed in front of Cal. Come in, she said, don't just stand there in the hall, come inside.

Surprise? Maury's smile flattened. Patti, he didn't tell you?

Patricia's smile, also faltering.

Cal stood behind her, his hands in his pockets.

Tell me what?

He didn't tell you. Maury slapped his forehead. I can't believe he didn't tell you.

They both looked at him.

Cal just stood there, half grinning.

Uncle! the boy suddenly blurted. Can we play WILD games?

You're supposed to be babysitting tonight, Maury said. It's a sleepover.

You're kidding, Patricia said.

He was supposed to tell you. I called, like, a month ago. *And* yesterday. He said—I knew I should have—

Oh dear, she said. I have so much—a paper due, on Monday—I didn't—he didn't—

Look, Maury said, maybe we should just—

Uncle! WILD games! Can we?

No, no. If he said we would, then we will. HE bloody well will.

UNCLE!!

That's enough, Danny, Maury snapped. We're not staying. We have to—Uncle and Auntie Patti can't— because—

The boy's face. He was going to cry.

No, she said. Of course we can. Honey, we're going to have a wonderful time.

The boy: WILD GAMES! WILD GAMES!

Maury considered his watch.

It's a dinner thing, kind of an awards thing, you see—that's why I'm in this monkey suit.

Maury peeled back his trench coat to show off his black bow tie.

Go! she said. Go! We'll be fine, really.

She took the boy's hand.

———

They played wild games.

Cal chased the boy.

The boy giggled. The boy ran under the kitchen table. Cal got down on his knees, reached for the boy. The boy laughed, put tiny hands over his eyes, retreated. Cal wormed under the table, to grab the boy. The boy fled. Around the couch. Past the easy chair. He lumbered after the boy. The boy's white basketball sneakers—perfect mini-replicas of the ultra-expensive real thing—slapped and squealed against wood and tile. Cal stuck his arms out in front of him in order to seem zombielike, undead. Urggh, he groaned. He lurched after the boy. The boy scooted behind the stereo unit. He had not known there was space for a boy behind the stereo unit. He lurched in that direction. His arms danced in front of him. His face twisted. He groaned something about getting the boy. The boy giggled. Urgghhh, Cal cried. The boy was trapped. Trapped between the stereo unit and the couch. Cal reached for the boy. The boy screamed. Gonna get you, Cal groaned and moaned. His arms waving. His fingers dancing. The boy screamed, looked on with expansive brown eyes—my eyes, Cal thought as the boy peeked through sweaty little fingers fanned over a miniature face.

Got ya! Cal proclaimed.

The boy started to cry.

A mournful howling filling the house.

No no, he muttered, putting the boy down, backing away.

He bumped into Patricia. She held a sheaf of papers.

What exactly is going on here? she said.

She walked around him to the boy. Cal could smell her smell. He was suddenly tired. He thought of the long night ahead with the boy.

She took the boy in her arms. Sweetie, she said. Danny. C'mere, honey. The boy buried his wet face in her sweatshirt.

Cal watched this.

It's all right, baby, she said. She stroked the boy's soft head. Your uncle was just kidding. He just got a little carried away. He isn't scary, is he? No, he's just a big baby. Who's afraid of a big baby like your uncle?

The boy looked at him, giggled.

She put the boy on the couch. The boy swung his short legs in the air. Cal sat next to the boy on the couch.

Good boy, she said, hovering over them. Now Auntie's gotta get some work done. Auntie's going to the library. Can you say library?

Libwawy.

That's right. She smiled. Leaned in and touched one of the boy's pudgy cheeks. Uncle isn't going to scare you while I'm gone. No more wild games, okay? She looked at the boy, at the wall behind the boy. Uncle's going to order a pizza for your dinner. You like pizza, don't you? And he's going to read you some stories, brush your teeth, wash your face, put you in your pyjamas and put you to sleep in our big bed, because you're such a big boy.

The boy received this information in silence, his eyes amazed.

Your uncle is going to put you in your pyjamas and if you want to play games you have to play quiet before-bed games, okay?

She was smiling.

No more wild games, the boy said sweetly.

Auntie has to study. Auntie didn't know you were coming to visit. Auntie's going to the library until late. And when Auntie comes back you'll be asleep in the big bed and Auntie's going to sleep in the big bed with you and Uncle's going to sleep on the couch tonight.

Cowch?

That's right, honey. She ruffled the boy's hair. You're so cute, she said. I could eat you up. She crouched in front of the boy. Pretended to bite a cheek. The boy giggled, squirmed. She kissed him, smoothed his hair. He was sitting there too. She didn't look at him. Okay, you have fun now with your uncle. But no more wild games, okay?

Neither of them answered. She was putting her coat on. They watched her, transfixed. She put books and papers in her knapsack. She opened the door. Bye sweetie, she said, blowing the boy a kiss.

The boy kicked mini-sneakers through the dangling air.

The door closed.

He ordered the pizza.

Cheese, he said.

Just cheese? the pizza lady said doubtfully.

Cheewse, the boy said, imitating him.

He got the boy in his pyjamas. Should the boy be put in his pyjamas before or after the pizza? The boy didn't seem to care. The boy didn't seem hungry. He had probably ordered a cheese pizza for nothing. Spent the cash for no reason. Though he himself was hungry. He thought about her going to the library. He thought about what she meant when she said *late*.

The boy's chest was smooth, a reflection. Put your arms up, he said. He covered the ethereal skin with a spaceship pyjama top. He didn't want to think about it. The boy: see-through, miniature, barely even there.

The boy allowed his bottoms to be snaked off. The boy wished to continue wearing his dinosaur underwear.

Do you have to go? he said. Do you want to pee-pee?

The boy shook his head.

Are you sure? he said. Do you want to just go and try?

He was happy that he had thought of the boy possibly going. It was something Patti might think of, like gloves and hats and scarfs.

The boy shook his head emphatically. No.

Okay.

He pulled the spaceship pyjama bottoms over the boy's gently waving legs, up over the dinosaur underwear.

There, he said, setting the boy upright. He closed his eyes. He tried to picture the boy as a man. He could not. The buzzer rang.

Pizza, the boy pointed out.

———

The boy watched his uncle eat pizza. The boy looked down at the two slabs on the wide plate in front of him. The slabs were attached, grooved but not split. The boy's eyes were wide with wonder and mystery at the fan of pizza occupying his plate.

I dought dou diked dizza, Cal said, chewing.

The boy swung his feet.

He swallowed, pointed at the boy's plate. Just take a bite, Cal said.

The boy smiled too, shaking his head. He had rows of tiny white teeth. They seemed to catch the light in the kitchen and glare.

So, he said, do you or don't you like pizza?

The boy shook his head. Yes or no, maybe. Glaring smile.

Just take a bite.

Kicking his feet and shaking his head, the boy hefted the Siamese slice. He used both hands, guided the curved triangle to his wet, round, grinning mouth.

Good, good, Cal said encouragingly.

But the pizza was too big. It slipped out of his tiny fingers, slapping the boy on the chest. The slab split apart as it went down, separate pieces splatting on the linoleum.

Now the boy's plate was empty.

Oops, the boy said.

No shit, Cal said. Cal took a bite of pizza, chewed until the thing in his mouth lost taste and consistency. A kitchen in a rented apartment. Nothing special about it, cabinets, fridge, stove, toaster oven, coffee machine, small white table. He could have been anywhere. He was where he was. What if nothing ever changed? What if things that happened kept happening? Shit, the boy said.

Don't say that.

No shit.

The boy stood on his chair.

What are you doing?

The boy was all smiles.

Juice now, the boy explained, starting to climb onto the table. Cal could hear the white shiny running shoes squeak. The boy stood next to the open pizza box on the small table. He had a red splatter clearly visible on the sky-blue spaceship pyjama top. He had another series of red sauce stains less visible on the lap and leg of his darker blue spaceship pyjama bottoms.

Juice, the boy announced, spreading his arms out like a miniature god.

Get down from there. What are you doing?

Cal had eaten three slices of the pizza. There were two on the floor. Ten slices in a box. Five left, he thought, without counting them. He could eat two more. That would leave three for her. Fuck it, he thought to himself. And fuck her too. He would eat all the pizza. The pizza was soggy, had the consistency of raw flesh.

Thirsty, the boy proclaimed, arms out, dancing in a slowly revolving circle.

Get down from there, he said.

The boy's smile was mesmerizing. Blinding.

Will you get down from there?

Juice?

I don't negotiate, he said.

Shit, the boy said. The boy licked his smiling lips with a pointy pink tongue.

He circled the table, ignoring the boy. Opened the refrigerator. Diet Coke, water in a Brita pitcher with a filter last changed before they moved into the place two and a half years ago, a carton of something called Silk Soymilk vanilla flavour all natural with calcium supplement.

He reached in and pried a can of Diet Coke out of its plastic six-pack holder. He popped the can, offered it to the boy.

Here, he said triumphantly.

Jooose? the boy said suspiciously.

Oh yeah, he said. Super juice. Better than juice.

Suwper juice?

Come down from there.

The boy, dizzy from his orbit, tried to step back onto his chair. His small leg extended, the sneaker waving in air. The boy pitched forward. Cal grabbed the boy, catching him as he fell from the table. Diet Coke sloshed, a brown wave soaking a shoulder swath of spaceship pyjama top.

Fuck, he said.

He sat the boy on the chair. The boy swung his feet cheerfully.

Here, he said, offering the can. You want this?

The boy reached out.

Both hands, he said.

The boy grasped at the shiny can with both hands.

Cal let go of the can.

The boy held the can, raised it to his lips, then threw it on the ground next to the discarded pizza.

Want juice! he said.

His lips fluttered and curled. His face turned red.

Juice!

He was screaming and crying.

Diet Coke gurgled out of the can, a fuzzy brown river.

Hey, Cal said. Stop that!

The boy jumped out of his seat, began trotting around the kitchen.

Juice! Joooooooce!

This is what boys do, Cal told himself. He thought about that sentence. He thought about typing it up, printing it out, copying it fifty times, giving a copy to Bob, to Bookburger, to Apollo, head of the Jim Franklin's Traditional Bourbon sales and marketing team. *This is what boys do.* He wasn't sure, though. Was it? The boy was spoiled, brought up wrong. That much was clear. The noise was incredible. Unbelievable. The noise could not be tolerated. The noise was intolerable. This is not what boys do, he thought to himself. He couldn't hear himself think. He typed the words, his fingers playing an invisible keyboard. He felt better.

Hey, he yelled through the boy's screams.

Joooce! Jews! Juice!

Hey.

He clapped his hands together.

Joooce! Juice! Jews!

I'm talking to you.

Juiceyjuiceyjuiceyjewsyjoooce!

He crouched down in front of the boy. He put his arms around the boy. He wrapped the boy in his arms. The boy, maybe, at first, thought he was being comforted. Hugged. He squeezed the boy. The boy realized he couldn't move. The boy tried to squirm. The boy's arms pinned to his sides. Gasping now.

He kissed the boy. He kissed the boy on the head, on the eye, on the cheek, on the chin, on the lower lip.

Bedtime, he said.

The bad times were over. He had to keep telling himself that. The good times were here to stay.

He stripped the boy. The boy, he reasoned, would sleep naked. The boy could not sleep in his pyjamas, and that was the boy's own deliberate fault. The pyjamas smelled like pizza, were wet with Diet Coke and tears and snot and sweat. He moved the boy and the boy stayed where he had been moved until he was moved again. He was gentle with the boy. Raised his arms up over his head. You have to be firm, he thought. He left the dino underwear on. Took everything else off. It was still early. He could wash the pyjamas in the tub, then dry them with a hair dryer, then put them back on the boy before Patti or his brother or even the boy himself knew what had happened.

He lowered the mostly naked boy into the bed. The boy smelled of wet cheese and mucous and something else, something he recognized but could not quite identify. The boy said nothing, watched everything he did with those eerie brown eyes—like looking in a mirror, Cal thought. He paused before shrouding the boy with the comforter. The boy was thin, white, fragile. His nipples like two fading chicken pox, his body a leftover disease, white and pale and soft, a little boy body. The boy breathed methodically from the centre, as if he was afraid to make too much noise. The boy breathed as if he was thinking about breathing.

Cal frowned down at the boy.

Who's your favourite uncle? he said.

The boy stared straight through him, breathing in that weird old man way.

He's tired, he said. Is he a little tired?

He's cold, he said. Is he a little cold? Does he want the covers? Here come the covers, Uncle's gonna tuck you in real good.

All at once, the boy pissed himself.

You little—

The boy seemed to smile without smiling.

He reached for the boy.

The boy moved with speed, scampering across the bed. Cal stayed in place, clenching and unclenching his fists.

You little, he heard himself say.

He forced his fists into hands. Made himself smile.

Come out, he said, stepping into the hallway on his way to the living room. Come out come out come out.

He turned into the living room.

Uncle's not angry. Uncle's not mad at you.

He stood in the centre of the living room.

Uncle's not mad at you. Come out come out come out.

—*come cum commando cock coo-coo crazy*—

He strode over to the stereo cabinet, kneeled down. The boy squealed, another jet of urine darkening his cotton crotch.

Cal snaked a hand in. Grasped the boy's foot. Skin skidding against hardwood floor. The boy's mouth opened and closed. Cal leaned over him, trying to strip him of his underwear. The boy kicked, small foot slamming into Cal's nose. He could feel the pain and heat rising in his face. He pinned the legs, ripped the underwear off. The boy sprayed piss. How could he have so much piss? Piss splashed Cal's face. This should not be happening. The boy should not be pissing on him. The boy should be having fun. Fun with his uncle.

He held the boy down. He had to wash. He had to wash the boy. He had to wash the floor. He had to wash the pyjamas. He had to wash the sheets. He had to hide the underwear and hope nobody wondered why the boy was no longer wearing underwear.

Fuck, he yelled.

He dragged the boy across the floor. The boy, wet, left a slippery trail. Cal opened the hall closet. Shoved the boy in.

Cal stood there, breathing—panting. Peering into the partial darkness.

ARE YOU SCARED? Dr. Reivers asks Maury.

No. I'm—

What are you scared of?

Maury gets out of the bed. Stares out the window.

What it is, Maury says, it's that— He exhales. It's that everyone's got something for sale. You know that—right? But you just walk on by. It's a given. You don't stop. You just keep walking on by. You just go on with whatever you're doing, no matter what, no matter what's for sale. You go on. And you keep walking. You tell yourself you're saving up, picking your battles, waiting for the right exact situation. Then you'll stop. You'll stop buying. You'll start—I dunno—doing something else. I don't know what. *Making a difference.* Only the thing is, you get used to it. You get used to saying whatever about everything. Whatever whatever whatever. My son has a thing about saying things three times. Thinks it'll make what you're saying come true. Saw it on TV or something. Who knows? Maybe it works. When the time comes to put your foot down, you don't even know it's time. So you just walk on by, looking at where you're going. What you're going to buy next. And you keep saying it: Whatever. Whatever. Whatever.

You finished? she says.

He's looking out the window at the grey city. She ruffles her hand through his thick hair. You have great hair, she says. You know?

He shrugs her off. My wife used to tell me that.

She doesn't any more?

He'd like to hear it himself, how it all came to be, how the cards look laid out face up on the table. Maury needs a personal counsellor, an advice hotline, an official spokesperson. He needs someone to field inquiries and deny rumours. Maury's left home. His skyscraper office is gathering dust. He's on the trail of some bigger prey, big game hunt for sanity and family. What is he doing here? He knows he won't find his brother in the streets of this city shellacked with smog, home of perfunctory mental patient care. Maury's paying a perfunctory visit, following a trail of fucked-up doctors all the way past the point of history, of sense, of good done wrong.

Doctors.

His son in some kind of a—coma.

Reivers knew his brother better than anyone. Maury wants to imagine it might be possible that someone knew his brother, cared about him.

Did she sleep with my brother? Did she fuck Cal? How could she? But then—how could *we?* Why did

I—? It just—happened. Isn't there some kind of rule, patient–doctor type of thing? I'm not a patient. Why did we—

Proxy screw, Maury thinks. The one that got away replaced by the one who comes a-calling. She's the expert. She should know.

Maury pulls his pants on. The doctor makes coffee. They sit in the kitchen of her apartment brandishing chipped steaming mugs.

So do you want to talk about him?

Talk, Maury says. I—

Dr. Reivers smiles, blows ripples across the dark hot water.

What is it you want to know?

Maury breathes in thick air, tastes hops and barley and molasses, feels fermentation bubble tickling his nose. This is a distillery town, huge liquor factories foul the riverbank, smoke crowding the air.

It isn't over with Dr. Reivers.

On the street, Maury steps past bodies, past a woman streaked with dirt holding up both ends of a weighty conversation. This is where all the crazies live, where they ship them, how can the doctor stand it?

There's no one to complain, no one to notice, just bulging brewery workers and aging busty barmaids and state health care professionals doing whatever they do behind closed locked doors.

Anyone can be convinced to buy anything.

He's staked his life on it, repeated it at desert resort

trade shows and guest speaker awards banquets and executive-level client meetings.

Maury lets the door swing closed behind him, checks the window of his motel room. It's all the way shut. But the room still stinks. Percolating pre-liquor. The rank belching odour.

He looks through the window at the bar across the street. He doesn't drink. He stands at the window, watches a flickering neon Jim Trad sign.

Jim Franklin's Traditional is the local distillery's most popular brand. Give me ten minutes, Maury thinks, and I could increase their per pop consumption ratio five percent. Like that, Maury thinks. He stares out the window. He snaps his fingers. He licks his lips. No. Ten percent.

But he's not a senior vice-president head consultant any more. He's had a job his entire life, except when he wrote it, the book, fresh out of college.

He's quit his job. In the middle of the ketchup campaign.

It's more than a sauce!
Taste the difference!
Try it with shrimp! Try it with souvlaki!

Souvlaki, Maury thinks. So what's he supposed to do? Beg his wife to forgive him? Or is it vice versa, the flip side of the coin? He almost killed their son. Came here. Why did he come here? That's easy. It's the last place his brother was seen alive. Last night—with Dr. Reivers. The air between them fouled and soupy. How can she stand it?

He turns the taps, lets the hot water run. The bathroom fills with steam. He peels off his clothes, folds them neatly, puts them on the shelf above the sink. He can smell the sex still on him. It's his first affair. He's had opportunities. Secretaries and interns and junior staffers.

Dr. Reivers has big breasts, white pendulums. He unzipped her slacks, she stepped out of them. Her pubic hair was scant, blonde, not the thick patch Maury was expecting. The details, what makes one thing different from another thing. He's got to start taking notes. He's got to start working it all out, writing it all down. He'll write another book. Take it all back. Take *what* back?

He steps into the shower, has the water going full blast. Maury wills his hard-on away. Becky—hates me. Of course she does. I left, and Danny, on a respirator—how could I—

He's still hard.

He'll go back to see the doctor; he won't find his brother there, eyes closed, supine on the proverbial leather couch, hands folded peacefully over his chest.

If you really want what you want, you'll go farther. You'll lean into the grain rot cloud of a river and you'll disappear. You'll think: this is where he did it. And you'll jump too.

Maury switches the TV off, tries to get some rest. If he's dead, where's the body? He left with his little boy still in hospital, what kind of father would—

Surprising himself, he falls into a deep sleep.
Disappears.

Maury wakes up.

The phone ringing.

Yes. Hello?

Maury. It's the doctor here. Dr. Reivers. I feel awkward about yesterday. I lost my perspective. It was the shock of seeing you. You look so much like your brother. Circumstances got out of hand. I apologize.

Doctor?

Yes?

I need to see you.

I've cancelled my appointments.

I'll come to your place.

I don't think that would be a good idea.

Then where will we meet?

She sighs.

Doctor? Doctor?

At the wharf. Just get in a cab. Ask for the end of Wharf Street. In an hour.

An hour?

Maury? Are you all right?

He hangs up.

She doesn't know where he is now. Why would she know? That's not what Maury is here to find out. The thing he wants to know is . . . did he—to Danny—

Maury can smell himself. He flushes the toilet. Gets in the shower again. He considers himself clean.

121

Consider yourself clean!

Can't stop thinking in slogans. The doctor smelled of soap and tears. He knows he'll never smell anyone like her ever again.

She knew his brother. She tried to help him.

Dr. Reivers looks older. Fragile and heavy at the same time. Like he could crush her into a brick and toss it down the sluggish river. Or it's just the light. Afternoon soup sticking to everything. The breweries, hulking sepia buildings, line the other side of the river. Maury compares the scene to the latest Franklin's Traditional Bourbon campaign. Where are the snow-capped mountains, the wild animals, the sun-licked lakes?

Maury—are you all right?

She touches his arm. Maury shudders, has the feeling she's talking to someone else.

Did you ever touch my brother like that?

She pities him with a smile, her freckled forehead wrinkled in mute laugh lines.

Is that what you think? Don't be ridiculous. He was a sick man. He was sent to me for help.

I just thought— He stares across the river, at the bobbing garbage, bobbing birds. Look, you have to understand I didn't come here to—I don't even care— but I have to know—for my—

Family? She smiles. She knows what he's going to say. She's beat him to it, put it better than he ever could. There's a current stirring in the air, blonde wisps dancing off her ears. She's alive, Maury thinks. She has that much. She's older than him. She'd have to be.

I wanted to help him. I tried my best.

Did you really, Maury?

God, he groans. It stinks here. It's making me sick. How can you stand it?

The doctor smiles.

I'm sorry, Maury mutters. I—

Go back to your wife, she says, her voice even. He's gone. And there's a little boy. Isn't there?

Maury grabs her. What did he tell you about him?

Your brother is gone now.

Dr. Reivers steps back, out of Maury's grasp.

He talked about the boy?

Your son?

Danny. He's—in the hospital.

I'm sorry to hear that.

He fell.

Dr. Reivers twists a wan lock of hair in her fingers. She looks at him like he's part of something, this pathetic place she'll never leave.

I'll tell you something, Maury. He wanted to hear from you.

Maury makes a noise. Doubles over.

What's wrong? Here, sit here. Just sit down.

She pulls him to a bench. The sky is low.

Put your head between your knees and breathe, the doctor says. Don't close your eyes. Quit trying to talk. You'll just make yourself dizzy. Keep your mouth shut and your eyes open. She laughs a short bark. For once, she says. There. That's better. Just relax, take it easy.

She touches the back of his white damp neck.

Who's gone? Maury pants. What do you mean he's gone?

I'm sorry, she says. Her hand on his neck.

He's dead? He's not dead. Maury heaves at the air, almost falls forward. She grabs him.

It's just upsetting you. Try to calm yourself. She squeezes his neck.

Maury gasps. Take me home.

I'm sorry, the doctor says. That's not a good idea.

She stands up, shifts away. She's tall, strong. She's the sort of woman who starts a hostel for victims of abuse or preaches Jesus to lost souls.

He lurches up. Sways. Can't seem to hold on.

I need to know.

She pushes into him. Her warm buried bones. Go back to your wife. Your son.

A bird pulls a plastic beer cup out of the slow river flower, flaps, sqwacks away.

I've read your book, she says.

Maury totters along the boardwalk, breeze pushing him. It's a place no one visits on purpose. You have to end up here. Maury moves past rundown homes. He feels hollow. He passes an old billboard. It's fading down to nothing. Weather-beaten man on a mountain fooled into monotone. Jim Franklin's Traditional, Maury makes out, peering at the sign above him. He shudders. Keeps walking.

The boardwalk narrows to a strip of sidewalk. Rusted railing angled over the eroding bank separates Maury from the murky water. He looks and almost doesn't see his reflection. The dizziness is just a passing thing, he's Maury Stern and there's nothing wrong with him. Maybe a little funny in the heart. Runs in the family.

Why did she do it? She took off her top and pulled him into her.

After, the good doctor said: Go back to your wife. Your brother is gone.

Clapboard houses push against each other squat on the edge of the path. Windows are shuttered against the charcoal panorama. Fifty years ago it was equity, Maury thinks, it was a good buy for the value. Beautiful home on the river. Now they'd have to pay *you* to live here.

He thinks of his mother, still living in their childhood home. She watches TV all day. Says she doesn't even notice the commercials.

Gone? Gone where? He isn't gone.

Maury unzips his jacket. Up ahead the path plunges to the river where it narrows to a curve, picks up speed, heads east to the ocean. Maury stops, suddenly recognizes the place. His brother wrote him a letter once. Just once. Talked about a room in a house. Point overlooking the river.

A yellow house.

Maury didn't answer the letter. He burned it.

His brother's tiny tight handwriting.

You see. I am getting better!

―――

125

Old lady opens the door and stares into him.

No, she says. She's already shaking her head. Blinking desperately.

Please, Maury says. I was—I'm—his brother.

The woman draws back, raises a heavy arm, crosses herself.

Maury pushes in.

God help us, she whispers. You look just like him.

In an attic room of angles, sharp slope corners, triangle windows giving way to the pulsing river. Look down and it's all you can see. For a moment Maury feels dizzy again. He grabs on, thinks: There's nothing wrong with me. The smell is hot wood, insulation in cotton-candy tufts.

Pale drawn figure in the doorway: I just left it. Kept it as it is. After him, I didn't take in any more of . . . of . . . them.

Maury nods. He should ask her if she knows—no—she wouldn't know. How would she know? She was supposed to watch over him. She took him in. This was his—what do they call it?—halfway house.

The last place he lived before he disappeared.

A cot in the corner, smeared sheets in a scatter fold.

They used to share a room. Maury always made his own bed. Then his brother's bed.

That was a long time ago.

Halfway, Maury thinks.

He just—changed, the old lady says. Just like that. I said: Where are you going? You aren't allowed to— and he grabbed me—he grabbed me—my—

Two-by-fours jut into head space. Small rusted sink. In the winter the wind would sweep right through, you can feel it already, smell the pea-boil river.

Maury can't breathe.

Dusty blue sheet in his hand.

Don't, the old lady says. I don't want you to—

Maury shakes it out, smooths it back, tucks it into the corners.

You should leave now. I want you to leave now.

No, you don't understand. I've come a long away. I need—another minute. Just another minute.

Maury walks to the small desk, words cut into the hard wood with a penknife: *Jerk*. He traces the letter J with an index finger. A sliver of sun cuts through. Maury shudders. The woman holds her arms in a tight fold. Maury opens the desk drawer, looks in at his own yellowed face. The back of his book, paper-back edition. *Get With the Program: The Power of Slogans*. Maury opens it up. His own inscription: *To my little brother. Everything you never wanted to know.*

I think it's better if you leave, she says loudly.

He's still getting royalties. They published an updated version.

You can leave now. She's yelling, practically.

Maury pulls the book to his chest. He wishes he knew a prayer, a hymn, a psalm for lost lives. Go back, the doctor said. How can he?

He slides the drawer shut. Turns to face the old woman.

I'm sorry, he says.

You look so much like him, she says.

There was a time when Maury could snap his fingers and get what he wanted, pixels of possibility floating on a screen, all he had to do was close his eyes and talk and the art boys made it happen, presto, the picture he saw in his head, the one he wanted to see.

So what changed?

Melting plastic chip bag spewing plumes of stinking smoke. A boy's smile, never quite right, bright shadows, fumes drifting past pine tree boughs and a lapping lake, nothing changed, nothing wrong with anything, just Maury trying that trick he used to do, opening and closing his eyes, and waiting for the fragments to appear as whole and real.

If he was at home right now, he'd be arranging the storyboards for the ketchup campaign. He's quit. So what? Does the world stop turning? Does ketchup lose market share to mayonnaise and mustard?

Maury sits on the bed of his motel room staring at the blinking Jim Traditional sign in the window of the bar across the street. His bags are packed. He's ready to go. Home to his boy, his wife, his mother. I'm sorry, he'll say, and he'll mean it and it will just have to be good enough.

Jim Traditional. In flashes.

I don't drink.

His bags are packed.

I'm sorry, Ma, I couldn't find him. They don't know where he is.

Maury's got his brother's copy of the book. Cheap paperback propping up how many basement collections? Maury's missive wedged between *What Color is Your Parachute?* and *The Joy of Sex.*

He flips through the pages. A postcard falls in his lap. Faded image of a group of kids sitting around Willy Wolf. Willy Wolf is clowning for them. In the background, Magic Castle all lit up, the sky the colour of rainbows, cotton candy, confetti.

Maury grips the postcard hard between his finger and thumb. He turns it over. The other side is blank, just the cardboard yellowed with age, and the caption: *Fantasy Kingdom.*

He stands in the shower rubbing the wet crumbling bar of soap deep into the crevices. The water so hot it hurts.

Across the street from the motel, Maury orders a Traditional. Then another, and another. He buys rounds for the regulars. They ignore him, simply nodding. He buys a drink for the woman who comes to sit next to him. Darla has a tattoo of a rose on her white skin shoulder and frosted blonde fringes that curl up over her wide empty forehead.

Maury tells her he's in town on business.

What kind of work do you do? Darla asks.

Nothing important, he says, and laughs.

Darla laughs too.

What about you? Maury asks, gulping another mouthful.

129

That's cute, Darla says. She puts her hand on his thigh. She looks around the bar. It's late on a Tuesday night. A couple do the fat hip shuffle. A man sits in the back, nursing a long-neck and watching the sports highlights.

You're really not from around here, are you? Darla says.

Maury laughs again. Her hand on his leg through the slick fabric of his trousers.

I mean, she says, we could go back to my place, if you're lonely, you know what I mean? She laughs, hot sweet air moist against his stubble cheeks.

Fantasy Kingdom, Maury thinks, draining his drink.

While he fucks her, he imagines the doctor. He fucks hard, sweating and panting. The doctor's big body over his, suddenly light, suddenly lost.

Maury's never paid for it before. He's drunk. Is he supposed to care about the woman under him? Maury alternates between grunting savage thrusts and long soft strokes. Darla makes a sound through her nostrils, keeps her face pointed at the wall. Maury tastes his own breath, tepid, warm, sweet, Jim Franklin's Traditional.

Dr. Reivers stands looking out her window, across the oily startle of black water moving.

You can't stay, Darla says, pulling on a terry cloth robe.

Maury puts eighty dollars on the nightstand.

———

He drifts down to the wharf, passes out on a by now familiar bench, dreams of the ceaseless river, the black soot smokestack dispersing the churning mushroom clouds of effluvia that envelop the town. At night the odour down by the river is at its thickest, its most potent. Maury wants to leave the way his brother did. At night, under cover. The stink of the distillery will slap him conscious. He'll stand up in a stumble. In the dark, he won't notice the doctor perched in her bay window. Flawed sculpture, weeping statue. He leaves the postcard in her mailbox.

Cal wanted the weather to be severe. He wanted to feel the wind press into his face.

How cold do you think it is? he asked Maury. They were just boys then. The road ahead bleached by frost.

Dunno, Maury said. Not that cold.

I'm sooo cold. It's minus fifty out here.

Minus fifty out here, Maury mimicked.

They walked a few more blocks. Cal thought of the programs on TV at this time, the after-school special, the cartoons. Plastic figures, mouths pantomiming.

Where are we going? Cal whined.

Maury smacked him on the head. Cal staggered back, tripped over his snow boots. Fell against the hard emerald crystals of someone's front lawn. He blinked fiercely, the blue sky, the cold snap of the air rushing against his hot cheeks.

Well, Maury yelled, do you have to talk like that? What kind of shit is that? You're thirteen now, remember?

Maury walked down the road. Stopped. Turned around. Came back.

C'mon, he said, pulling Cal up.

What'll we do when we find her? Cal asked.

Maury slapped his mitts together. It is kinda cold, he said.

The two boys trudged toward the smudge of the city. It started to snow. Cal didn't know where he was. The snow coiled around their faces, whipped their exposed necks. They walked closer to each other. The shoulders of their parkas brushed, made a tickling noise. The snow held on to the street, formed a slick wet skin. They panted their breath into the air, hard clouds, solid shadows. Cal's teeth chattered together. He seized his jaw, hissed air out between clenched teeth.

Outside a corner store, staring longingly into a steamed-up window. Cal took a shuffling snow-boot step forward. Maury hooked him back, padded arm scarfing his neck.

We haven't got any money.

We could ask. Just ask.

Ask what?

The silence of the snowbound city all around them.

Ask what? Maury said again.

We could go in and pretend we were buying something and ask if we could stay and warm up, he blurted.

I know where we are, Maury said the way older brothers always say things to their young ignorant siblings. It isn't that far now. Are you going to quit being a baby?

They shuffled down a narrow side street. Cal looked back but couldn't tell where they were, where one block ended and another began. The snow drove off angled roofs. Ice chips hit his lips. Cal thought of frosty cones, of certain brightly coloured flavours. He licked his lips for the taste of it, his dry tongue catching in the cracks. He followed his brother. If she wants us, he thought, why doesn't she come get us?

He closed his eyes. Can't see anyway, he thought, putting one foot in front of the other regardless.

Suddenly Cal was tripping over something soft. His limbs scrabbled, useless parka swishes. He opened his eyes, the lenses of his glasses sticking in snow. He inhaled powder through his nose, coughed it down his throat. He tried to get up. His limbs slid, like he was treading water. Underneath him the soft thing rustled, groaned. Hugged. Caressed.

The afternoon suddenly hot. He screamed. His screams eaten by the sidewalk snow. He pulled his face out, gasping. He smelled piss and sweet cloying breath. He thought, suddenly, of his mother kissing him good night, slopping her lips over his face. He always pretended to be asleep. It was late, wasn't it late?

Under him, a bum. A *meshugana,* his mother would say, frowning in disgust as she pulled him to the safety of the other side of the street. Cal squirmed. The man held him tight, leaned in. Cal felt a warmth in the hollow fold of his ear. Then wet. A tongue. He stopped struggling. He was paralyzed by the probing strangeness.

Then his body pulled from the hot stink. Yanked by one snowsuit arm.

Get up, his brother yelled. Get up!

A skeletal creature protruding out of a sleeping bag. It looked away from them, mouth grinning.

C'mon, his brother said, screaming at him. They ran. Cal felt the wind in his wet ear, blinked furiously at the way the buildings tucked into each other; the fluctuating absence of distance.

In the after-school-special version, the brothers don't fight. They stay together, comfort each other, hold each other in the wordless night, huddle under the cold stars listening to the distant howl of wolves. In the after-school special, the boys persevere, they never give up, they make their way out of the forest onto the deserted highway and are picked up by a benevolent policeman who has been spending his off-duty time looking for them in order to adopt them into his own happy family.

Maury and his little brother already had a family.

Cal couldn't stop shivering. His teeth bounced against each other, sending tiny vibrations down his throat. Maury walked half a block ahead, didn't look back.

Cal hurried to catch up.

He couldn't stop shivering. Didn't care. Wanted the wind lashing his face, wanted freezing air scouring his flesh. Snot out of his nose in elaborate crystalline layers. His lips salty and cracked.

Cal looked up to see his brother, but it had gone suddenly dark and the snow was all over everything making shadows and pockets and buried moments. He couldn't tell where the sidewalk met the road. He couldn't feel the point where his skin met the air. He clawed at his mittens, the inner lining clinging to his sweaty hands. He shook them off, let them fall. Ran his hands against his cheeks, rubbed his eyes with his fists. He cried through his hands, hot tears seeping.

This is it, his brother said, grabbing hold of him. Hey, Maury said. Stop it now. You're almost fourteen. Stop that right now.

Cal sniffled, opened his eyes, looked through his hands.

They stood under a street lamp flickering indecisive, the gloom between night and day.

This is it, his brother said. Six tall steps up. A crumbling foyer, a dead plant, the taste of salt and melting snow coursing over a swollen tongue.

Cal stopped crying when they got into the lobby. A dead plant. A full ashtray. The hum of normal moments. His glasses fogged up, so he took them off and held the plastic cold against the inside of his moist palms. He couldn't see anyway.

She wanted us to come? he asked.

Maury didn't answer, just kept punching the up button for the elevator.

Cal blinked through the dim haze, felt his breath caught in his stuffed nose. The elevator opened.

SITTING AT HER DESK, Patricia traces blue veins in her pale arm with a sharp-tipped pen. The phone rings, but she doesn't answer. The phone always rings. She looks down at her arm, at the intersection of angles. She's glad she's wearing long sleeves. She rolls them off her elbows, does up the buttons at her wrists. Her smooth small wrists. Her wrists end in big hands with jutting fingers and frayed nails. She's otherwise small, perfect; she would never consider it, hurting herself. She's seen it and knows it never turns out the way you think it will. You can only cry for help if someone's listening. Underneath her perfect translucent skin her heart beats pumping hot blood. She won't do anything to hurt herself. Why help the bastards out?

Patricia deals with the bastards. The bastards with their triplicate request forms and procedural processing protocols and their by-written-decision-only arbitrary commandments. It's part of the job. If she left, throwing herself off a bridge, slicing wedges into those narrow white wrists, taking a position with regular hours and regular duties and nothing to think about but next month's holiday and the boss's new hairdo, then they would win, and it would give them too much satisfaction to win. The bastards.

Patricia picks up the file on top of the files on her desk. Files cover her desk. Fall leaves in a forest, always rustling underfoot. She's given up trying to keep her files in some kind of order. It would be impossible, a full-time job itself, the paperwork. Her solution is to keep order in her head. She scribbles the details in cryptic shorthand. A series of spiral notebooks she keeps in her deep desk drawer. The notebooks are methodically dated, arranged in an order she never deviates from. She can always find the name of the mother, or the precise day and hour a child revealed a dark secret, a spreading bruise, a broken smile. Patricia taps her forehead with her pen. She stares at the groove where the wall meets the ceiling. A spider once built a web and trapped a beetle in that corner. Years later, the carcass still dangles there, has been hanging in place since just after Patricia came on the job. That desiccated shell suspended in a grey clot of web.

Today, she's meeting Jimmy Corrigan and his mother. Jimmy and his mother are both fat and slow. In her department the fat always seem thin, desperate, see-through, invisible. They drag their huge ballooning carcasses into Patricia's office. They arrive unannounced. The receptionist at the desk out front doesn't see them. The security guard reading his magazine doesn't see them. Office gossip Janice, hunched over her desk scouring the Internet for bargain flights to hot destinations, doesn't see them. Patricia sees them. She's the last to see them. Then they disappear, like a balloon expanded too far. Pop.

Patricia taps her pen against the side of her cheek, sifting through the heap. The Corrigan file, a recent addition, is somewhere near the top. At what point do the files stop mattering? The words are the same, but up close Patricia knows every case is particular, unique. She knows you can't count on anything, and what happened last week or last month or last year doesn't help you get through today or tomorrow. You've run the race once, and you have to keep doing it again and again and again. The route is never the same, and the finish line is always shifting. Are you trying to finish? Are you aiming to place? Tenth, fourth, first—what's good enough? Personal best? Best overall? The crowd cheering, the loudspeaker trumpeting her name.

Nobody cheers for Patricia. She's not an athlete, a doctor, a lawyer; she's not even a financial planner bestowing largesse on middle-class clients anxious to lengthen their lives and swell their savings. She is not the recipient of handshakes and thank-you-so-muches; a basket at Christmas, to keep the lines of communication and good favour open.

The case of Jimmy Corrigan and his mother comes to Patricia the usual way: mandatory report from the Goldstein Children's Hospital psychology department, which received a referral from the local school guidance

139

counsellor who, for her part, was answering the desperate plea of an overworked harried teacher unable to deal with another disruptive, obese, failing child whose inability to live up to even the lowest standards of public school in the city's poorest and by extension dumbest district clearly indicated a need for a diagnosis. With a diagnosis, Jimmy Corrigan could then be branded "in need" and shipped to special ed.

At the hospital, standard questionnaires prior to performing the learning disability battery reveal an absent father and an out-of-work mother herself functioning at a "diminished" level. Asked if she drank alcohol or otherwise ingested substances such as crack, glue, heroin or marijuana during pregnancy, Jimmy's mother shrugged. Some, she said. Further probing revealed a pattern of a few beers or more nightly throughout the pregnancy and finally an admission of steady heavy drinking over the final trimester as Jimmy kicked and squirmed in her belly and Daddy slipped out the back way, squirrelled down the fire escape into the night and was never heard from again.

Patricia adds these tiny details to the picture in her head. She adds flat brown to the mother's beady eyes, gives Jimmy a hint of a dark spotty just-pubescent moustache. She's heard it all before. It could be day one or day 2,036. Most don't last. She's senior in her department. Her thin delicate wrists attached to those long spindly ungainly hands. A scratch of black pen following a dissipating vein past the cuff of a blouse. She bends her head low, her brown hair framing the page, so that all she has to see is the Jimmy Corrigan file.

Upon the news of Jimmy's post-conception heavy drinking being noted, Jimmy's dossier is sent down to the pharmacology and toxicology division, a process that takes no less than four full weeks. There it sits in the stack for another three weeks. At which point the program coordinator reviews the reports enclosed. Jimmy is then selected as a candidate for testing for Fetal Alcohol Spectrum Disorder and given a two-day appointment two and a half months from the day that his file is evaluated.

When Jimmy Corrigan and his mother turn up months later at 9:43 a.m. (almost an hour late) it is evident that the family unit is under considerable strain. Jimmy stinks, and has chocolate smeared all over his big face and sweatshirt, having apparently been lured to the hospital by a series of candy bars delivered at intervals on the trip (on the sidewalk, on the bus, outside the building). The mother also gives off a palpable odour, and both, Patricia surmises, are at this point fatter than ever before. The standard pre-test questionnaire delivered by a nervous young intern wading her way through graduate school reveals that Jimmy has been suspended (or possibly expelled, Jimmy isn't sure) from his junior high school. The plan, Patricia later discovers after talking to the principal, is to keep him out of the school until the tests are done. Once the tests have been conducted, the school assumes they will have the necessary paperwork from the hospital to transfer him to special education. While he, admittedly, won't learn much there, he at least won't prevent an entire class of kids—of whom a few might be going somewhere, though most couldn't care less—from learning to read and write and multiply. On the home front, Jimmy is left in the care of Andy, his mother's latest boyfriend, while Jimmy's mother works the breakfast and lunch shift at Lindy's ultimate all-you-can-eat pancake house.

Over the course of the two-day testing period Jimmy is variously truculent and impish, uncooperative and over-friendly. Two months later, the test results are finally tabulated. The results reveal that Jimmy is just smart enough *not* to be stupid enough to qualify for special education plus the other interventions, assistances and benefits that the state has available to bestow on troubled children. However, the social/emotional profile suggests a familiar pattern: a child unable to function in a classroom setting, probably suffering from some variety of Fetal Alcohol Syndrome (though no one can be sure) with symptoms including impulsiveness, hyperactivity, aggressiveness coupled with a lack of self-awareness, a high level of naïveté and an inability to make differential judgments about good or bad. Something has gone seriously wrong with Jimmy. Without intervention he will no doubt end up an addict, a sexual deviant and a general pariah praying mostly on himself. Since the scores do not qualify Jimmy for special education, it is recommended that he be returned to the classroom, where he can avail himself of extra help from the teacher after school, subject to availability.

All this is pending the recommendation of child social services—Patricia. Because when the senior psychologist reviews the final report, she concludes that Jimmy Corrigan and his mother are sufficiently, as they say, "at risk" to warrant a mandatory investigation. Jimmy's poor hygiene, his questionable diet, his mother's "low functioning" and the presence of boyfriend Andy all suggest an "at risk" scenario. This scenario is further advanced when, in the part of the test where Jimmy is asked to draw a picture of his house, he draws a picture of himself sitting on Andy's lap on the living-room couch. Andy has a bottle in his hand that Jimmy helpfully identifies as "Trad." As the report concludes: *Possible neglect and/or abuse. Immediate report to child social services.*

Patricia stops reading. The phone rings. It's 11:23 a.m. The appointment with Jimmy Corrigan and his mother is in exactly seven minutes. She knows from experience they will be exactly on time, this first and only time. She closes the file, crosses her gangly hands over the manila folder. She licks her dry lips. She stares at the corner, that beetle shell swinging.

Finally, reluctantly, she answers the phone.

Patricia Stern here.

Patti?

She doesn't speak. That voice on the other end. —it can't be—

he's—

Hello? Hello? Patti? It's Maury Stern calling. I, ah, I'm—

She doesn't hang up. Maury, she says calmly, talking to a ghost through a void of time and memory, I have an appointment in five minutes.

Patti—it's—great to hear your—

I go by Patricia now.

Okay. No problem. Patricia. The reason I'm calling is—I'm just wondering, because, you see, well, I mean, I'm sure you haven't but—I've been having this feeling, lately, that Cal is—that he might be—

Your brother?

Your ex—my brother. I think he might be . . . resurfacing.

Really. Patricia stares at the pale skin of her wrist.

It's—I haven't—seen him, but, well, I know you don't want anything to do with—I mean, I figured. But you're his—I mean—you were . . . and I—

Maury, I have to go. I have a meeting.

Patti—Patricia—but—I just want to know: have you heard from him?

Goodbye, Maury.

She hangs up.

After work—consisting of two meetings with "clients," notes in her books, several official memos to be sent to various departments under the euphemistic title Progress Reports, and seventeen phone calls from various frantic parents, teachers, agencies, societies and "clients" including a fourteen-year-old recently placed in a group home and now claiming to be suicidal (Patricia promises to visit the next day)—she meets Aveek at the bar.

It was supposed to be a drink before dinner, but Patricia strongly suspects, without looking at her watch, that she is very late, that perhaps it is too late for dinner. She walks briskly down the sidewalk. There are nights when she wonders why she bothers, why she should be the only social worker who works until nine every night then goes home, takes a long shower and runs through all the futile, desperate, hopeful encounters of that day, not to mention the day soon to begin, the day perpetually looming on the gloomy edges of the illuminated city.

Aveek has the corner table and is working his way through his fourth beer. She slides into the seat across from him, at once smelling her own perfume and sweat, the bar's smoky air and the air all around him, bristling as if about to burst into flames.

Sorry, she says. She wants to say something else. He holds up a hand to stop her. They just sit there like that, looking at each other. Aveek has dark red-brown skin, intense hazel eyes dwarfed by bushy black eye-brows, thick thatches that furrow together when he fucks her.

They're not exactly boyfriend and girlfriend, though they're not exactly not that either. There should be a word, Patricia thinks. One that would come after boyfriend but before husband. One that would mean lover without implying permanent partnership or illicit attraction. She's been married once, when she was younger.

She doesn't talk about it. It's nobody's business.

Maury—what did he mean?—*resurfacing*.

Aveek runs a finger down her forehead, down the bridge of her nose, over her thin red lips, off the crest of her chin. Close your eyes, Aveek suggests. She blinks at him. Come on, he says. She closes her eyes. He strokes her cheek, her forehead, her lips. He takes her hands, runs his fingers over her palms. You're one hour and twenty-two minutes late, he says gently, almost whispering. His accent comes through now, rich like a spice, exactly the way he intends it. Your faithful and eternally obsequious houseboy had dinner on the table at the appointed time as requested. But now, everything is cold. The fields are dark, the coolies trudging home, their week's wages—less than you spend in a week on chow for your purebred Staffordshire terrier puppy—jingling in their pockets. Tonight they'll spend it all on drink, cursing your name before heading home to screw, beat or cry to their women. But your house at the top of the hill overlooking the plantation will be quiet, as always. So quiet. Just the squeal of the macaws and the rustling of the mango trees and the cries of the teeming monkeys. Houseboy paces, adjusts the cutlery. He can't relax. He's agitated. He's angry, furious with you for missing dinner. He loves you. The truth is, he has to have you. He'll have you on the kitchen table. He'll have you on the floor. He'll have you over and over again until you like it. Then he'll strangle you with your own silk scarf, and take all your money and jewels and flee to the mountains until he can arrange passage to the emancipated New World. You're late. He has no idea when you are going to show up or even if you will show up. All he knows is that he can no longer contain himself. He pulls down his tattered pants and begins working his ropy dick over the cook's speciality, a Yorkshire pudding that tastes, like everything the cook does, of vindaloo.

Patricia laughs, opens her eyes. He's leaning in close. Hot breath against her face.

He jerks off in my Yorkshire vindaloo? Patricia asks.

Aveek nods, delighted. And? he says.

And . . . I catch him. He tries to cover up. I take his hands away, soothe his hot dark member with my cool white fingers.

And?

Patricia puts her long ugly hands gently over Aveek's face. Checks to make sure he's got his eyes closed.

He closes his eyes, she says. I stroke him from the shaft up. I squeeze the head, I find his bursting hairy balls. He's never come before at the hands of a woman, only done it with the goat out back. He moans, swings in his spot over the pudding. Just before he explodes, I push him forward. He falls, plunging his rigid member into the burning spice of the Yorkshire vindaloo. He shrieks with pain. My swifty one-eyed butler comes running. I exit the dining room.

She hefts his beer, finishes it.

Hey! he says.

Let's get out of here, she says.

He's the city's only professional Indian comedian. She's never seen him perform, though she has a pretty good idea of the material: horny perverted house-boys, arranged marriages, the conversations Gandhi and Vishnu have over beers, the Bombay beggar/taxi driver/carpet salesman.

He doesn't invite her to his shows. There's a line they don't want to cross.

She takes him home, sinks into him. It doesn't have to be explained. It doesn't have to be perfect. Foul-mouthed comedian with bulging eyes and a skinny chest. Afterwards, they lie together and she begins to talk, at first about nothing, then about everything— almost everything—about Jimmy Corrigan and his mother and the fourteen-year-old in the group home and the way her office seems to be getting smaller. And then, again, she comes back to Jimmy Corrigan, because one look at Jimmy and his mother and she knew it was true, that the boy was neglected, abused, destined for a life of repeat performances.

She says: Jimmy's got four chins and a kind of fuzz growth on his upper lip. The mother tries to make her face pretty with makeup. They both wear sweatshirts covering up their spotty rippled skin. There's some love between them, I can see that right away. I know if I take him away from her, she'll fall to pieces, they both will. The mother's got a big bruise on her arm, says she slipped in the kitchen at the pancake house. We both know what really happened. So I ask Jimmy how he likes Andy. He just shrugs. I say, what kind of stuff do you and Andy do together while your mom is at work? He shrugs again. The mother starts bawling and yelling: He's a good boy, he's a good boy, he doesn't do nothing wrong. Jimmy shrugs, won't look at me.

So what will you do? Aveek asks. He's half asleep, lured into the violence of her story, to him no more real than a snake charmer comedy sketch.

She doesn't answer. She had forgotten he was listening.

Come away with me, he says. Let's take a trip. A week. A few days even.

No, she says.

She puts her head on his chest. He's too thin. She falls asleep, instantly, completely.

The phone rings. Patricia ignores it. If she closed her eyes and put her head on the sheaf of papers covering her office desk, she would sleep through the day, through the phone ringing, through everything.

She's tempted.

She doesn't take vacations. She doesn't get much in the way of rest. Her whole life, she's only gone away that one time. It was when he—the ex, the little brother, she doesn't know how to think of him, doesn't want to think of him—asked her to marry him. The time they got lost and later, as the sun set and a baby moose nudged against its mother in the shallow reeds just across from their campsite, he asked her to marry him.

Did it really happen that way? Could it really have happened that way? The sunset blinded her. She shaded her eyes.

It doesn't matter now. He's—gone.

A long time ago, a long long time ago, she said yes and her bony hands fluttered to the sides of his face and they kissed and how small she was then, how alone in the world, how desperately perfect. The blood through her veins, those tiny white wrists, those big hands scratchy and not at all soft.

She never went away again, to the lake district, or to the ocean, or to an island on an ocean, or to a castle on an island on an ocean, or to a castle in a theme park even.

The phone rings again.

What if it's—

She doesn't answer. She makes a list on a scrap of paper. It's something she does every morning. She makes a list. In order of priority. Number one priority. Number two priority. She tries not to have more than five or six priorities. After that, it gets ridiculous.

Number one priority is to get Jimmy Corrigan back in school so that he has somewhere to go during the day other than the small space on the couch thoughtfully provided for him by boyfriend Andy. Number two is to get Andy out of the Corrigan household. Number three is to meet with a suicidal fourteen-year-old having trouble adjusting to life in her group home, not that you'll be there forever, Patricia will assure the girl, just until things settle down. This is what she'll tell the girl though they both know the truth, that nobody wants her, that she is to be permanently unloved, unsettled. They both know it. Kids are tough. They figure things out, they adapt. Or else they fade into nothing, disappear behind the thin veil of premature adulthood.

The phone rings.

This morning, she left Aveek still sleeping. He stirred as she dressed for work. She wanted to slide back under the covers with him, straddle his wiry body or, better yet, lie on her back and let him thrust into her.

She did up the buttons of her blouse. Kissed his bristly chin.

When the phone finally stops, she grabs it before it can bleat again. She calls the school district adviser who, having referred Jimmy to the hospital some six months ago, has since forgotten all about his existence and has to be patiently led through the case, valuable minutes wasted as she massages his ego—as I'm sure you recall, Mr. So-and-So—while the messages pile up on her line and the cases arrive on her desk.

She calls the school's counsellor, who, thankfully, remembers Jimmy Corrigan but seems unbothered by the boy's status in educational limbo; he is, after all, the fat, the poor, the see-through, the hopeless, the invisible. All of this is true and Patricia does not deny it.

Next, she tries the principal, with whom she uses phrases like *one more chance* and *new-found maturity.*

The principal agrees to a possible conference and a potential rescinding of the expulsion. He suggests she ring the teacher to get her, as he puts it, on board. Patricia hisses air through her front teeth, a tiny gap. Her large awkward hand sweats against the plastic of the phone. The teachers are impossible to call, since they teach most of the day and after class they seem to bolt out of the school and disappear (except in the posh areas, where they are forever engrossed in extracurricular enrichments). Either way, Patricia knows, you can never get a goddamn teacher on the phone, though she doesn't blame them, who is she to blame them? She agrees with the principal that she should try to get the teacher on board and she pleasantly recites several of his key proclamations back to him, such as *temporary reinstatement,* and *deserves another chance,* and *some good in the boy,* that mantra of catchphrases mixed in with bureaucratese that, who knows, may just alter the arc of a Jimmy Corrigan's imploding life.

She doesn't blame the teachers or the mother or Jimmy or even boyfriend Andy.

Those thin wrists containing her pulse.

What if she did go away?

The phone rings.

She once asked Aveek how it was that he was the only Indian comic in a city full of Indians and comics.

There was one other, Aveek said. He was terrible. His Vishnu sounded like Gandhi and his Gandhi sounded like a Pakistani taxi driver. He couldn't do a

three-hippy-college-kids-trek-Mount-Shrikhand-
Mahadev-to-ask-the-swami-Sri-Aurbindino-the-
meaning-of-life gag to save his pathetic Bengali life.

So what happened to him? Patricia wanted to know.

I set him up.

What? Like, you had him killed?

You really don't think much of me now do you
Patricia Stern?

I was just kidding.

Sure you were.

So what happened?

I got him a gig.

I don't get it.

I got him a gig working the crowd before a Bombay
pop sensation—sexy broad, can't sing worth shit, but
they have a line of backup singers and most of it's on
tape and she sure knows how to fill out a sari.

Is there a point to this?

Yeah, okay, so I get him a gig. At this big concert.
Filled with displaced Hindus searching for a way to
connect with the motherland.

I still don't get it.

Ah, what do you white people get?

Okay, so I'm ignorant of your culture's exotic ways.
Enlighten me.

Let me try. They were all Indian. Every single one of
them. Living here, in the New World. But still they
have their brown skin, their apartments stinking of
curried cauliflower, their singsong accents. They don't
need—or want—to be reminded of it. The act we do,

it's not for them, it's for you. It's for white people who can laugh at it because they're not in it.

So . . . they hated him?

Of course they hated him. Not a single laugh. You could have heard a pin drop.

And after that?

A bunch of kids beat him up in his dressing room, smashed his cellphone, the whole business.

That's awful.

Yeah, awful. He disappeared the next week. Nobody ever heard from him again.

Aveek smiled a proud glowing smile.

The phone rings. Patricia jumps. She's alone in her office. The phone always rings.

The phone. Maury's voice, so much like—

She shakes her head.

Jimmy Corrigan. Remember?

She'll need the cops.

She slept with a detective once, during the course of a particularly harrowing abuse case, but she couldn't stand his moustache and he was greatly exaggerating the extent of his "trial" separation. It was all very television. They still keep in touch.

She'll call him up and tell him the situation. Does our man Andy have a record?—of course he will have a record—and can he be spoken to on his way out of the apartment to pick up his daily supply of bourbon and Pepto-Bismol? And if he is picked up, maybe a warning would be in order, that they know what's going on and he should be thinking about finding another desperate single mom waitress living in a one-room apartment and sleeping with her son on a fold-out sofa who might be willing to take in a deadbeat ingrate with a spotty past encompassing any number of undisclosed crimes and ongoing grievances against the state and Mommy.

She doesn't put it quite that way, but her detective friend knows what's needed and doesn't mind wandering over and having a talk with the fellow.

It won't be enough.

The phone rings as soon as she puts it down.

It always rings.

She told Aveek: Don't even try to call me at work. And never ever come by to take me to lunch. I don't do lunch.

They—her co-workers—they do lunch.

Janice sometimes asks her to join them.

Patricia checks the time, the watch loose on the slim wrist of her right hand. Time for one more phone call before she takes the subway and bus across town to meet the girl who, currently confined to the home, is having trouble adjusting. She's worth worrying about, Patricia thinks, trying to justify the trip, which isn't really part of her job. Once they're in the home, it's the home's job, but whom is she kidding, as if anyone anywhere does their job. I can't forget about any of them, she tells Aveek, they're in my head. She knocks a fist against her skull.

One more call, she says to the peeling paint of her office wall.

She picks up her ringing phone and replaces the

receiver. Before it can go again, she hoists it to her ear, punches buttons. The man answers. Andy.

Yup, he says.

This is Patricia Stern calling, she says, from the Children's Services. I'd like to speak to Deborah Corrigan please.

Uh, Andy says, as if stunned. In the background she can hear the chant off the TV game show: *Wheel* . . . *of* . . .

Deborah Corrigan, Patricia prompts. She keeps her voice pleasant.

Uh, Andy says. Debbie?

I'd like to speak to her.

In the background she hears the boy, Jimmy's high-pitched wheeze: Is that my mom?

Shut the— Andy blurts, then catches himself. I'm trying to—I'm talking to—

Can you put Deborah Corrigan on, Patricia insists.

Uh, Andy stalls.

She's not in? Patricia taps her pen against the cardboard of a file.

Uh, Andy says something incomprehensible.

Is she there?

Naw, he admits. She's at work.

I see, says Patricia. And you are?

Uh . . .

Your name, Patricia says.

I'm her . . . boyfriend . . . Debbie's, you know . . .

I see. And you are living at the residence 6943 Dufferin Street, Apartment 12D?

Well, I'm, no, you know, I'm, uh . . .

You would describe your status as cohabitant?

Co-uh-what?

You live there?

Me, I'm, I got my own, pad, you know, I stay around.

You stay around?

No, I mean, yeah, sometimes.

You stay around, you mean, when you're needed, to help Deborah out, is that right?

Yeah.

Look after things while she's at work? Babysitting, that sort of thing?

Yeah, sure.

She hears the boy again, his pathetic squeal: Is that my—

The boy cuts off with a gasp. Patricia doesn't say anything. Imagines Andy's greasy hair, his undershirt, his bulging gut, his goatee. The gesture he makes at the boy, a finger draped across his throat or a fist swinging in the dark stinking air.

Well then, she finally says. Thanks for your time.

Yeah. Yeah, sure.

She hangs up the phone. Opens the drawer to her desk, removes a Memo 344a, to be filled out in triplicate. She notes the details of her phone call, time, date, the stunned disoriented stutter of Andy, bourbon drinker, felon on parole, babysitter.

She takes the train across town. She waits impatiently on the platform. Is there another way to wait? She watches people stroll around, slouch against walls, slump on the benches; the placid conducting their affairs, unhurried, inefficient. Patricia is truly mystified by them. The train finally comes. She sits down. She makes mental notes for her plan regarding this visit with the girl, Erin, at the group home. She prioritizes her priorities. One: reassure and calm Erin. Two: re-establish contact with group home staff and director. Three: drop in on the other occupants of the home whose cases are still active in her files. She recites their names, and tries to form a mental picture of each of their faces.

Instead, she sees the face of her former husband, suddenly appearing on the guy sitting in the corner of the train.

She rarely thinks about him. She kept his name. Stern. She likes the name. She hates him.

Why should she think about him?

His brother—calling—

If she's shocked to see him sitting there, she doesn't show it.

After they sent him away, she vowed never to wonder or regret.

If it's him, then she's wrong about everything.

It isn't him.

She gets off.

The group home is at the top of the hill, a sloped road ending in a cul-de-sac. The houses here are big, dilapidated, no one can afford to fix them up. Though the area was once considered prime real estate, it's been supplanted by the cheaper, less complicated uptown suburbs. Patricia takes the warped steps two at a time, feeling her muscles stretch, the tiny jets of air coming through her nostrils. The home looms above, smells like blood trapped in a pad, hospital food, sweat, cigarettes.

Patricia rings the bell with an optimistic stab. Talk to Erin, make the rounds, still have time to rush back to the office and make a few calls. Nothing happens. She rings again. She hasn't telephoned ahead, prefers to surprise the staff, get a glimpse of what's really happening. Abuse is infectious. You have to guard against it with spot checks and unannounced doses of civility, propriety, what's left of the rule of law.

Yes? The home supervisor scowls.

Hello, Patricia says, beaming. I'm Patricia Stern from Children's Aid. She extends her hand.

The woman snakes a few fingers into a cursory shake, doesn't introduce herself. What can I do for you? she says.

Well—the smile slips away from Patricia—for starters, I'd like to come in.

The woman doesn't budge. You're coming in? she says sourly.

Certainly, Patricia says.

You're supposed to call first. Make an appointment.

Patricia takes a closer look at the woman. In her fifties, gaunt, with no breasts or shape to speak off. Lank black-grey hair, wears a purple cardigan over a nurse's smock.

Well, you see, Patricia says, I had some business around the corner and I promised Erin I'd stop by and check on her, and so I remembered how close I was, and here I am.

Erin, the woman mutters, reluctantly stepping back.

Thank you. The voice she uses is loud, cheery enough to be abrasive in the sarcophagus silence of the foyer. They stand there for a moment. Patricia can hear creaks in the wooden steps. The rustle of the wind outside. Where's the TV drone, the rap music, the endless games of cards? In her past visits Patricia barely stepped through the door before the catcalls and bitter chatter of teenage girls gone hard before their time slapped her in the face.

Quiet, isn't it?

Yes, the attendant agrees.

Patricia waits.

I sent 'em all upstairs. The girls. She says it like she can't believe she let them out in the first place.

Upstairs?

To their rooms.

Patricia starts to say something, coughs. Excuse me, she manages.

Ah, the woman says, they're to keep quiet, up there.

Patricia, calmly: I'll just—I'd better—check on Erin.

Oh yeah, the woman says. New girl.

Patricia waits for the woman to lead the way upstairs, but she doesn't move. Finally, Patricia takes a tentative step up.

Which room? she says.

The woman fumbles with the keys on her ring. You'll need this, she says, extracting a key.

You've got them locked in their rooms, Patricia says.

The woman drops the key in Patricia's outstretched palm.

Patricia marches slowly up the flights of stairs. Erin's on the fourth floor. She wants to run, take the stairs two at a time. She doesn't run.

She stands outside 412, raises a fist to knock. She thinks of the man she saw on the subway. Her ex-husband riding the trains through her mind. It couldn't have been him. He's dead. She's decided he's dead.

And Erin? Erin's got black hair cut in a bob with bangs across her forehead. She's got tired, imprecise blue eyes and red cheeks, and an awkward oval body that makes it seem like she's always about to fall over.

Hello? Patricia says, sliding the key into the lock.

Tinny pop harmony on the radio.

Hello?

No answer.

Patricia doesn't go into work the next day. She doesn't go in the day after that.

Her absence is met with shock, amazement and glee. Nobody wonders: Why this girl? Why this case? It's enough to know that it finally broke her, happy chatter in the coffee shop, lipstick smiles revealing protruding front teeth gone double-double brown. Everyone is so busy talking about what happened, nobody really bothers to find out what really happened.

Patricia thinks to herself: I'm—

disappearing.

Aveek comes over. He kisses her. Her closed mouth. Hands loose at her sides. What is it? he asks. She doesn't blame him. He looks at her with bemused anger, a flash of lust and disgust, rickshaw driver pulling a pair of New World college girls in tank tops through the safe parts of the city.

Patricia shrugs.

What happens happens and no one changes anything.

Fuck me, she says.

Afterwards, she tells him she'd like to go camping. Canoeing.

Camping? Aveek says. He makes a joke about the bobbing bodies of holy cows caught in the polluted rapids of the river Ganges. He had something more exotic in mind for them. Something more comfortable, with a pool and waiters and dark-skinned men with machine guns guarding the lobby kiosk where you change your money. A country of poor brown people where a well-to-do brown man and his white woman would stand out. That's how he'd write it up for his routine, my vacation with a white woman, though, really, he doesn't consider it funny, and what he wants is exactly that—only not that at all.

You'll love it, she says. She says it like it's take it or leave it.

He kisses her forehead. Okay, he says. Okay.

She packs for the outing. It's a dream she's in. Somebody's else's fantasy. A dream she thought she had forgotten.

Look how big my fingers are. How far away they seem.

She rolls a sleeping bag into a portable bundle. Look at the tiny wrists, how do they keep those big gangly hands attached to my arms? Look at that. Isn't that something? And will it be very cold? Will there be bugs? Will the days become porous wet nights?— water lapping against the rocks, sky thick with stars—time-delayed beacons arranged in mythological constellations nobody remembers any more. One million and one, one million and two, she'll count all night, she'll count to make it last longer. It's amazing, how many stars there are, how we can see each other in the starlight, pass each other in the dark where the trees beckon you further into the forest. We make our decisions and they take us over and it's like we never decided anything, like someone else decided. He only hit me once. The ex. The little brother. The man I married who went crazy and did terrible things.

They paddle through the twisting river.

The past is just the past, she tells Aveek.

Until you're reborn as a mosquito, he says, slapping his arm.

Neither of them knows how to canoe. They keep

hitting the sides of the narrow waterway. The current is against them and if they stop paddling they end up wedged across, Aveek making jokes, Patricia scowling like she's late for an appointment.

Can't you steer? she says.

Not really! Can you?

The river narrows, twists, branches off. It's supposed to reach a lake, eventually. A place where sundappled beaches meet tree-shrouded campsites.

It never ends, Patricia says.

It must end, Aveek says.

But Patricia doesn't care. What is she doing here? She'll wake up in the middle of the night in a terror, remembering a different night, a different dream, a different dick forging its way through the twisting stream of her need.

Sex in the tent is uncomfortable. Aveek does it behind her, knees and elbows padded with sleeping bags. He grasps her hips, works her back and forth, his fingers digging in.

She doesn't come.

Afterwards, he's tender. She stiffens, shrugs. He grins his showman grin.

He tells her about growing up in Uganda, about the house on the hill and his parents and their arranged marriage and the small repressive Indian community there. He tells her how he hated them but now misses them dearly, would give anything to see them again. He describes a longing more powerful than any memory. Some nights, Aveek says, he wakes up and doesn't know

where he is. It could be the night they set fire to the shop
and his mama cried, or it could be the morning he flew
away to study political science and international rela-
tions at a mediocre Midwestern university prone to
doling out scholarships to brown people from poor
countries. It could be one of those fleeting climactic
moments, or it could be something permanent: the
rainy season, the taste of his mother's honey-drenched
sweets, his father's barking voice cutting through the
humidity like a scythe.

The mosquitoes outside the tent sound like a highway. Moths dive-bomb the fireproof, waterproof
walls, driven mad by the dull ebb of Patricia's
flashlight.

I thought you grew up in Bombay, she says.

Just an act, Aveek snaps.

Patricia nods, a sharp shadow.

Is he dead? She can't remember now. She thinks this
must have been where it started. Mother moose and
baby moose. Holding hands. Sun going down. So
happy she cried.

She would know if he was dead.

Aveek leaves the tent.

The water laps against the rocks buoyed in the gentle wind.

Why now? Why in this horrid tent distended by
the condom smell of rubber, the kamikaze moths, the
leaves on the tall thin trees swaying over the weedy
lake slowing draining into the maze of a river? With
Aveek she paddled until her arms hurt and her palms

blistered, and the only wildlife she saw was a dead tur-
tle, on its back, green belly bloated. Will I ever again
see a baby moose nuzzling a mother moose in the heat
of the summer's twilight? Somewhere else it's breakfast time, the day's promise coming alive, the sun
lurching into the sky like it's been tripped. Patricia.
Patricia Stern. Stern Patricia. She kept his name. She
thought she was done with all this, she thought she'd
seen it all—haunting the halls of the hospitals waiting
for the outcome of a pumped stomach or sewn wrists
or stitched torn petals of sex, her own parts throbbing,
thin translucent wrists full of dark blood. Is it him? It
can't still be him. She blames herself, the blood, the
thin wrist attached to wraithlike mummy hand spreading across the page as she scribbles her notes, her day's
agenda of priorities and outcomes: the pale blue eyes
of Erin swinging or not swinging, locked in her room,
back and forth, free to come and go, no longer
plagued by memories set to radio melodies sung by
apple-cheeked fifteen-year-old twins, nursery rhymes
on the electric guitar, corporeal voices already haunted by their temporality. How else to be free of it? He
did what he did—it wasn't really him any more. It was
some trick of chemistry, some imbalance in the neuro-
transmitters, some serotonin-spewing sleight of hand.
Now you see me. Now you don't. Not boyfriend
Andy's lumbering casual methodical destruction, but
something else entirely, she doesn't know what it was,
not some boring pedestrian self-obsessed evil taking
the well-worn path with predictably dire results, but

something else, something more like the ethereal moment when, Patricia tells herself, Erin died while I chatted with the house supervisor; light and invisible and locked in her room she died and floated down the stairs past me. And I knew it all along, didn't I? Because I'm one of them too, look Ma, no scars. Just a pale sullen endless capacity to accept whatever happens: our hearts pumping blood to thin wrists and awkward big hands, too big, which he loved, then crushed, and I wore a cast and everybody asked, but by then wasn't it obvious?

I could have written him. Visited. But I just wanted him to be—

dead.

Patricia opens the blade on Aveek's bright red new army knife.

Jimmy Corrigan takes it in the ass, the mouth, the ear.

The bastards.

part 3: **ontology**

In Bubby Stern's dream, she is going for an operation. She is having her lungs replaced. She is calm. It is the day of the operation. She meets with the doctor. She discusses the operation, then suddenly recalls that, in fact, there is also another operation she is meant to have under the auspices of another physician. One operation is bad enough, but two operations! The lung doctor tells his assistants—two young happy boys—to take Bubby Stern to his office, where she can call the other doctor and get the details of this other operation. They can be performed together, he explains. Performed? Bubby Stern exclaims in her dream. It isn't a show!

The young boys lead Bubby Stern to the office. She places the call. Soon after, Bubby Stern finds herself in a series of anxious situations. She's in another woman's apartment, the atmosphere dense and sexual. Thick red curtains billow out of an open window. Then she is discussing her health with the other doctor, who cannot remember her name but nevertheless recommends a complicated procedure involving the fat tip of her nose. Finally, she sees her younger son Cal unconcernedly moving past the slab of flesh that is Bubby Stern, Bubby Stern lying naked on the operating table, skin peeled back to reveal the twin sacks of her lungs, gently undulating like a butterfly's wings. Bubby Stern's beseeching eyes rolling in their sockets, tracking his progress.

The day after this dream, she feels watched, observed. For the first time in a long time, she allows herself to think about him: her youngest. Cal the crazy. The *meshugana* as they used to say in the old country.

Bubby Stern is still robust enough to live on her own and pay regular visits to her late husband's grave.

Bubby Stern doesn't need a remote control. She doesn't need cable. She doesn't need a new TV. She's happy with plastic wood panelling, rabbit ear antennas, four channels, two of them only visible in the late evening, at which point she watches the late show, sneering at the lady guests in their tight tops and lipstick.

Bubby Stern watches the game shows, the soap opera, the dramatic hour-long shows that come on at nine or ten, and the late show, at eleven-thirty or twelve.

What is this television world she lives in? It is a world with a plan. A precise world of time, where nothing can be wasted because nothing really happens; everything is predetermined, already figured out. A godless world. I'm an old lady, she tells herself, what else is there for me?

The thing that bothered her most when her youngest got sent away was the thought of his time wasting. The thought of him doing nothing, just sitting there.

Bubby Stern has her television.

Temple is the star of the soap opera Bubby Stern watches every day, Monday to Friday, at three in the afternoon. Bubby Stern never talks about Temple. Bubby Stern believes she is not one of those lonely old people who has lost the ability to discern reality from encroaching fantasy. Bubby Stern thinks of Temple as a friend, as an inaccessible long-distance pal. She would dearly like to have influence on Temple's doings, but she knows she cannot; Temple is on TV, bound to the script and the commercials, tied to the arc of broadcast temporality with its sweeps weeks, repeat summer doldrums and season finales. And anyway, even if Temple could hear Bubby Stern's advice and was not permanently preserved in the amber of the small screen, Bubby Stern knows that she would be ignored, because Temple doesn't listen to anyone's advice.

Temple is headstrong.

Temple is beautiful.

Temple's family is dead, killed in a tragic accident.

Temple is alone in the world.

Temple is a survivor.

Nobody tells Temple what to do.

Bubby Stern does not care about the actress who

plays Temple. Bubby Stern would never seek out her autograph in front of the lingerie store at the local mall, and wouldn't even mind if the actress who plays Temple left the show, so long as she was replaced with another Temple, a just-as-good-as-the-last-one Temple.

In the last five years, there have been three Temples.

How does that make you feel? inquires Bubby Stern's analyst.

No, Bubby Stern does not talk to her analyst about Temple. Bubby Stern does not go to an analyst. Temple goes to an analyst. Temple is having an affair with her analyst. Bubby Stern sometimes imagines that she too is visiting Temple's analyst, her problems carefully stroked and caressed—not an affair, she's too old for an affair—but something like an affair. Bubby Stern watches Temple splayed out on the analyst's couch, her bosom heaving, her cheeks wet with silky tears.

Bubby Stern started watching TV the way everyone started watching TV. An hour here, an hour there. It was like committing a kind of suicide, walking into the cold lake and the ice freezing over you, trapping you with the fish and the fingers of slimy weed frozen in motion until the long winter is over.

The long winter has just begun. The days are as slow as hibernated heartbeats, as prolonged as a repeat of *Who's the Boss?*

7 a.m. *The Breakfast Show*

8 a.m. *This Morning It's Your City: The News with Donald Daddy*

8:30 a.m. *Live with Susan Slotti*

9 a.m. *Chris Chevers Shoots from the Hip*

11 a.m. *Founder's Heart*

12 p.m. *A Cry in the Dark*

1 p.m. *Talk Talk Talk! with Dini-Betty Cindy Lou*

2 p.m. *The Clock is Always Right!*

3 p.m. *As the Hours Go By*

4 p.m. *Just for the Fun of It*

4:30 p.m. *M*A*S*H*

5 p.m. *Roundup with Paul Fitzwillis*

6 p.m. *Sudden at Six: The News with Souhana Martinez*

6:30 p.m. *This Evening It's Your Country: The News with Doug Saunders*

7 p.m. *The Simpsons*

7:30 p.m. *Fashion Television*

8 p.m. *Laser*

8:30 p.m. *Ain't That Pet Amazing*

9 p.m. *LAPD: Life in the Hood*

10 p.m. *911 Emergency Rescue*

11 p.m. *Nightly Night: The News with Sahara Savage*

11:30 p.m. *Wow! It's Live! with Archie Wellman*

12 a.m. *The Good Night Show with Danny Super*

Bubby Stern varies her schedule and doesn't honestly mind missing any of these shows much. Sometimes she plays cards with Marlyss her cousin on her father's side who lives in a nursing home but is still sharp as a rusty nail. Tonight, she notes, *Wow! It's Live!*—with that loudmouth Archie Wellman (who's definitely Jewish)—is doing a special segment on some young man who claims to be half-man half-computer. Calls

175

himself a cyborg. Just another crazy. Bubby Stern sighs, leans toward the filtered glow.

The one time she visited him the sky was clear blue and the sun was shining. It was not the kind of cloudy drizzly day that she wanted it to be. It was not, as one would expect, immediately after the sentencing and the transfer to the hospital, but, rather, six months later. When it finally happened there was a sense of relief, the dread spilling out of her until she was empty.

She was already an old woman; a grandmother, an artifact, an antique whose worth could be calculated in her relative rarity. How many were left who survived the war, and after the war, and the pilgrimage to the New World, all the while maintaining their unique singularity? (In Bubby Stern's case, thick Yiddish lips and an ardent pragmatism demonstrated by her propensity for boiling and hoarding food.)

The sky was blue, and the sun was shining.

Bubby Stern was wearing her peacock-blue suit with the matching ruffled blouse. It gave her the air of an ailing queen. Her neck was already giving her trouble, her head more comfortable on a permanent angle, just a little crooked.

The cab dropped her off and sped away without waiting for her to march resolutely up the twelve stairs and into the lobby of the building. Inside, it was much darker than the day behind her. She stood blinking. The ceiling was low, pushed down by madness, painted a peeling aquamarine. The lights were fluorescent and dour, the walls thick and claustrophobic. Bubby Stern put her hand in front of her mouth, as if to assure herself she was still breathing.

There was a large grille, locked. Behind it was another door, also locked. In the space between the grille door and the locked door was a guard, in uniform, sitting on a chair.

Bubby Stern stared at the guard trapped in between those two doors. How could he just sit there?

She didn't hear the woman behind the counter call out sharply:

May I help you?

Hello, ma'am, can I help you with something?

Excuse me, ma'am! Is there something I can—

The other guard, the guard not between the locked doors but standing with the receptionist behind the lobby counter, finally left his post and gingerly approached Bubby Stern. He touched her elbow.

Ma'am?

Was she sure where she was, at that moment?

Perhaps she imagined herself back in the mines, at the mercy of a lean stubble-ridden nineteen-year-old Slavic soldier, his rifle unloaded, barrel aimed futilely at the endless steppe of the sky?

She allowed herself to be assisted to the counter, where a lady in a polka-dot blouse looked at her with practised disgust and said: Yes, can I help you?

Whereupon Bubby Stern explained, in her thick English, that she had come to visit her son.

The guard and the lady exchanged grimaces.

This is not the normal situation, Bubby Stern said. She spoke slowly, breathing heavily between words. This is not the time for the visitors to come.

Yes, the guard said.

The lady looked at him. Frowned.

The lady explained that what Bubby Stern had come for was impossible. She listed the set visiting days. She noted the complex procedures that taking advantage of those visiting days required.

Bubby Stern waved a dismissive hand and turned so she could look the guard in the eye. She said: You understand. I am old and I need to see my son. I have come from long way to see my son.

She had no colour in her cheeks, except smears of rouge applied so crudely you could see the streaks of her fingers.

Who would say no to this old woman with her thick ankles and awkward white plastic pumps, with her matching blue skirt-and-blazer suit, with her hollow haunted eyes and lipstick-flecked teeth? The guard was sent scurrying into the bowels of the building, ostensibly to pick up the appropriate forms, though no one was going to fill out any forms; there should be no record of accidental kindness, of spontaneous shifts in the routine, let the paperwork only reflect the way things were supposed to be done, not the clickety-clackety sound of an old woman's unsteady gait as she proceeds down a dark long corridor on the way to see her mad, incarcerated child.

In time the guard returned, nodded to the woman at the front desk, who had spent the minutes urgently whispering on the phone, seemingly intent on keeping busy so she would not have to contemplate the countenance of the waiting Bubby Stern.

Or she really was busy, this visit being absolutely extraordinary; never done before, never to reoccur under any circumstances.

They led her, two guards, one black, one white, both middle-aged men with well-built, slightly stooped bodies that at once hid their bulging torsos and suggested a ceiling lower than the low ceiling pressing down above them.

Bubby Stern kept her eyes straight ahead, did not look up. The second door swung shut behind them. Her heart beat. Her arthritic fingers made fists. Her cheeks paled, the rouge like fresh wounds.

They shuffled down a narrow hallway. Locked doors were opened by a giant ring of keys. Bubby Stern was not surprised by the number of locked doors. She breathed regularly through her nose, felt her nostrils flaring as she inhaled. The smell of trapped air and boiled meat and urine disinfectant was not altogether unfamiliar—a smell from the past, from the old country; claustrophobic reek of the locked away, those perpetually housed in the permanence of temporary accommodation.

They entered a chamber with rows of benches along the walls, rings in the concrete—the room looked like a cross between a stable and a classroom. The door behind them swung shut. For the first time Bubby

Stern allowed herself to breathe heavily through her mouth.

The white guard, balding and sallow, spoke into his radio, received an unintelligible reply of static and feedback.

They're bringing him down now, he said.

The black guard took his hands out of his pockets. He smiled at Bubby Stern, then abruptly grimaced and turned away.

The door on the other side of the room opened. They led him in, two more guards. Now the long space seemed crowded, with the four guards and the one inmate—patient—and the visitor. Everyone moved very slowly, as if hypnotized. Bubby Stern wanted to take some decisive action, a slap or a kiss or a hysterical outburst, ears ringing and sharp nails clawing. How could he, her son, be here? And what portion of his fortune did Bubby Stern pass down to him, cause him to inherit?

They brought him across the room, toward her. He was not manacled or otherwise restrained, but he walked slowly, allowing himself to be herded the way cattle are led to pasture. He stood in front of her without speaking. Then grinned, showing missing teeth. A guard put a gloved hand on his shoulder, pushed down. He sat on the bench. Bubby Stern lowered herself slowly. They faced each other like lovers or soulmates or best friends. Bubby Stern felt a sudden sharp pain in her neck, the muscles objecting to the angle of her head. She ignored this pain, determined to relish her waning flexibility; in a year or two her neck would be a stiff column. The guards retreated to the far corner, produced crumpled packs of cigarettes out of creased beige uniform trousers. They stuck the cigarettes in their mouths but did not light them.

Bubby Stern opened her purse and, after some rummaging, extracted a red-and-white striped mint. She held the candy out to him. He plucked it out of her hand without touching her palm. He unwrapped the mint and put it in his grinning mouth. He closed his eyes. Faint red rash like freckles across his cheeks. Sucked on the mint.

Mmmm! he said.

You're so skinny, Bubby Stern said.

When Bubby Stern was a young girl, everyone in the shtetl called her Knish after the savoury stuffed pastry, eaten only on rare occasions because hers was a mean town, mean in the sense that it had few luxuries or amenities, though the young Knish knew joy there, perhaps for the first and last time. The town was split between the Jews and Catholics, both sides dirt poor, each side adept at ignoring the other except when business was to be conducted. The Jews were experts at tailoring, moneylending and crafting all kinds of intricate but useless objects. The Catholics did the farming, the bricklaying, exchanged a cow and five sacks of potatoes for a set of gold candlesticks decorated with the symbol of their god's son's crucifixion by the fine steady hand of Yacham, the goldsmith.

The Jews could not own land, but it was not something young Knish concerned herself with. The terrible stories, the slaughters and rapes, were whispered and rumoured and even warded off with fervent pledges of devotion to the one god of her people, but no such event had taken place in Knish's young life, and indeed nobody thought it likely, given the current climate of what could be described as near calm, near interdependence. Where would the Catholics be without the canny Jews? Where would the Jews be without the brawny Catholics?

In the end it did go bad, and most did die, including the young Knish's parents and brothers and sisters and almost all of the Jewish residents of their hardscrabble town on the edge of a forest soon to be full of blood dripping off branches.

Bubby Stern is eight, and it is bath day. Once every two weeks the women go to the bath, naturally not every woman in the town at the same time, there is a very elaborate system, but it works out to one hot bath every two weeks—unless of course the woman is bleeding between the legs, untouchable, there is a special bath for her, but Knish has only the vaguest notion of what goes on between the legs in the special bath.

Young Knish is very much a fan of the bathhouse, where the children run and splash and squirm and cry with exaggerated fervour when they get the tiniest drop of soap in a bright eye.

The bathhouse, the bathhouse, the bathhouse, Knish

sings, skipping down the dirt street ahead of her mother and grandmother, pulling along her four-year-old sister, who plunges forward with plump abandon. She too sings: *Badhouse, badhouse.*

Of course, all this takes place in another world, another time, another language, one not quite dead to us. It is a language that Bubby Stern never hears on *Talk Talk Talk!* or even the late night *Wow! It's Live!* though the producers and writers and hosts and guests all seem to be Jewish. The language is heard only at the Golden Age where she plays cards with Marlyss and all around them come the ancient peasant rumblings.

Bathhouse! Bathhouse!
Badhouse! Badhouse!

It was a special trip to the bathhouse. The next day, Friday, the day before the Sabbath, would be the day that the Great Rabbi would arrive from the Great Yeshiva in some giant foreign distant place that Knish had never seen but often imagined. It was, she knew, a city of Jews, a place of learning and elegance. Imagine! A whole CITY of Jews! Imagine! The Great Rabbi coming here. Here! The entire town was preparing. The men were in fervent prayer and discussion of the proper greetings and honours to be bestowed. The women decorated challah covers with beads and prepared an elaborate feast to be served cold after the service on the Sabbath day. The Great Rabbi was coming! This was no ordinary bath day. The shtetl was already scrubbed clean, as clean as a mean little town with dirt everywhere could be. Now it was time for the women to take the soap to their little ones as if they were nothing more than floors and walls and kiddush cups.

Despite all the excitement, little Knish could not stop thinking about the dream she kept having. In the dream, she was standing in a green field. The field was lush and hot, the grasses swaying. In the dream, Knish wore a white dress that set off her dark brown hair and wide hazel eyes, the pale of her skin pressing tight against the soft fabric so that even she, the wearer, could not tell where the dress left off and her skin began. The dress was the softest thing Knish had ever felt, softer than her mother's touch, softer than the tender shoots of grass trampled under her delicate bare feet. Young Knish stood there all night, in the dream, smiling like Yakovitch the *meshugana* who stood in the corner of the market and sucked his one tooth, hooting and grabbing as the children darted past him. Yakovitch never stopped smiling. Perhaps that was why the dream was so disturbing? It was the smile, the smile plastered on her face, a wide empty grin of mad desire.

Knish woke up terrified, a damp sweat coating her. Ignoring the whimpers of her sleeping sister, she pushed the coarse cover off and looked down, relieved to find she was not still wearing the clinging white ethereal dress, but her grey shift gone soft with the endless number of times it had been washed and wrung out to dry, her nightdress, her only nightdress, smelling of wind and sun, smelling of a little girl sweating through a bad dream of summer.

She told no one about the dream.

In the bathhouse, they stripped naked. Little Knish giggled as the water tickled.

Stop that, snapped her mother. She thrust a rough sponge and a mass of soap at her. Wash your sister.

The women, even today, took some time out of their labours to relax, ignoring the children and pouring ladlefuls of warm water over each other's shoulders as they gossiped:

The Great Rabbi will be bringing with him many young men.

Ah, young men.

Disgusting creatures.

Godly men, Knish's mother reminded the group. Men of god.

Yentach made a face.

Everybody laughed and Knish did not understand what was so funny.

Furious at being left out of the joke, she held her sister firmly and brutally scrubbed at her chest. Her sister screamed.

Stop that, Knish's mother said, not even looking over. Do under her arms.

Knish wanted to hear what her mother and the other women with their heavy breasts and dark patches of fur between their thighs were saying, but there was so much laughter and her sister was whining and splashing, she couldn't hear anything.

She pinched her sister hard. Her sister started to cry, tried to slip out of Knish's grasp. Ended up with soap in her eyes.

Quiet, you, Knish hissed.

Her sister cried louder.

Quiet!

All at once a bucket of water doused both their cries.

Mama stood over them, shaking her head.

The Great Rabbi is coming, and you two! Carrying on!

Bath time was over.

The Catholics were suspicious of the bathhouse, and often accused the Jews of doing unnatural and even supernatural things in the large building. The fervour of these accusations came and went, depending on how many of the Catholics died of whatever plague was claiming victims that particular season. The Jews, too, died, though in much cleaner smaller numbers, which clearly suggested some unnatural congress with a foreign god—an unholy unwillingness to share with the Catholics the burden of man's fall from grace.

Actually, the Catholics had a whole day set aside for them to come and use the bathhouse, as custom decreed, but, again as custom decreed, only a few ever came and rarely without being mocked by their farmer peers: Goin' Yid? went the vodka-tinged cry, yellow teeth protruding in a crooked leer.

Many of the Jews noted that it was a waste to have the bathhouse sit empty that day, it already sat empty the entire Sabbath, but the practice was never altered. It was generally assumed that the availability of the bathhouse was one of the things that prevented Catholic anger against the Jews from becoming vengeful.

Perhaps there was something else at work, some other unknowable shift governing the coming years, a dark rift in the sky like lightning before a storm?

The day passed in games and housework, the house smelled of challah and soup, and Knish, clean, revived, pretended to forget her dream. She spent her time contemplating what revenge she might enact on her sister for making trouble in the bathhouse the day before the arrival of the Great Rabbi from the great city of Jews so far away.

That night, exhausted after performing Mama's endless litany of chores, she fell asleep with her sister's warm skinny body pressed against her in the narrow bed. She dreamed, again, of the gorgeous green field, and the white dress, and the wind gently caressing her long brown hair. At first it was a pleasant dream. Then, as if standing outside herself, Knish noticed the stricken smile, the red wax of her lips. She was a statue, unable to move or change expression. But did she want to move? Her bare feet, rooted to the soft grass, the soles purring. Knish felt alive in the dream. More alive than she had ever felt before. As Knish dreamed, she lay prone, not tossing and turning. The dream had incapacitated her, an invitation to some distant horrible place she could not decline.

On the Sabbath morning, Knish put on her yontef dress and helped her sister do the same. Gently, she brushed her sister's hair, smoothing down the fat curls with a wet palm. Then she combed her own long dark brown hair, even letting her sister help.

Do you know who is going to be in the *shul* today? she asked her sister.

Yeth.

You baby, you don't know.

Yeth, I do know.

Do you know everything?

No!

Why don't you know everything?

Only *Hashem* knows everyfing!

Who is coming to the *shul* today?

De rebee!

The rabbi is always at the *shul*.

No! De GREAD Rebee!

Ah, the Great Rabbi.

Yeth.

And why is the Great Rabbi GREAT?

Bedause, bedause, the Gread Rebee is gread bedause he comes from FAR AWAY!

My, you are a clever little girl.

No!

You're not a clever little girl?

No!

No?

Not liddle.

The two children fell silent for a bit, listening to their mother yelling and sighing and prodding their brothers to action.

Listen, Knish finally said.

Yeth?

Why does the Great Rabbi come here today?

I know! I know!

So tell me.

To bring us, dhe, dhe, dhe Mesheyach!

The young Bubby Stern put down her comb and pulled her sister to her. Do you know what the Mesheyach is?

Knish's sister buried her face in Knish's lap.

The synagogue was crowded like it had never been. The old building burst with the shtetl's residents, every man, woman and child, the ancient and the newborns, the sick, the stupid, the brilliant, the town Communist, the town Zionist and the town drunk. The men were like a flock of ravens in their long black coats and black pointy hats, their beaks dipping back and forth as they fervently prayed. The women, in the screened room to the left, looked on proudly: You see Chaim's hat? That fur around the edge, I made that special for today, god provides for us, to send us the Great Rabbi and fur for Chaim's hat all at once!

The huge room stank of sweat and the pages of ancient books and the passion of proximity to the shtetl rabbi and the Great Rabbi and even, many believed, to the Messiah himself, who might at any time slip in among them to test their devotion and, if he likes what he sees? Who knows? Who knows? It was too much to contemplate. The women fainted and the men raised their arms to heaven, reaching for the redemption and peace all men pretend to long for. A hand over a beating heart, a woosh of sudden hot breath, eyes closed, just you and god, no words, no world.

Knish wandered through the scene, her big eyes sunk against her pale cheeks as she scampered with the other children through the rows of davening men— their fathers—then out into the hallway and down into the adjoining room where their mothers would grab them, smooth their hair down, pull them onto their laps and tell them to be still. But they would remain for only a minute or two before squirming off and, once again, rushing out into the hall.

On a normal Sabbath, Knish would expect her father to scoop her up and hold her high above him as he muttered a prayer, his favourite little girl aloft and that much nearer to the blessings of god. But today her papa ignored her. Knish was glad that he did not pull her to him, raise her up to the naked glance of god. Would her father ever touch her again, if he knew where her dreams had taken her? Where she had been? Where *had* she been? Knish knew that she had been singled out for some horrible pollution, some fate far worse than merciful death and a lengthy tenure in the heavens above at the side of the one true god who watched over all the Jews. A thrill to her loins, a hot feeling in her gut—this, more than anything, was what the dream gave her. The dream was a sin; damningly intoxicating, bearing a solitude that could no more be revealed than forgotten. And yet she was just a little girl, free to run back and forth while others saw to it that she received the necessary benedictions and prayers.

She paused for a minute amongst the men, contemplated her older brothers Yossi and Chaim, twelve and fourteen respectively. At that age they were expected to pray amongst the men, and, she thought contemptuously, they acted like they were already men—though they were still just boys. In a few years Knish also would be expected to comport herself as an adult, sit with her mother in the back room and contribute her silent exhortations while the men loudly sought a good word, a sign, a blessing, praying always praying, always ignoring god's mute response. Knish herself ignored the fact that soon she would be too old to scamper through the halls and rows of praying men, in and out of her mama's wide soft lap.

She wanted to tell her best friend Etel about her dream, but she could not.

Did you hear? Etel whispered to her. They were in their favourite spot—a dark closet holding the mops and brooms used to clean the sanctuary.

What? Knish demanded.

After Musaf, the Great Rabbi will say a special prayer for the children. We're all to gather together at the ark.

All the children?

All the children. Etel clasped her friend's arm. I want to be in the front, she whispered, as if afraid god might overhear this desire, a sin, surely, though what kind and why, she did not know.

Etel didn't say it, but she was secretly hoping to be noticed by one of the serious young men who had joined the Great Rabbi on his journey. Of course it was true, as her mother told her, she was too young to marry. But perhaps they would notice her all the same, speak to her father—a holy man himself, the shtetl butcher, the shochet!—and make arrangements to come back. In a year or two or three, Etel thought ruefully, contemplating the loose fabric hanging over her chest. But it could be! It could be! The Great Rabbi presiding over my *chuppa!* God forgive her these thoughts, but couldn't it be?

Isn't it exciting! Etel cried, throwing her arms around her friend.

Knish pushed her away.

Late in the afternoon, the announcement was made: all children were to come forward for the Rabbi's blessing. The Jews of the shtetl cast about for their young ones. This, more than anything, was why they carried on, why they worked till they hurt, why they turned the other cheek to Christian taunting and threats, why they prayed until they fell down exhausted—so that their children could have a better life, grow up to be rabbis or the wives of rabbis, all living comfortably in the great city of Jewish learning and refinement. My life is already over, Knish's father the tailor often told his customers when they asked about his children, but theirs, god willing, is just beginning.

It was a time of calm, of dirt poor prosperity, of

grudging ignorant tolerance and neverending grunting toil.

Knish's father made sure that all his children had gathered—he even pushed fourteen-year-old Chaim forward, much to his son's embarrassment, for was he not a bar mitzvah, a man? But let him take the blessing, what harm could it do. Only the girl missing, his elder daughter, his favourite; just like her, he thought, to be causing trouble on this day of all days!

He quickly strode through the sanctuary, calling her name. When he did not find her, he moved out into the hall. It was empty. He stood breathing, listening to the fathers shoving their children forward, some already beseeching the Rabbi to begin, begin this most important brucha of all, please, begin, begin before the children wander off or are uprooted from their position at the front where the Rabbi is most likely to notice them and grant them special favour, begin before the Christians come and bar the doors and set fire to the walls and burn them to ashes, all, of course, according to god's will and wisdom.

Papa heard a faint sobbing. He strode down the hall, threw open the closet door. And there was his daughter, her nose running all over her yontef dress. He pulled her hard from the closet and slapped her face.

The Great Rabbi comes just once. Just once in a lifetime, he hissed. She fought him, but he dragged her down the hall. His rage was a terror: the Rabbi would notice his daughter's bad behaviour, god would not find favour with his eldest girl. Little Knish knew the truth: her father's fear now would be a greater torment later, magnified six million times in the eyes of god, who punished not only the wicked Haman but also his wife and his sons and his relatives, until there was no trace of his roots left and the Jews lived in peace in Persia for five hundred years.

The Great Rabbi had not yet appeared to do the prayer. He was huddled with his advisers, making sure that the exact words, the perfect brucha, could be uttered over the heads of these little children, the future of the Diaspora Hebrews. Perhaps, perhaps, and even he dared not think it, but perhaps the messiah—*the Mesheyach!*—could even be among them, for did not god love and honour the holy poor above all his minions in the kingdom?

Knish remembers Papa roughly wiping her face with his handkerchief. She remembers being shoved through everyone and right up to the front, all the children around her pushing and pulling and pinching, prodding for position, desperate to catch just a little extra of the Rabbi's attention, to be that much closer to god's blessing, which comes, after all, only once in a lifetime. Knish remembers slowly reciting in her mind the names of the town's children—first her brothers and sisters, and then her friends, then the others, those too young to be her friends, or too old, or too, god forgive, ugly and stupid. But it didn't work. She felt her loins pulsing, her face turning a revealing pink.

The Great Rabbi emerged from his huddle and faced the gathered children. His lips pursed with passion. He spoke directly to god on behalf of these poor ragged children living on the edge of nowhere, on the edge of a poor ragged world. Knish could not move. As in the dream, all around her was the field of grass, every single swaying blade eliciting a sensual shudder. Suddenly the Great Rabbi loomed over her, boring into the depths of her dream. He snapped his eyes closed. Too late. He saw it. The abomination: Desire. God's purity turned perverted premonition by the mind of a little girl. Knish screamed. The Great Rabbi had recognized her horrible vision. He saw it too. In recognition, it became inevitable. God's will. A revelation. A dark cloud came over the *shul* sanctuary, night settling too early. The Great Rabbi cried out and fainted.

That must have been very disturbing. Can you tell me how it made you feel?

Why should it bother me? Why should I be afraid, now, of death or of anything?

Are we getting to the root of the problem with this sort of approach?

The root! What for! You think there are roots?

Bubby Stern's analyst sighs. He scratches the skin under his beard. In another life he might have been a rabbi, a religious man, a commentator on the Torah. In another life at another time, he might have been something else, something better or bigger or truer.

Why come here, if there are no roots to explore?

What do you care? My son pays, no?

You think I do this for your money?

I'm an old woman, doctor, but you don't have to yell. The heart is going, but the hearing is still good.

Why did you tell me about this?

Doctor, I'm alone. A widow. I had two brothers and a sister. Dead. Kaput. Ashes, smoke, maybe even soap. I have seen things. I have dreams—what would you do? You want I should kill myself, throw myself maybe off a bridge, maybe?

No, I only meant—if we could go further into it, the experience.

I've gone far enough, doctor.

Bubby Stern's analyst resists the urge to stroke his beard. He finds it is often interpreted as an erotic gesture. He saves those for Temple. Suffering siren, she'll be the end of him, he'll lose his licence because of that one. So what? The doctor adjusts his trousers. It's worth it. Anything to get his mind off this old crone. The same thing every week. Her dead relatives, the son that married a convert and never visits, the son that married the shiksa and went crazy.

Last week, he finally says, the dream about the operations. This week, the dream about the dream. What is the common denominator?

Bubby Stern nods. Please, go on.

Guilt, the analyst pronounces triumphantly, watching Bubby Stern's shrivelled face. Guilt! he says, as if this was the first time he presented her with this idea. Is the breakthrough imminent? Or, just as beneficial, the breakdown? Guilt, he hisses. You blame yourself, of course.

Bubby Stern nods her head in agreement. So tell me, doctor. What did I do wrong?

Please, Mrs. Stern—we've talked about this, gone over it, over and over it. Perhaps your sense of abandonment goes deeper, back to when you were a little girl.

I was fourteen when I left. I was an outcast, I had to leave. My parents sent me away. It saved my life. A few months later they slaughtered everyone. Like pigs.

Yes, exactly. This profound dream you purportedly had as a little girl, it evokes deep anguish, fear, guilt. You've lived in guilt all your life, and still today you seek to—

Please, doctor, don't tell me about fear. What can you tell me about fear? When they sent us to the frozen lands? When we ran away to cross the border and they shot Chaya? When we waited six months in a camp to find out if they would send us across the ocean to a country where we'd never been, where almost no one spoke our language, where they didn't want us, and we didn't even know that all our family was dead and we would never see them again, no matter where we went? So why should I be afraid now?

But that's what you are. You're afraid. You're terrified. And your fear drives everyone away from you. You smother them with your denial of your guilt. You consume them.

Bubby Stern watches the credits roll. She sighs. What's on next? Shuffles to the kitchen to make herself a cup of tea.

———

It's 5:38 and Bubby Stern is watching *Roundup with Paul Fitzwillis*. In the last four days she has left precisely twenty-three messages for her older son and his wife the convert. None have been returned.

The doorbell rings. Then a knock. Bubby Stern starts, forgetting that her neck doesn't turn so much. The fossilized muscles grate.

Knock knock on the door, Bubby Stern's heart pounding. Will it be them again, with their uniforms and questions? Mrs. Stern, mother of Cal Stern? You'd better have a seat . . . We're sorry to inform you . . .

No, she can't go through that again.

Ma? Ma?

Bubby Stern hooks a hand on her neck and freezes. Is it him, the younger?

Ma? Ma?

No, of course not. Bubby Stern hoists herself off the old couch. At the front door, she works the locks with frail fingers.

The door swings open.

Ma!

She's stiff in Maury's arms.

She steps back, surveys him, her elder son. The one who made good for himself, the one she always claimed to be proud of. He's wearing a dirty suit without a tie. His curly salt-and-pepper hair is matted. He gets his hair from his father. He smells like a Howard Johnson's restaurant; Bubby Stern sometimes goes, to treat herself, takes a cab, takes Marlyss.

He's gaunt, his belly an empty thing, hanging under his stained white shirt like a burst balloon.

Ma!

She can't bear it. It's too much for an old woman all alone.

My son, she murmurs. Maury.

They embrace again, her nose against the lapel of his jacket, the scent is of perspiration and grease, she'll forgive him, what choice does she have? Let that nosy Applebaum woman across the street have a good look at this!

They go inside. In the dusk, her small house seems neither here nor there—not the dim cozy retreat hiding behind night's cloak or the bright cheery domicile for a Jewish grandmother with activities and hobbies, passions and interests, the sun dappling along the wall of a kitchen smelling of sugar cookies and blintzes.

They stand awkwardly in the gloomy living room as Paul Fitzwillis sums up the day's current events. *Back to you Leslie.*

They both speak at once.

Ma—I—

Maury—

Ma—I have to tell you—

Bubby Stern's voice is the potent one, a peasant voice burdened by survival.

No. Wait. It's not so important. Not now. You're so skinny. Since when did you stop eating? Listen, Maury, listen to your mama. You go upstairs, you take a bath, you put on that nice purple sweatsuit I bought you, you forgot it here last time you visited, what was that, two years ago?

Ma—

No, never mind, you put on that sweatsuit, it's in the closet in the guest room, go Maury, go get yourself cleaned up, I'll make us something, if I had known you were coming, you could have called—

Ma—

Never mind, never mind, of course god knows you're always welcome. Bubby Stern moves to the kitchen, opens the refrigerator, begins to pull out its guts. Let's see, what can I make—

Ma—

Go, go, listen to your mama, go take your bath.

Maury stands mute, looking at his mother. He can see his own reflection in the mirrored plaque hanging on the wall. They got it for her birthday, five years back, had it made special. *Bubby Stern's Kitchen,* it says in pink letters. He kisses her on a doughy cheek. Goes upstairs to clean up.

In an hour, Bubby Stern has chicken soup, kreplach, she has the greasy oblong meatballs—klops, Maury's favourite—she has the coarse grainy kasha, she has a pot of boiled potatoes, she has—her one concession to modern cuisine—a plate of iceberg lettuce and grated carrot doused in bright orange syrupy dressing. Where did it all come from? Bubby Stern believes in being prepared. Keep rows of kreplach frozen and at the ready, a pot of chicken soup, who doesn't have a bissle chicken soup in their fridge?

Bubby Stern's seen the way it's done, watched the bubbies on TV, big loud women who love to pinch their flinching flock of grandchildren then offer them hard candies from a crystal bowl. She pours Maury a bowlful of soup, the thick kreplach dumplings bobbing against each other and slowly rising to the surface, floating on a greasy sheen of translucent gold fat, eat, here, nah, eat, Bubby Stern says, putting the bowl in front of him.

She watches carefully, waiting for him to pick up the spoon.

Ma? he says, his voice strained.

She turns to the old white gas stove. Eat now, she says, not unkindly. Eat. One by one, she fishes chunks of soft potato out of boiling water.

She wants to tell him that Temple's analyst was right, she's been afraid all her life. Guilt as a kind of fear. And now it's too late. Passed on to her children, it has become something else, something unconquerable, inoperable, indescribable. And does Maury have it too? Will he also suffer from what went on in the nightmares of a little girl, in the dark cold forests, in the sprawling steppes of the hinterlands, in the squalid calm spring of the displaced persons' camp? He will. She knows he will. Why does my son come to me now, when it's too late? He has always feigned optimism, ignorance. But something has changed, Bubby Stern can see that now, just looking at him, his hair everywhere like a wild man, his bones showing through his face. Why come to me now? What's done is done, she wants to say. My analyst— Bah, it's all garbage. She doesn't have an analyst. None of it means a thing. So you make things up. That's the way it's done. How else, otherwise, does one go on?

Bubby Stern makes them both instant coffee. She sits at the table, turned so she can face him despite her rigid neck.

It's getting worse, he notes.

Bubby Stern stares at him.

Your neck, Maury continues. You're seeing your doctor?

What does the doctor know? Pills for this, pills for that, pills for the pills. What does the doctor do but give me pills?

Ma. C'mon. Those pills are to help you. Maury looks down into the brown of his instant coffee. Ma, he says, I came here because—Ma—something's wrong with Danny. He's in the hospital.

Oh my got. Oh my got. What is it? Is it that cancer? Cancer on the brain, like I saw on television with the shaved heads? Got forbid.

No, Ma—

Her thick hand clutches her breast. Got in heaven, my grandchild, my only grandchild.

Ma, please, don't get emotional. Everything is—

Yes, yes, we can't get emotional. We can't even pick up the phone and call, so why would we get emotional?

He's in a coma, Ma. You understand me? A coma?

He hit his head? He's hit his head and now he won't wake up?

Something like that, Ma. I don't—he hit his head.

Oh my got. This is what happens. This is what happens.

What are you talking about? Ma? What do you mean?

Maury, in the morning, we'll go to him.

No, Ma, it's—

She watches him, waiting while he blows on his already cold coffee with ripe middle-aged lips. He has his father's lips.

I've left Becky.

Now? Your wife? At a time like this?

I know, Ma. I know. But I had to. It's . . . him. It's like he's still around, you know. He's waiting for me. So he can—I don't know, Ma. I don't know.

He's your brother, Maury. Your only brother. *Cal.* Not some *him.*

I know, Ma.

You can't change it.

Ma, I know. You think I don't know?

Blood, Maury, it's in the blood.

Ma! Stop it! It's enough already.

He's still alive, Maury.

He is?

I'm his mother. I'm both of your mothers. You feel it. When they killed my parents I was thousands of miles away, pregnant with you, I was in the mines—but I felt it, Maury, you think I didn't feel it?

No, Ma, of course—

When you were just babies, you and your brother once ran away. Do you remember that? You were looking for me. I was visiting with my cousin Marlyss. We were frantic. We didn't know what to do. The police were searching everywhere. Your father—got rest his soul—searched everywhere, like a madman. I waited at my cousin's apartment for news. Then, a knock on the door. Who can that be? I said. We opened the door to the apartment and there the two of you were. Frozen like snowmen. But there you were, got knows how you found me.

In the morning, before he wakes up, she stands in the living room holding the book her elder son wrote. She keeps it in the back of a closet stuffed with mothballs and old dresses. She's never liked it. It was the book that made him famous. It was a best-seller, she mentions it when anyone asks after her family. My boy the author—that book of his—they're still buying it, after all these years, can you believe it? But even as she speaks she feels the hollow truth behind the words. Maury's book, she never read it. There's something wrong about it, a crudeness, a sense of disconnection between who she knows her son to be and the way the book, well, not exactly looks, but *feels*. There he is on the cover, a young man in a pink tuxedo suit, smiling like some kind of shyster used-car salesman. The words in great big bright bubble letters: GET WITH THE PROGRAM! What kind of book is this, Bubby

Stern remembers thinking. A book should be dignified. A book should be—never mind, that was the year it all started, anyway, the year Maury's brother—

She knew the book was no good from the beginning. It was the younger one she thought might have been a writer, an artist. She could never bring herself to read it. She thinks of it as something unnatural. Why does she keep the book? She'll burn it. The book is a portent, a figment, an apparition, a lie come true. She should show it to someone, just to prove to herself that it really exists. Whom could she show it to? She doesn't want Maury to see it. She hides it behind a hat she hasn't worn in twelve years, the hat she plans to wear to Danny's bar mitzvah. What if my only grandson dies? she thinks. After everything else, this too?

Maury stands on the doorstep.

You sure you'll be all right?

Bubby Stern shrugs.

How's Etie? Maury looks at his feet as he talks.

Dead.

And Shertl?

Gone.

And Rubie?

Passed away.

What about your cousin? Marlyss?

She's in the Golden Age home. We play cards sometimes.

Tell her I said hello.

She kisses his cheek, leaves a mark.

Bubby Stern left them once. Her boys. Her husband. Maybe it was for a week, or a month, or half a year.

It could have been just a weekend.

She imagines herself getting off the bus, going directly to the hospital, embracing her daughter-in-law and, with that act, finally reconciling herself to Becky's goyishe beauty, her straight blonde hair, thin lips and tiny tits, just another burden god has chosen for her to bear. She sees herself succouring the infirm Danny, eyes rolling in his coma haze, sweat burning off his smooth brow. He's sweating, she'll say to her daughter-in-law, it's good, he's sweating it out. It isn't a fever, Bubby Stern, Becky will snap. Bubby Stern will stand, primly, beside her supine grandson's bed.

She'll be like Temple: stalwart in her convictions, perplexed by the way things never seem to turn out right, escapee from destruction, star of the show.

She left him once, her husband who died of a heart attack at thirty-nine. She went to stay with her cousin Marlyss. Marlyss was a wild girl at the time, a scandal who lived in a low-rise downtown. The apartment had the kind of faded glamour appropriate to leaving your husband—carpeted elevators and a dead fern in the lobby next to the ashtray. The smell of perfume and stale smoke.

Why leave him, after everything they had gone through together?

But she did. She threw her tattered dresses in a suitcase that came all the way from the old country. She marched off to the bus stop, took the 7C downtown to Marlyss's gloomy apartment with its dust and reverberating silences and thick red curtains. And it was winter, too, cold, the snow swirling in crystal crumbles.

It was because her husband, who had seen all the horrors the world had to offer, who had worked in the mines, who had lived through the most desperate times, refused to go to shul. It was because her husband no longer believed in god.

Every weekend, every major or minor holiday, Bubby Stern would prod him: It's the Sabbath. Why not daven for an hour or two? What harm will it do?

She remembered her father, a man in a black suit disappearing into the rows of men in black suits.

And look what god gave them, her husband pointed out.

Never mind, she screamed. Never mind.

She put her hands over her ears, and her husband—a simple man, a tailor—made no attempt to speak again.

And late that night, after she had consented to be used the way a man must use a woman, she allowed him to hold her and she whispered in his ear: for the children, for the children.

He pushed her away and fell asleep.

So Bubby Stern left him, refusing to live with a man who did not believe in god. Never mind the children, let him take care of the children, for a change, for once, if he was sure he knew everything, let his godless hands cook for them and wipe their spills and smooth their hair as they fall asleep at night. Let him do all that and then tell me there is no god.

But her husband was adamant. He had seven reasons, he kept saying, one for every day of the week. Seven brothers and sisters burned like diseased cattle.

Did he send the kids to find their mother?

Or did they just show up one day, overcome by the awesome loneliness of their own little lives?

They came, their faces frozen, their mitts stiff with ice, the little one—not so little any more—hot in the crotch where he had wet himself.

Soon after, Bubby Stern went back to her husband.

Something happened that day or week or month or year, and Bubby Stern was never again the wife or mother she had been. She didn't light the candles Friday night after serving the chicken soup and kreplach and lochshen and sweet eggy challah. She never again told god's stories, the stories her father used to tell her. She watched her programs and she dreamed of giving away all her secrets, whispering them into a stranger's hired ear.

Bubby Stern takes the bus to a city three and a half hours away. She wonders if she will be too late, if the boy will die. She wonders if she will ever again have the strength to say it, the kaddish, god's hymn to the dead.

Twelve years old.

Danny is writing a program, learning himself a new language. He's amazed at the clarity, the way grammar turns one thing into another:

```
<this>=<that>
```

One thing. Then another. Feelings into words. The same only different. Better. Created and, so, controlled. Danny wants to do the same to himself: create, reinvent, re-imagine. Flesh and blood, what can be erased, what can be adjusted. Stops. Thinks about it. Types:

```
<body>
<text>
<ref= now>
<img="/images/boy?">
(width=" " height=" ")
<text> "invisible (no text)"
<this>=<that> (what if?)
<ref=
```

This equals that? Boy? Invisible, disappearing, reborn into a new language delineating a new world. Could

be anything. Everything. What does he want? Nothing.
Start over. Starts over.

As he works, he leans closer to the screen, dangles
his body over the keyboard, forgets he even has a body.
He breathes steadily, thinks of—not nothing, but of the
murky otherworld he is creating, a world he knows
well: a no thing; a someday that will exist simulta-
neously as image and event, elusive depiction of a connection between multiple reals that never happened.

Didn't they happen?

Where did his father go? Where did those lost
weeks go, when Danny wasted away in a coma more
real than anything he had ever known?

Until now. This new hobby of his. This ordered
chaos:

```
<ref=then
<img="/images/boy">
```

—not a *boy*—

```
<img="/images/man">
```

—*no*—

```
<text> "being again, in between, wolf boy, man-
wolf, baby body TV daddy deadly"
<this>=<gone; down; back; begin being again;
no>
<img="/images/???">
<ref=
```

He interprets and intercepts, takes steps forward
that only serve to pull him back past the interlocking
complexities of creating something from nothing.

```
= no thing>
```

Danny lurches out of the screen. His stomach distends, contracts. Sweat on his brow. Walls and ceiling press in. Danny throws his arms out—to steady his balance or keep from being crushed. Air swirls through and out of him. Cheeks hollowing as he gasps. It lasts forever—a few moments. Miniature relapse, tornado comas he tells no one about.

When it ebbs, he stands. His legs, soft under him.

He wants to keep working. If he can put it on the screen, he can make it real. If he can make it real, he can make it go away. Erase. Delete. Would you like to save this file before shutdown? No. *No.*

He gropes forward, pulls at the blind, which curls up into itself. Afternoon. Sun bright through the window. He can see the blue sky, white clouds and, underneath, the houses extending in rows, each house with its lawn going green, awaiting the eager attentions of a thousand different moms and dads.

His mother in the garden. Digging with a spade.

His father disappeared, then returned, then disappeared again.

Danny was in a coma, woke up to the reek of Bubby Stern's thick perfume, the feel of her gnarled hands encircling his soft ones.

The months after he got out of the hospital were the worst ones. There was no yelling or screaming the way parents who are splitting up on TV yell and scream and carry on. Maury brought in the computer—stolid in cardboard and styrofoam like some frozen Arctic fossil. Maury said, Well, here, son.

Danny slams his fist down on the keyboard.

A present from his father. The monitor on his desk, bulbous and alien in the bedroom. His father is gone. Has been for the better part of two years. During that time the computer sat in the bedroom, staring at Danny. Danny stared back. Didn't touch the thing.

So what changed?

A charge when he fingered the power button that first time. Danny felt it, some surge of energy, released yearning. It was there all along, he suddenly knew, was in him—with him—all along. Just waiting to be turned on. He began to teach himself how to recreate it. The past. The unknown. What happened without happening. What he fears—and needs—more than anything.

He wipes the sweat from his forehead with the sleeve of his sweatshirt. Shivers. It's bright in the bedroom. Why did he open the blind? Pulls it down. But with the gloom his dizziness returns, lured into the open by the shadows, soft footsteps muted by the furious pumping of his heart and the steady whirr of the computer's hum. He stumbles to the bed, buries his face in his pillow. He shuts his eyes. The half-grey darkness. Familiar swell into which he falls. His breath rushing past him.

Not even a teenager, Danny is taller than either of his parents. Where does he get it from? Becky, short-hunched over the earth, works her shovel in the backyard. Early spring, the weeds just starting to push up. She feels it under her skin. When you're pregnant, she thinks, they say your skin glows. Becky isn't pregnant. She thinks she feels it anyway, torpid, sluggish, inevitable. She has no intention of starting again or over. In fact, she tells herself, I have no intentions at all.

She's not like Maury. She doesn't need to search for what isn't there. And who is he kidding anyway? If he wants to forget his family and career, run off to some banana republic to play hero, Becky isn't going to stop him. Right up until he left, she thought it was just a phase, this thing with his brother something he needed to work out. Part of a mid-life crisis, Becky thinks. That's what it is. Or was. He isn't coming back. She wants to explain it to someone. The whole ugly story. From the beginning. Page one. Maury's younger brother. Always a bit weird. Keeps getting fired. And then—some kind of breakdown. No one ever really does figure out what exactly is wrong with him. And Danny. That night Maury left her four-year-old son alone with his crazy creepy brother. Nobody knows, nobody can say what exactly did or did not happen. But something happened. Even if nothing happened. After that, it was never right. Between Maury and Danny. Between Maury and Cal. Between the world and Becky Stern. Then the coma, and Maury leaving, coming back, going crazy too, Becky thinks. That's it. That's her life. She wants to tell the story and have it all add up; but what does it add up to? What numerical value, how many pages, how many dollars, how many days months years? She'll call Suze. She's stopped call-ing Suze. Why don't I call Suze? She wants someone to know that she knows. What does she know? Maury isn't coming back. He'll never see Danny again.

So now what? How will she live, alone, with the boy? Will they still be Jewish, light the Hanukkah candles, prepare for his bar mitzvah? She converted for the sake of the marriage. She was faithless herself, went to church a few times a year with her parents but otherwise never spoke of it. Jewish was serious, she knew, but serious like a joke she couldn't quite get, no matter how many times it was explained to her. But isn't she stuck with it now? She imagines the church of her childhood: claustrophobic pews, the preacher's yellow teeth and hollow eyes. Is that what I want for Danny? The day is beautiful. The sun is warm. But who made the day? Who made her husband leave her? She tries to remember what the Jews say about fate, what it means when bad overruns good people. Is she good? Isn't it all god's will, in this world or the next? She is good. Why not? She's done things, but nothing so— She thinks of the smooth chest of Jack Hodgins, like a fire in the distance. I didn't—that was—coincidence. So what was she supposed to do? In the old days, in Maury's mother's shtetl, they would have stoned her or at least cast her out. But these aren't the old days. There's nothing to cast her out from. And I'm not the one who— Is there even a god? Could there be a god? She imagines an aging bearded bloated cherub, swollen penis dangling between his legs, his arms around a bevy of beautiful virgins. Sure, why not? Makes as much sense as anything. Why did her son wake up? Why did her husband disappear? Some kind of trade, a deal she made without even knowing it.

Becky stares up at the house. Danny's room, overlooking the backyard. He's probably on the computer. Maury bought it for him before he left, a logical, calculating surrogate father. She shouldn't have allowed it. Danny has enough problems without spending all day on a computer. She should drag him outside, have him help her turn over the garden. But she wants to be alone. It wouldn't do any good, she reasons. Nothing changes. It doesn't matter how many hours he spends staring at the computer screen, the weeds keep coming, the sun too. The days pass and what happens happens.

She digs the shovel in, throws dirt. Shadows in his bedroom window. The blind up, then abruptly down again. The boy doing whatever the boy does. The hours passing regardless.

At school.

Danny moves in a dream. Thinks in illuminated floating symbols. A language only he speaks. Invented, really, so he could write it. *It.* The Program. Half game, half he doesn't know what. That's the problem. He doesn't know what it is. He's like a fanatic drawn to the cause, whatever the cause may be. Can he finish it? He was in a coma once. Was it like this? He touches a pencil, feels it pass through him, though it digs into his palm when he presses down, leaves a scratch where point meets palm. He turns the pencil around, it's like he's not even there, the pencil moving all by itself.

Grey numbers on the white page, copying the problem on the blackboard. Numbers. Just marks. Create and erase. This or that. Danny imagines going through the world, his finger on delete. None of it matters. None of it adds up to anything. I was in coma. And before that? Numbers are just numbers. Like the distance between things, they stand for no thing—indivisible, irreducible, impossible to represent and, so, pointless. But—not pointless. That's the thing, that's the whole point of the thing. The Program.

At lunch Danny sits alone, feels himself floating off the cafeteria bench. He doesn't eat. Takes his peanut butter sandwich out of its Baggie and passes the forty-five minutes running his fingers over the sandwich Baggie's thin permeable plastic creases. The din of children talking—an empty buzz in his head. His temples pound. The room shifts then rights itself. He gets up, staggers as the hallway contorts then opens like a stutter.

He makes his way down the hall. Trails a hand against the wall. He's afraid of his locker, the combination a sudden mystery. Don't think about it, he thinks. But how can he not think about it? Cold shudder washing over him, his throat constricting to the point where he has to beg himself to swallow.

Spit in a warm mouthful down his esophagus like string.

He closes his eyes. Breathes.

When he looks down, the locker is open, the combination dialed.

But what about next time?

English class, Friday. Second-last period of the day. Danny's turn to read aloud. He's done it before, his cheeks red, his voice unsteady and faltering on simple words.

They think I'm—

The teacher is Mrs. Jenkins, heavy-set and aggrieved; nonetheless, she believes in inspiration, fantasy, poetry. And so on. Fridays, they read out loud from a text that won't be on the end-of-year exam or the grade seven placement test. It's about words, children, she always says. The way words can tell a story. Isn't it amazing?

Words are just a kind of number, Danny thinks. Words and numbers. The Program isn't going well. He's stuck on the surface. He doesn't know how to go deeper. If he could just—

Danny, Mrs. Jenkins says. We're waiting for you.

The words sit on the page in clusters. Words and more words. Words! Smothering him. His father's words. *Well, here, son.* His hands on the spread pages of the book. His hands far far away from him. This isn't real. Don't think about it. Delete it.

Mrs. Jenkins looms above, her mouth a hole, her greasy mane of curls obscuring light. Danny feels his tongue writhing, trying to read, trying to make a sensical sound. His throat closes. Saliva pooling. Dark in the classroom. No light. No air. Mrs. Jenkins over him, Danny Danny Danny do you hear me?

Don't think about it.

He can't help it. It's happening.

Don't—

Shadows. Can't breathe. Some dark creature. Looming. Descending.

Fingers around the pencil, moving right through.

Danny! Danny! Danny!

Stabs at Jenkins. Nothing.

<No thing.>

Becky's first instinct is to tell Maury. Who else is there?

She leaves her newly suspended son in front of that goddamn computer. Goes to work. Comes home. Puts a frozen lasagna in the oven. Sits on the couch in the evening gloom playing her old jazz LPs on Maury's record player. Every time she gets up to turn the record over, she thinks: Too cheap to get a CD player. That fat—

She calls Danny down for dinner.

So how was your day, kiddo? Inside she cringes. *Kiddo?*

Danny shrugs.

You're using that computer a lot lately. You been playing games on it?

Danny nods.

Don't feel like talking much?

Danny pokes at his broccoli.

You going to eat that?

Danny puts his fork down on the table.

I've got that meeting with the school tonight.

Danny stares at his plate. At the light bulb glare dancing an invisible current in his glass of water.

I guess things are kinda screwed up now, huh?

Danny leaves the table.

Becky turns the light on in the garage. It goes poof and dies. She stares up at it, fading afterglow, she can't remember ever changing it before. Maury must have. Does it take some kind of special bulb? She should change it now, it'll be dark when she gets home. Is there a spare bulb? With Maury there's always a spare bulb. But even after two years she doesn't know where he keeps things. She ponders the cluttered interior—rakes, shovels, hammers, scattered screws, a cracked plastic sled, the detritus of a past decade—she'll clean it out, get rid of all this junk, Maury's junk, it's on her list, a project, Maury was always the one for the projects.

You'll be late for the meeting, she says out loud.

She gets into the car. Takes a deep breath. New car smell, only a few months old. Her first major purchase on her own. Head of the household. Ha. When she thinks like this, about Maury and being alone, she feels a nothingness, a burst blister drained of its juice. So she's alone. An empty flap of rubbed-raw skin. She considers calling the school and telling them she can't make it. Why not? Why shouldn't she? What's done is done. She can't change what happened any more, she thinks, than she can change what is going to happen.

You're going, she tells herself. But she doesn't start the car. Why should she go? Why should she do anything?

If things happen for a reason, then whatever happens happens outside of her control. If events are random, Becky thinks, the same holds true. There's something fuzzy about this logic, but she has adopted it nonetheless. The meeting will happen, its outcome will occur and this is all she really wants to think about—occurrences and outcomes, a planned-out program for the future. That's all there is. There's no point in going off on some search for *what it all means*. And what does Maury think he'll find now that he didn't find when he was gone all those weeks with his son in a coma? There was a time when she would have taken him back.

Becky walks calmly down the bright hall to the principal's office. It's been four days since the incident. Danny's been in his room most of the time. She tells herself she's giving him space. She tells herself she can't imagine what he's going through.

The principal, the guidance counsellor and the school board official all rise when Becky enters the room. They have that grave look about them, a funereal countenance that seems out of character in the principal's office—brightly painted homage to the power of positive thinking. A giant yellow smiley-face poster leaps off the lime-coloured wall. Beneath the red grin the predictable admonition: *Smile!*

She does. Shakes hands. Takes the seat offered to her.

Well, the principal says. He opens and closes the file on his desk. As you know, a very serious incident occurred last week involving your son Daniel.

Becky nods, keeps smiling. Smiling is all wrong for this meeting. She lets her face relax into neutral.

We want you to understand, pipes in the guidance counsellor, that we're here for Danny and you, regardless. This isn't about punishment, it's about what's best for the child.

There's silence.

Of course, Becky finally says, folding her arms definitively.

The principal begins, once again, to talk about the serious nature of the incident.

Becky stares over his head. Smiley with his crescent currant grin.

The school board representative picks up where the principal leaves off. Violent, she says. Shocking. Cruel.

Becky nods as if to the beat. What's wrong with me? She wants to shake her head, clear it, bang her skull against the green wall. She wants to care the way these people clearly think she should be caring. She thinks: It was only a pencil.

Disturbed, the guidance counsellor says.

Becky and the happy face. Staring contest to the death. She just wants to go home.

Mrs. Stern? the principal says.

His tone surprises her. There's no need to snap. Yes? she says.

The way they are looking at each other. Like she's not even there. Am I here? It occurs to Becky that she is making a bad situation worse. What can they do? What's left for them to do? She's taken him to doctors,

Maury never went, refused to go, just sat in his soft chair high up in his office tower and waited for her to call. *So?* he'd say, as if he was too busy to even formulate the full question. *So? What did they say?* What do they ever say? Was the boy— Did Maury's brother— nobody knows, nobody can *say* for sure.

How is Danny's home life? the guidance counsellor inquires.

Fine, Becky says.

Fine?

Becky nods.

We understand, however, the guidance counsellor says, lowering his voice to confidential, that there was not that long ago—a separation—

I'm not here to talk about that.

No, no, of course not, we're just trying to—

Mrs. Stern, interrupts the principal, perhaps you don't fully understand the gravity of the situation?

—it was only a—

—it was only—

—it was—

She feels the way they are looking at her. She's looking at Happy, his lascivious leer.

What's wrong with me?

She closes her eyes. Shakes her head. They're watching her, she has to—

Mrs. Stern?

Are you—

Can we get you a glass of water?

She opens her eyes. Finally meets the principal's

gaze. Her face flushing. I'm fine, thank you, she says calmly. I just—Danny is—we've both been—going through a bit of a hard time.

The room nods. Relief permeates. This is the language they need to hear.

It's been a difficult time for us, Becky says.

Of course, murmurs the guidance counsellor, shifting his chair a little closer.

Becky leans toward the principal: How is Mrs. Jenkins?

She'll be fine, the principal says. It was really just a scratch.

There was a lot of blood, notes the school board representative. Not to mention the shock of it.

It must have been horribly frightening, Becky says. Please extend my best wishes for her speedy recovery. Danny is just distraught about the whole thing. He doesn't know what came over him. It was an accident, really. A horrible horrible accident.

She could have lost an eye, notes the school board woman.

Terrible, Becky says.

—it was only a—

Given the situation, and the, uh, recent home life disruption, the guidance counsellor says, I don't think disciplinary action is advisable.

His grades have been slipping, however, states the principal, carefully ruffling through the papers in his folder.

Well, says Becky.

You've been under considerable strain yourself, the guidance counsellor offers.

Have you ever considered having Danny see someone? the school board representative wonders.

—it was—

Becky allows herself one last look. Happy the smile clinging to the lime wall for dear life.

Later, she'll kill the engine. Shove her cold hands in her lap. Sit alone in the dark garage.

A CAR DOOR OPENED, slammed shut. Let me off here, Cal wanted to say. The baby, Danny, sat stolid, stuffed in a snowsuit too big for his squat limbs. Cal tickled the baby. The baby stared straight ahead.

Quiet, his brother's wife hissed. He's sleeping.

I didn't say anything. His protests sounded like whining. He could see Maury watching him via the rear-view mirror.

Maury, hunched over the steering wheel, makes a noise in his throat.

Of course there was traffic: a parade. Roads closed. The beat of palms against a plastic wheel. Cal was in the back seat. A twenty-three-year-old man in the back seat of a car next to a baby. The next time they stopped, the baby slumped forward against the straps of the plastic seat. The baby's ripe head dangling. The baby's mouth opening, emitting a squawk of annoyance.

Cal could feel the two of them up there in the front. Eyeing him. Thinking about him: Why does he tag along? Why doesn't he get a life?

A job. A girlfriend. Then, later: a wife, a house, a promotion.

A life.

A child.

Cal looked at the baby. Danny drooled, made a noise, ineffectually waved his arms, trapped in a padded mini-parka. Cal closed his eyes. He wasn't with them; he had never been with them; he didn't know them. Hordes of parade-goers swarmed the side streets searching for a superior vantage point. The day had just begun. He could imagine jumping out of the car while it was still moving. He would take the baby with him. The baby cradled in his arms, cantaloupe head protected. Together, they rolled in the snow reduced to wet unlovely slush. Together, they slept while people gathered around them, laughing and clapping as giant-sized cartoon characters paraded past—Willy Wolf and Mrs. Funny Lamb waving and calling out special greetings just for them: *Hello Cal! Hello Danny! HELLO CAL and DANNY!*

They arrived at the gallery. There was a fee to pay. His brother and sister-in-law huddled behind him, waiting. He said he would pay and now he was paying. After, he patted the empty walls of his wallet through his pocket.

First the baby had to be settled in the stroller, freed of his sausage snowsuit, comforted, soothed, tricked into the kind of behaviour preferred at art galleries.

How many hours have gone by? he wanted to know.

What does it matter? Maury snapped.

They don't like him. They've never liked him. But he is still the younger brother. He is family, despite everything, despite all appearances to the contrary.

He paid. He didn't mind paying.

The baby squealed alarmed laughter.

They checked their coats at the coat check, included in the price of seeing the art. He felt revealed without his coat. There was a stain on his sweater. They noticed it immediately.

In the shadow of a giant portrait the baby smiled. Maury swooped the baby up. You like that, he crooned, does baby like that? You like that big big picture, that picture of man-man? Baby likes that?

They entered the special exhibit of the now-famous dead painter. There was a sentimentality to this exhibit that had less to do with the art and more to do with the painter's death, which was not so long ago. His effects—notebooks, letters, mementoes, snapshots— were encased in glass. People peered at them with squinty eyes, then stepped back to give others a chance. Cal too took a quick look. Stuff from someone's life. Cal felt cheated. Just stuff. I paid for this, he thought. There were many young women looking at the art. Cal saw them, but it was more than that. He wanted them. He needed them.

He took the baby from his brother. He held the baby under his armpits and brought him up to face a painting. A naked man with an erection spraying cartoon-devil sperm. He said, If you wanted to buy a picture like this, you'd have to pay tax on it. There's tax on paintings. The baby gurgled, tilted his round head back.

You could never afford these paintings, his brother said.

These paintings aren't even for sale, his brother's wife pointed out. She extended her arms for the baby.

He stepped back, propped the baby up above his face like a shield. See the art, he said. It's expensive and your uncle cannot afford it. He spun on his heels, tucked the baby into his chest. Ran for it.

He came to a dark corner room where the objects were all lit under fluorescent strobes. Everything glowed like stars. A sign on the wall explained: the artist loved disco dancing, mirror balls and glamour suits opened at the neck. He breathed heavy, held the baby against his chest. There was dance music against air, the beat of a tiny heart. He wondered how anyone could appreciate art that costs so much, that is assigned a value so beyond its worth. He wondered if he would ever have a girlfriend. The dark room reminded him of his basement apartment. Of his job washing dishes in the basement of a restaurant. His brother had written a book. Cal washed dishes. He told the baby that art was a chimera, a vision no one could see clearly, obscured as it was by taxes, electronic drumbeats and blinding strobe lights.

Turn it down, he yelled into the nebulous swirl of music. The baby felt wet, pressed against his T-shirt. There was a bar stool. It was painted with graffiti scribbles and little oval devils with sharp teeth. It was cordoned off from the public by a braided white rope. It was art. He stepped over the cord. He put the baby on the stool. The baby looked around warily. He pulled off the baby's shirt. Cotton stuck on stubby arms. Then lying the baby on his back. Squeals when the soft baby skin touched the cold wood stool. Pants off. Everything off.

He retreated past the rope. The baby perched there. Art.

When Becky was pregnant, Maury took her to a fancy inn, two hours out of the city. She didn't want to go, but he insisted. He didn't know what to do with her. He didn't know how to touch her, how to talk to her. It was like she had become a different creature overnight, a creature of moonlight, dispersing everywhere, constant, encompassing.

Maury told her jokes, slogans from his new hypothetical campaign to sell pregnancy to the common man:

Don't be afraid, your wife does all the work!

When they're thirteen, they'll mow your lawn!

Becky smiled but didn't laugh, kept her hands on her belly. Maury had trouble looking at the belly.

Other slogans Maury didn't try out on Becky:

What if it's dead!

What if it's ugly!

What if you like it better than me!

Children: they cost too much and they always end up hating you!

230

Maury remembers coming out of the shower and finding Becky leaning over the wooden railing, staring down into the waterfall burbling just outside their room. It's so pretty, she said.

Hey, be careful, Maury said.

Becky smiled. It was cute, the way he was being.

Come in, Maury begged. You'll catch a cold.

The first night at the inn, they had dinner in the pod, a private booth overlooking the river. It was extravagantly expensive, even without the wine that Becky couldn't drink and Maury never touched. He remembers ordering the rabbit, sitting there with her, floating out above the river. Neither of them felt like talking, or seemed to have anything to say. He loved her then, and hated her too. He wanted her to tell him everything, but she just sat there.

The second night, she had pains.

Maury dialed the obstetrician's number. His hands were shaking. He kept getting it wrong.

The doctor said, It sounds to me like you're going to have a baby.

They packed and left.

Maury looks over at the empty seat next to him. The spot where his wife once sat, jumping at the bumps and grooves of the road, telling him to be careful.

He hasn't called home.

—Danny—

Abruptly, Maury pulls over to the side of the road.

He spills out of the car. Dry heaves in the dusty air. For an instant he thinks he's not breathing. He thinks he's dying. It's only a hangover. He's not dying.

Instead, he drives. What would he do if he ever found him, this mythical horrible brother of his? Maury imagines just standing there, tears slipping down his cheeks, the credits rolling.

He uses a nail to excavate dried skin from behind his ear. Flicks it forward in the vicinity of the dashboard. He wonders if the old car is up for the drive. A few more days, no more, and then he'll turn around, head home, wherever that is.

He should at least call. He has nothing to say. He told them at the hospital: Nothing happened; he slipped, tripped, fell over the edge.

Kids, you have to watch them every second.

Wolves! they're not really your friends!

Wolves! they eat your children.

He can't go back. But he has to. Of course he has to. His job, his child, his marriage, his mother. All falling apart. Danny's little hand disappearing into his brother's spotty paw. A sense of panic and delirium, like being locked in a ride that seems not to be ending. What happened and what didn't happen.

He can't stand the thought of it. He can't stand not knowing.

He wants to change everything, make it all different and disappeared. He wants to eat organic, exercise, bake his own bread, use his talents for the propagation of good, whatever that is.

He pulls off into the rest stop. Orders the chicken sandwich, large fries and a Coke. Drive through.

Maury thinks: Thirty percent of all children eat fast food once a day.

He drives through. Parks and wolfs it down. Special sauce running down his chin.

When he's done, he still feels empty. Considers going back. It's as simple as driving around the parking lot again, speaking into the smiling plastic face.

Consider going back!

He pulls onto the highway instead. Wipes his lips on his sleeve.

The lines of the road and the afternoon sun make his head heavy. He slaps his face, the sting a reminder. Becky's hit him, over the years. She broke his glasses once, back when he wore glasses, before he got the laser surgery. He deserved it. Because he didn't see it coming. Considered it a wake-up call. A reminder of what happens when you, as they say, take your eye off the ball. It's an advertising mindset, one of the directives of his book: you don't wait for things to happen, you *make* things happen. He bent down and picked up the smashed frames and held them out to her, an offering.

He can close his eyes and see her naked, her skinny rib cage, the shock of short sharp curls covering her sex. He closes his eyes and sees the night they returned home. He thought Danny was asleep. But when they pulled into the driveway, Danny wouldn't wake up. He ran to the house and pounded on the door and called her name. Becky wasn't there.

Horn bleating. Maury opens his eyes, catches his car just veering into another lane.

In the doctor's soft big bed, it all made sense. And again with Darla, her face in a permanent pout, her mascara just slightly smeared. *You can't stay.* If Darla hadn't said it, he would have stayed. He would have closed his eyes and fallen asleep.

The sign divides the highway, and Maury recognizes the name of the next town. His old college town, as a matter of fact. They're always asking him for money. He follows the turnoff bend.

Maury creeps down a two-lane highway he vaguely remembers. Colourful markers point the way to the university. There are signs now, there never used to be. The farmers' fields are gone, replaced by giant parking lot complexes featuring the kind of discount stores that pay somebody to greet you at the door.

Maury passes a Hooters. He passes a Rock-n-Bowl, twelve lanes, open twenty-four hours. His gut rumbles, the grease congealing in a lump in the pit of his belly.

Twenty-four-hour bowling?

Finally, he reaches the campus. They've taken down the modest wooden sign and put up a garish banner.

Maury pulls up in front of an ornate manor. His old student residence, the Manor House, a refurbished mansion, part of the university's original heritage. Now a sign in front of the building says it's the ITM Residence. And he can see that they've built an extension, an awkwardly attached warren of small rooms that seems to have been fashioned entirely out of plastic and concrete.

Maury stands on the sidewalk.

So he's here. Now what?

A car pulls up behind him.

Hey buddy, someone says. Hey, buddy! You're parked in the fire lane. Mister?

A tapping on Maury's shoulder.

Maury finally turns. It's just a kid, stiff and uncomfortable in his campus security uniform.

Mister, the kid says, you got a visitor pass?

What is this? Maury says.

Can I help you, sir?

Maury shakes his head in amazement.

All visitors have to check in at registration.

What?

Sir, the kid says, grabbing Maury's elbow, if you'll just come with me. We can—

I'm not a fucking visitor, Maury snaps. He pushes the boy away, maybe harder than he meant to. The boy stumbles back.

Maury gets into his car.

Hey, the kid yells.

Maury drives off. He cuts down a side street, searching for a way back to the highway. But the road goes past a new business faculty complex and circles around into a dead end. Sirens fill the air, students stop to gawk. Maury puts it in reverse. Campus security screeches around the corner. Blocks the way.

They pull him out into the sunshine. He waves wildly with his fists.

They handcuff him and push him into the back of a car.

Campus security is a prefab hut filled with battered wood desks and the smell of cold coffee.

Maury takes deep breaths.

Get these things off me right now, he finally manages.

Sir— one of the pimply-faced security personnel says.

You little fuck. You don't know what the fuck you're dealing with.

The captain—

You get these things off me, you rent-a-cop under-graduate shit—

Sir—the captain—

Maury lunges at the boy, head down like a bloated rhinoceros. I'll fucking—

The captain appears, just in time to calmly and pro-fessionally put Maury into a chokehold.

Settle down now, old boy.

Old boy, Maury thinks, spluttering, still trying to yell something, anything.

The captain pushes him into a wooden chair.

Maury looks down at the grooves in the metal floor of the security hut. Finally, when he catches his breath, he says: You in charge here?

For now, you're in our custody, says the captain.

You can't arrest me. I'll—

Trespassing, assault, reckless driving. Not to mention peeping.

Peeping! What the hell are you talking about?

Why don't you tell me what you were doing in front of the girls' residence?

Girls' residence! I wasn't— Do you know who I am?

Why don't you tell me?

Bradey. Head of the business school. Heard of him? You get Bradey over here.

The captain exchanges looks with his boyish deputy. Well now, the captain says, Dean Bradey is—

Dean Bradey, Maury says triumphantly. You go tell him you've arrested Maury Stern for . . . for . . . —he spits the word out—*peeping.*

Maury Sterm? The captain seems bemused. He nods at the deputy, who quietly moves to the desk, types something into the computer.

Stern, Maury yells. What, are you fucking deaf?

The captain looks at the deputy, who shakes his head, shrugs.

The captain sighs. Look, Mr. . . . Stern, why don't you just tell me what it is you're doing here, and then we'll see about clearing up this situation.

Arrest me! Get the *real* cops! Otherwise, get Bradey over here—

The Dean is a busy man—

I don't care if he's on fucking sabbatical in fucking Timbuktu, Maury yells. Get him over here.

The captain scratches under his nose.

Maury stands up, his chest heaving.

Sit down, the captain says.

Maury stands there. Hands twisted behind him.

The captain sighs again. He turns to his deputy. Look, Dan, he says, why don't you go over there and check with the Dean's office about this Maurice Stern.

Dan nods, heads for the door.

Maury, Maury bellows. He stares at the captain.

He sits down.

When the kid finally unlocks the cuffs and draws quickly out of lunging range, the first thing Maury does is look down at his shoes, spattered with flecks of dried mud.

He's in the same rumpled blue suit he's been wearing since he left home. He's unshaven. The inside of his mouth tastes like dog food smells. The lush rot of booze hangs off his skin like some spoiled cologne. Christ, no wonder they— He closes his eyes, feels them hot and bloodshot, bulging under his lids.

He doesn't want to have to raise his head, take in the curious, incredulous Dean Bradey, who is doing his best to hide a smirk. Or the captain, arms folded over, just doing his job.

Congratulations, Bradey says. Gentlemen, you've arrested Maury Stern, pride of the college, a living legend.

Dean Paul Bradey, balding crown of his scalp bearing no hint of the long ponytail he sported when the two were roommates freshman year.

Maury picks his car keys off the captain's desk.

Gentlemen, Bradey says, nodding goodbye.

They walk out into the sunny afternoon. Maury inhales, exhales. Bradey watches him.

Jesus Christ, Maury finally blurts. What are you running here? A police state?

Maury, Paul says, let's get you cleaned up.

Maury flushes, follows Paul down a groomed path, ivy hanging off bricks, tree leaves shaking in the gentle breeze, in the sanctified quiet.

Paul lives in an old wooden house on the edge of the campus. The lawn is plush and green, the porch creaks when you step on it, white paint turned a lustreless grey. Maury balances his drink on the wooden railing, looks across the lawn and the road and into the strip of woods that runs parallel to the river.

Somewhere in there, Paul says. That's where it happened.

Jesus fucking Christ, Maury says. What's this world coming to?

She was a summer student. Described the attacker as a middle-aged white man, unkempt, wearing a tattered blue suit. That's all she said. Didn't get a real good look at him. Was terrified, naturally.

Jesus Christ, Maury says.

So you can imagine, when they saw you, staring at the girls' residence—

I didn't even know it was the girls'—it used to be our old—

Of course, I know. It was a misunderstanding.

Yeah, Maury says. That's awful. Some maniac. Shit. I hope they get him.

They look through the woods, shadows lengthening, a perfect early fall evening.

You're just lucky I was around. I'll be away for the rest of the month. Giving a talk in Italy.

Yeah, Maury says. I'm just lucky. He tugs at the sweatshirt Paul lent him. Emblazoned with the logo of his alma mater. It feels thick, encompassing. But hey, anyway, good to see you. You look good. I guess divorce has been kind to you.

Paul takes a prim sip from the neck of his beer. Maury's drinking soda water and lime. He can still taste the sour rise of his hangover, a ripe froth coating the back of his throat.

Aw, c'mon, he says. I was just—

Look, Maury, you don't want to tell me what you're doing here, fine. Maybe you need a friend right now, maybe you don't. Maybe I can help you, maybe I can't. But Maury, give it a rest, huh?

Maury sits down heavily.

Yeah, he says. Okay. I just meant—

Paul's always had impeccable manners. Came out of his mother's womb a genial liberal with a head for numbers. Maury used to scoff at his smug calculations. Maury believes that business is a sand castle in need of constant shoring up, an endless parade of ads and banners and billboards and phone calls and incitements to keep the greasy wheel from starting to squeak. For Maury, it was always about augury, abstraction, fakery, magic. They used to argue over that transcendental shift at the heart of the twentieth century, the miasma of promise impossible to separate from its gleaming package.

Paul used to laugh, called Maury a high-concept pessimist with an ear for catchy copy.

Now Paul's got tenure, ethical mutual funds, takes delivery of twenty thousand sweatshirts stamped with the business school logo, every single one of them manufactured in a murky factory in a murky country nobody's ever heard of.

There was a protest once. Dean Bradey promised to look into it.

He's looking into it.

You have to fight the small battles, he might say. Start what you can finish.

Maury's never believed that. Never really believed that you could start small and get really really big.

How do you like it? Paul says. Your meat?

Ah, Maury says. Rare for me.

He sits on a lawn chair on the back porch, watches Paul flip steaks. Splatters of grease flaring up in miniature arsons. Late fall, but it feels like summer here.

I got lost coming through town, Maury says. Couldn't believe it, the way it's changed.

Isn't it something?

Quite a difference. Had to follow those goddamn signs you've got all over the place.

Maury, you haven't been back here in, what, ten, fifteen years?

Something like that.

Things change. What do you expect? It's not just here. It's like this everywhere. More stores, more roads, more houses, more of everything.

Keep that economy booming.

That's one way of doing it.

The only way of doing it.

You know better than I do.

What's that supposed to mean? Maury says it without malice. He's suddenly exhausted, wonders if he even cares.

This is your world, Paul says. Our world. We built it. We made it. And now, we live in it.

Those steaks ready?

They sit in the living room.

Paul picks up the remote, looks over at Maury. You still a baseball fan?

Maury shrugs. Naw. I guess not.

Paul switches on the set anyway. What are we doing with our lives, Maury? Paul says.

I'm looking for my brother, Maury says. He doesn't elaborate. Stares at the screen, channels changing.

Almost immediately, Maury falls into a heavy sleep.

He wakes up.

He wipes sweat off his forehead with his bare arm. Mechanically, he puts on his suit, lying crumpled in a heap on the floor by the side of the bed.

Walks down the stairs, his bulk on the shrieking

wood. The door is unlocked. Small towns, Maury thinks, even now, even with— He moves through the night, the air wet and heavy on him. Crickets and grasshoppers, mockingbird coos, the distant hum of cars on the highway.

Maury puts his hands in his pockets, listens to his own breathing, stares at the thick trees, the path disappearing into the enclosing distance. He and his pals used to go down there at night, smoke pot, drink beer, mess around with girls. Nobody was afraid then. Now some animal, some fucking animal, doing that—here.

He crosses the smooth street. It was a dirt road back then, once upon a time.

Maury pauses on the edge of the woods, not as dark as he thought it would be, half moon, stars. He'll wander down the river, the way he used to.

The path is overgrown, branches of trees hanging low, long weeds slapping his thighs. Maury trips on a thick coiled root—looks behind him, the woods closed, the stars shut out.

He keeps walking. Maybe he's on the path, probably he isn't. Pine needles and leaves soft under his steps. Insects buzz around him, bouncing off his thighs, ricocheting off his chest. He breathes hard through his nose. Squints into the grainy darkness trying to see the progress of the twisting path's descent. He sees his legs, blue shadows merging with the thickening gloom as he moves forward.

It's what you can't see, what you know but don't.

That's advertising, Maury thinks, this night feeling in the woods, what we spend our lives trying to re-create in smiling illusions. Advertising is all we have left, the dream and the promise, P.T. Barnum's 200-year-old woman, Roman gladiators jousting in the hot sun while the young patricians cluster under an awning, the Little League, the World Series—what else is it if it isn't advertising for some other spectacle, deeper, truer, invisible but ever-present, not the thing itself but the thing we wish it could be?

Maury feels his shoes sink, stops suddenly, looks around him. He thought he knew where he was, now he's not so sure. He's near the river. The trees have given way to straggly shrubs, the soft earth a clinging sinking muck. He can smell it, too, a rich organic rot, the sluggish current carrying the scent. You don't swim in it any more. We used to, though. Late night skinny dip.

At the edge of the river he finds solid ground, the moon reflecting off the stolid current. The water looks thick, deep.

Maury unzips it.

He closes his eyes, pants in steady rhythm.

Back then there were—girls—

Panting now, he bucks his hips.

He's close.

Skinny-dipping in the past.

The bushes rustling in the hot wind.

Shiver on the back of his neck—

He spins.

Dick bobbing.

What am I—?

It's okay, just the wind.

Is there a wind?

Maury steps forward, throws his arms out, grabs for balance. Trips, lands on his hands and knees. Scrabbles to his feet, lunges at the shadow in front of him.

Fucker, you—

Maury hits, tumbles through, fists swinging.

Something gives: a gurgling noise, the river.

part 4: humanity

THE SUMMER COMES LIKE A GENIUS mad scientist bursting into the room cackling and hooting, eyes full luminous June moons, hair wild and thorny as a July blackberry bush, crazed smile white and glaring August thunder.

The summer comes hot and short, kills the old, stuns the young: toddlers dehydrate and shit their shorts.

Danny sweats in the air conditioning.

Actually, he prefers Daniel now.

There are six of them, riding a long escalator up to the foyer of the Gallorama Casino Games and Good Time Shopping Complex. The ceiling above them is rounded, shiny. Stained glass and velvet canopies muffle an opulent atmosphere, perfumed plump scent hiding under its lavish feathers the odour of dirty carpets, sweat and smoke.

Daniel stands behind the Professor. They ascend without moving, perched on the treadmill stairs.

Through his viewer, the Professor's wispy head of hair appears hazy, purplish, the unkempt mane merging with the arms of the black wraparound glasses.

Daniel raises a hand, waves it in front of his field of vision. The fingers stick, afterimages blurring together. He runs a pinky along the smooth plastic, the tip just tracing his flat smooth forehead. He made the visor in the lab, the Professor coaching him as he carefully aligned the laser portal point with the inner pupil, the exact spot where the lens flips light upside down to the brain.

It's the highest escalator he's ever been on. Don't look down. This isn't about heights. They're here to shoot what the Professor calls a meta-documentary, a work of performance art—though Daniel has only the vaguest notion of performance art.

He steps off the escalator. A moment of dizziness. The sudden motion of walking and the bifurcated computer mediation of the world around him come together in a liquid wave others find disorienting but Danny finds familiar, comforting like an old friend you rarely talk to but know is out there. Move with it, the Professor says, get used to it. But for Danny it's been there all along, a coma haze, a menacing smog gloom dawning over every possible action.

He pans the giant atrium, observer and camera. How many are watching right now? He pictures living-room Web browsers relaying the scene in blocky bursts of pixilated data somehow more compelling than the clearest high-density image. He frames his vision so that the unseen millions will have better access to what the Professor calls the ubiquitous gaze. He focuses for a moment on the lavish sprawling fountain that takes over the centre of the lobby like a half-dressed drunken beauty staggering through the end of a party. Daniel's gaze encompasses the entirety of the water-spouting monstrosity, then homes in on its grotesque particulars: the naked boy's penis shooting a constant spray of foam, the gilded mermaid's perpetual smile as she graciously accepts the cherub's never-ending load. He loses himself in the motion, moving his gaze back and forth, his head gyrating slowly, luxuriously, through the ceaseless pressurized jet. He doesn't notice the group moving off until he sights them past the mist on the other side of the fountain.

Shit, he mutters.

He runs after them.

Catches the group approaching the entry to the casino. The security guard slumped behind the desk eyes them. As they near the glass double doors, the guard rises casually, folds his hands over his belly. He blocks the entranceway, shifts from black loafer to black loafer. Daniel working his gaze-camera: close up, the guard's pale jowly face; wide view, the silver plastic hump hiding the security camera mounted to the ceiling above the heavy glass doors leading to the casino.

How y'all doing today? the guard says.

Calmly, the Professor unzips his tote bag, pulls out a video camera. He points it at the ceiling, at the opaque dome hanging like a beetle, blinking down at them. The red light on the video camera winks on.

I would like to inquire, the Professor states politely, as to the presence of an operational camera embedded within that dome of opacity?

Daniel opts for a wide view. He likes the image of the students in their protective semicircle behind the Professor. And in the middle their mentor confronts the ignorant standard-bearer of a mindless surveillance society. That's the way the Professor would put it.

Now, you see, sir, says the security guard, we've got a problem here. Cameras are not allowed in the Gallorama Casino. He uncrosses then crosses his arms like a period. You'll have to leave, he concludes.

Cameras are not allowed in the Gallorama? the Professors asks slowly, lowering his video camera so it points at the guard.

The guard nods emphatically. That's right, sir.

And yet, reasons the Professor, his voice a computer trapped in the strictures of logic, there is a camera in that opaque dome mounted to the ceiling, is there not?

I wouldn't know about that, sir.

As a security guard, you aren't apprised of your facility's security arrangements? The Professor adjusts his tone so that it sounds more confessional than stri-dent. As you can see, he says, we fully support the right to record images for security and safety.

The Professor gestures at the other students, all of them in their own tinted wired glasses, all of them, with the exception of Daniel, wearing T-shirts that state in red letters: *For the purposes of safety and security, I may be recording.*

A crowd gathers.

Daniel focuses in on a business type, compulsive gambler, blotchy red rashy face blooming from a cheap blue suit.

The security guard stares at the students, then back at the Professor and his video camera.

Hey, he says, is that thing on? The guard blocks the lens with a beefy palm. His arm outstretched, the pose somewhere between instinctive and as-seen-on-TV. You can't do that in here, he says, reaching for the camera.

The Professor pulls back. The two men tug at the appliance. Daniel frames the hands of the Professor, scrawny academic sporting dark wraparound glasses with wires sprouting through the edges like weeds past concrete. His hands, bony and white, the knuckles raw, red where the muscles stretch. The security guard wins the tug-of-war, triumphantly staggers back, stabbing at the eject button. The mechanism springs open. The cavity is empty.

What the hell? the guard says.

\<capture and transmit\>

What gives us the right to be human? the Professor asks. What quality separates us, distinguishes us, enhances us, elevates us to humanness? Is it free will? Is that our guarantee? What if we have free will but are prevented from exercising it? Do we become, then, unhuman? These are not just hypothetical concerns. The world has become mechanistic, we are trapped in the mechanism and, just like the bees, even those at the top of the hierarchy, the pinnacle of the food chain— the queens—simply go through the motions, each one pointing his stinger at the next: I am not responsible, I am not in charge, this is the way it has to be done, the way it is always done, and though I may object, I am not, as you might think, king, queen, president, prime minister, dictator, I am a process, a conduit for calculation, I am part of the machine. Is it, then, that we have lost the free will of the human? What if we have? Is that such an awful thing? Who will stand up under the banner of humanity and proudly proclaim their allegiance to this race of morons, rapists, terrorists, warmongers and, perhaps worst of all, voyeurs? Ours is the search for the post-human destiny, the point at which not only are we no longer human, but we are no longer what humanity has become. Let us merge with the machine, not to better facilitate our humanness, but to facilitate our *post*-humanness—to become the machine so that we might successfully corrupt the automaton that the human has become.

Daniel looks around him. The regular Friday afternoon meeting—what the Professor calls the HackFest—always ends with an impromptu lecture. The gaggle of students stare blankly at their terminals of code and graph, peer through tired eyes at kernels of data yet to reveal the misplaced numerals that turn a thing of beauty into a pile of crap. Daniel sits among them, lets the words bore into his consciousness as if he too can be programmed and reprogrammed, the tiny unavoidable errors slowly detected and obliterated in a process that takes years of tinkering and coding. This is Daniel's world now. Here he has found—not a home—but a temporary respite from his search for that place he's been, a nowhere somewhere he'll return to. Has to. How to get from here to there? The path is as fine and precise and potent as cords of data-transmitting wire, cameras small enough to balance on a thumbnail, the view through the computer a yawning tide of eddies and swells, the sensation equivalent to walking the plank, waves sucking you down, a sick sense of power and you stare into the foaming maw of it.

They are reviewing captures from last week's intervention at the Gallorama. The idea was to intervene into the most invasive processes of the techno-industrial state by exposing its security apparatus through what the Professor calls the Double Camera Quotient, in which video cameras with no tape are used as decoys while the entire proceedings are captured and transmitted live via secret wearable digital cameras to the World Wide Web.

The Professor engages the audio and the lab listens to the fountain's flowing purr, a woman's laugh, a conversation passing like a car on a highway, then, louder, Daniel's impromptu *Shit*.

Chuckles from the students scattered around their terminals.

Sounds fine to me, Daniel mutters.

The Professor says nothing, his expressionless visage somehow managing to convey a scowl.

The background noises—Daniel's breathing, the splash of the waterfall, the gabbling of passersby—drown out much of the dialogue. It will have to be painstakingly recovered, students searching through the muck of the audio wilderness for the remains of a digital path.

It's not a movie score, the Professor warns. We do not enhance. We do not fabricate. We simply adjust according to the aims of the protocol.

The Professor wants it real and ugly and dangerous. He wants to transcend the artificial by becoming it. What's more fake than the cyborg? What's more fabricated than the view through the cyborg screen, memory supplement, instant video moment? We're not making a movie here, the Professor proclaims. The Professor never watches TV, doesn't like movies. I am my own fantasy, he once told them.

Daniel fiddles with the keyer in his pocket, amuses himself by entering different sequences into the microprocessor that controls his visor. His view of the meeting constantly shifts and startles, upside down, on a thirty-degree tilt, negatively imagined so that black is white and vice versa. Daniel feels his legs under him, springs pulled taut. He wants to chase down the digital delirium—equations turned into words, pictures, grainy videos, memories.

The group disperses. The Friday HackFest is over. A few will slip away to meet friends, have a drink, take in a movie. But most will stay in the lab, work through the evening and night, order greasy 241 pizzas and stuff wedges into their mouths without even tasting them, their eyes on the prize—whatever the Professor wants them to do, each one assigned a task that stretches his ability to the limit, each one of them knowing that failure will bring about nothing worse than the Professor's disappointment and redoubled efforts on their own part to accomplish more faster.

Daniel, I'd like to see you a moment in my office.

The Professor's office is a corner cubbyhole at the end of a hall of cubbyholes. The tiny room abounds with circuits, transducers, thumbnail batteries, coils of wires in shapes and sizes running from small to micro. Reports are strewn in stacks, the white papers covered with illegible notes and microscopic equations—various versions of inventions in progress or limbo or abandoned altogether to make space for the next bright and risen inspiration. Daniel's muscles twitch and contort. He's bothered by small spaces. Also heights.

The phone rings. The Professor doesn't answer. Daniel's never seen the Professor talk on the phone, eat a meal, touch another person. He wears the same brown turtleneck every day. At night, alone, Daniel copies the Professor, stretches his face to form a look of detached confusion. Walks like the Professor, goose-stepping into the shadows of his room.

The Professor sits behind his desk. His long crablike fingers twitch over a pen, a pile of papers, a circuit board on its back, gut-wires obscenely splayed. Daniel watches those fingers on their methodical journey. The Professor's face: impassive and calm, eyes obscured by the ever-present dark glasses. Daniel imagines the eyes dancing like the fingers, tango saccades moving to the jitter of perpetual information. He's never seen the Professor's eyes. But he feels it too: the need for constant change, a desire for ever-fluctuating perpetually expanding space, an urgency so real you can reach out and touch it—it's not there; there's nothing there.

Sit down, Daniel.

He considers the only chair. Occupied by a steeple of documents.

Just put those anywhere, the Professor says.

Daniel shifts them to the floor.

They *encourage* me to write them, the Professor says.

Daniel thinks the Professor is making a joke. He isn't sure. He's never heard the Professor try to be funny. He doesn't smile. The Professor grimaces. Up close, he looks clean and boyish, though he is also unshaven, unkempt. He could be twenty, Daniel thinks. My age.

Daniel, the Professor says, I want you to know that I value your work in the lab. You are one of our most promising young interfacers. But, Daniel, our project is a difficult one. It demands constant attention and vigilance. The project of interface is one that others don't often understand. Your peers, your family members, they may seek to turn you away from the project. You may find distractions in the world outside the project. I ask you to resist them, to commit to us with the entirety of your self, because the project is not one of exclusion, it is one of inclusion and expansion, and only by giving it your totality can you achieve the completeness of experience that is the interface.

Professor, I—

The Professor raises his hand. Things are changing, Daniel. When the world sees our latest work, how far we've come— They used to stare at me on the street. When I was your age, they used to mock me, call me geek and freak and faggot. Now, Daniel, they don't notice me any more. They don't call me anything. They don't see me at all. Do you know why?

Because you look . . . normal?

Yes. Normal. Boring. *Pacified.* Daniel, what would you say if I told you that part of me longs for the past of metal-antenna hair sticking out of my head, my scalp encased in an aluminum Faraday conduction cage? Hate is pure, Daniel. Fear is pure. But what we have now—ignorance and ignorance's cousin, suspicion— Daniel, these are corrupting, dangerous emotions. Do you understand me, Daniel?

I—

When I was easily observed as a cyborg creature, I was hated and feared. I was a symbol of what many of us fear in ourselves. Now that I—now that *we* are hidden, we have become them again, we are too much like them. We interiorize their fear, and in due course they will seek to destroy us by killing themselves. This, you see, is the human tendency to self-destruction, to use technology to commit mass murder, a form of

self-loathing, a kind of suicide, each mind a concen-
tration camp, each heart a nuclear warhead. They are
out in the streets, Daniel, battling the slow secret creep
of their own technologically implanted desires, the protestor in cahoots with the giant corporation he pretends
to hate, but together they are a duality of dysfunction,
lost to themselves, disgusted at who they are and what
they've become. We are the dual embodiment of their
paranoia and self-loathing, we are the flesh-and-wire
construction of their fantasy, the real thing that proves
each and every agenda, the smoking gun permitting
the various conflicting factions to announce they were
right all along.

I don't—

Daniel, our interface project is not, as one might suppose, an issue of anonymity. Do we want to disappear?
Of course we do not. We want the option to disappear,
but we also want the opportunity to appear as we are.
As we are, do you see what I am saying, Daniel?

Daniel sees the wavy blue air around him. He sees
the constant flux of a video atmosphere conjured and
chewed, smeared and spit out into his eyes, a thick
saliva stew of floating particles. The office is dirty and
dusty. In the corner of his perception an ever-present
red flashing menu: stasis, status, record, erase, delete.
Words to become and be conquered.

I—

Daniel, you, of all my students, imagine yourself
caught between this world and the world we know we
cannot just reach but must first create. But in order to

make the final connection, to truly become one with that world in between, we need to acknowledge the truth, Daniel. Do you know what that truth is? That there is only one world. *Our* world. The world we create. We create it out of the past, Daniel. And out of the present. And, finally, out of the future. Do you see, Daniel?

Daniel stops trying to answer. His face is hot, his eyes are burning where the laser portal projects deep past his retinas.

You understand in your own way, don't you, Daniel? The Professor sweeps a hand through the air like an incantation. You understand intuitively, that's what makes you such an asset to the project, isn't it, Daniel?

I—don't know.

No, of course you don't. Why should you? Don't worry, Daniel. You're just a young man. A child. Your whole life in front of you.

No.

No?

The room shrinking. Small spaces. He's standing. No, Professor, he says. The real cyborg is blind, Daniel thinks. The real cyborg doesn't need to see. Just knows. What does the Professor know?

The Professor claps his creeping hands. The sound is physical and real, startling like a punch in the gut.

Of course! His tone exuberant. Why would I have presumed that you were once a child? What is a boy, after all, in an age of instant limitless possibility? Your youth has been subsumed by your infinite potential for total destruction, total creation. Wonderful!

The Professor works the keyer suddenly in his hand, makes a note of something, sends an instant record of the conversation to—who knows where? Daniel has heard hushed discussion of encrypted worlds where the Professor floats totally and freely in a disembodied limbo of pure possibility. Hidden and completely safe, they say if he was to die then, to die suddenly, he could live on in that limitless world of immersed consciousness.

He's capturing me, transmitting right now.

You are not completely here, are you, Daniel?

Where is here, Professor?

Very good, Daniel. Very good.

The summer is an unfamiliar embrace, not unwelcome, just odd and maybe a few seconds longer than it should be. The city around him, the city in summer—all crumpled bedsheets, the ripped-open wrapper of the prophylactic, the lipstick-stained Kleenex, the underwear thrown so casually in the heat of the act, now strewn like an immutable sculpture, ode to the weakness of passion. Daniel, Danny, expectant virgin. He trembles on the sidewalk, taking deep gulps of air, opening and closing his lungs like making fists.

Behind him, the dark squat engineering building. Students arriving. Laughing. Pub night.

Daniel jerks into a walk. The sun sets slowly on his head, on his arms, on the back of his legs. Makes everything heavy. The world is false and flat, comes in floor model shades of chrome: silvers, blues, beiges, greens. The world is controlled, limited, predetermined. So what? Let the Professor think he knows. He doesn't— Does he know?

Daniel walks for a half-hour, an hour. He moves stolidly. The sun almost gone, he slows his pace, feels the way the heat of the day clings to him. He wants to sit down. He looks around him. Isn't sure where he is. He stops altogether, sniffs the air, the grey of exhaust, the bright green of cut chemical grass. He's only lived here since September. Ten months ago he was a different person.

He doesn't—

Daniel puts his hands in his pockets.

A car comes up behind him. He steps out of the way. Houses and lawns. A street light flickers on and off in the dusk shadows. He isn't really lost. How can he ever be lost? He could call up a path back to his room. In a minute he would have the fastest route projected over a view of the outside world.

He prefers to be lost. He closes his eyes. Lets the breeze, faint as it is, trail over him. It's the summer, he tells himself. His first summer on his own, almost over, though of course he's always been on his own.

He doesn't drink or smoke.

He doesn't have any friends.

He gets horny sometimes.

—don't think about it—

Jerks off with his eyes closed.

And the Professor lecturing: People talk about the brain as if it can't deal with the shock. They say the brain can't adapt, we'll go blind or mad or worse. They say we'll be trapped in a prosthetic prison of our own devising. (Here the Professor indicates the precise point where Daniel should apply the tiny flame, wielding the receptor input to the sturdy plastic, the apparatus painstakingly measured to fire its laser simulacrum directly into Daniel's pupil.) But the brain is a more adaptable processor than any computer, much faster, much abler, capable of stunning reversals and equally frantic leaps into the unknown. Give a man wings and the brain will come to recognize them, learn how to use them, provide the software for flight. Give a man a third arm and the brain will write the code, make it work, sensation, a hundred hairs waving in filament feeling, a billion calculations a second, neurons racing, nothing like it in the world, no robot or computer processor can compare. (Here the Professor nods approvingly as Daniel narrows the laser to a pinprick stabbing into the centre of his iris.) So why not turn a man into a camera, his hair into an antenna, his mind into permanent storage facility capable of instant recall? Why not free ourselves to be more ourselves, to attain the trans-human gaze we so desperately crave, to become the machines we worship and adore? Why not give a man special parts, turn the tables on invasive authority, see the world the way they see us, through the back of the head, through the side, through the predictable subjective objectivity of state-sanctioned autovision: you want to see me every-where and anywhere, I want the same of you, and why shouldn't we have it? (The Professor nods. It's as simple as a flipped switch. Vision explodes. Daniel closes his eyes.)

A woman comes out of her house, bare feet, shorts. She stands on her lawn and stares at Daniel, half his face lost behind the black wraparound glasses. Mutated crow perched on a perfectly tailored front lawn. Bad luck.

Excuse me? Can I help you?

Daniel jerks his head up from the pavement.

Me? No—I'm just . . .

Daniel has begun again. Started over. Returned to The Program.

How long has it been since—

He remembers being twelve. He remembers coming home from school and finding the computer gone. His mother took it away. His father gave him a computer and his mother took it away. A queasy eruption in his stomach: resentment, relief. He never saw the computer (or his father) again.

In time, he found a way to look at the world that allowed him to move through it. He shut himself away from what he knew: the mutable subjective temporary of words and numbers. He refused to think about it. Daniel refused to ask: how can they not see the truth? A truth everyone around him negated with stories and games and diversions—words codified and given credence by banks and books and their expert interlocutors. So he too sought to negate it.

He moved as if wearing blinders, commanded himself to see exactly what they saw: what was in front of him. He spoke when spoken to, shut his eyes at night and willed himself into simple uncomplicated darkness. How does one do such a thing? He doesn't know. He did it.

He went to class, studied for tests and quizzes, composed essays on the history of great people who meant nothing to him. He was never anything other than an average student. Kept quiet. People forgot about him. Daniel too took solace in forgetting. He forgot that he was once in a coma, that he once stabbed the English teacher in the cheek with a pencil, that his father left— so what? He was average enough to attend the average university of his choice, provided he did not require funding. He did not require funding. His father left him a trust fund. More than enough to fly to the other side of the continent away from his mother's anxious gaze, more than enough to buy himself a computer. He picked out an older model not unlike the one Maury brought to his room before going away forever. Took it home, refurbished it from parts strewn about the Professor's lab. His mother thinks he's studying psychology. He just wants to finish what he started. What has he started? All these years he kept The Program with him, lost language, hidden code, tabula rasa etched into the rock of his brain.

The Professor knows. Will understand. The gap between past and future. He'll do it for the Professor.

He was in a coma once, free fall through a world everyone suspects exists, though few visit. Daniel needs evidence. Something to mark his passing. I was there. Where was there? He's not alone, he sees that now. The Professor's been, is maybe even, waiting for him. Where? There.

And so. The Program.

Daniel's stopped going to the lab. He hasn't left his room in ten days. He's abandoned his assignments. They don't really need him, anyway. He's the least technical of the group, the rest are graduate students, computer science types who speak in Klingon about extinct machine languages they used in high school to write their own choose-your-own-adventure games. Daniel works intuitively, fiddles with the inner language—the language inside language, as the Professor would say. The Professor a voice in his head, a ghost over his shoulder. It isn't the technology that grabs him, it isn't the programming challenges; it's the space where the Professor lives, the space where the keyer and the computer and the visor all connect. You can't get there in a classroom. You don't get there by plugging numbers into numbers. You don't go there bit by bit.

All at once or nothing. Don't think about it. He doesn't think about it. He knows it. It's like a miniature suicide, without all the bother of pills or knives or pistols.

The Professor wants me to do this.

No one e-mails. The phone doesn't ring.

No one tries to stop him.

He's slipping away. That's what he's waiting for. The feeling of interiority, an inner folding into an outer. The endlessness scares him. He works to find a conclusion, thinks of it as building a fort in the wilderness—as much to keep things out as to keep things in. It's a language, yes, a way to speak to the world, but something else, a way to speak to one's self. It's a method of communication more awesome and encompassing than any mere program of connection and facilitation.

He's invulnerable. He'll live forever. The Professor watching over him.

Daniel's room in a shared house is longer than it is wide. Coffin-shaped is how he put it to his anxious mother, the line full of sighs as Daniel tried to put a good spin on living conditions that embody such traits as maximum affordability and solitude (so long as he doesn't have to use the bathroom or fry an egg).

There's a crack in the far wall above the door he keeps securely locked, not that anyone tries to come in. He's taken to staring at the crack when he masturbates. He sits in his computer chair, legs spread, naked except for the apparatus—visor, cranium monitor, keyer in his left hand, dick in his other. Sometimes he has the crack come alive, sway and contort, wink and wave. He has the crack pulse to the rising current of his brainwaves spiking frantically toward orgasm.

He shoots on his chest, wipes it with a sock.

Begins again.

The Program came to him during one of those lasting sessions. Back and forth till the skin was raw and he could barely feel anything. It doesn't matter, he likes it better that way. Doesn't have to feel it, can just act, go about his business.

It came to him at the precise moment of conclusion, sudden ropy heat on his scrawny chest landing like a heartbeat. At that moment he felt something. He thought he felt something. This is the way it begins. Nothing specific. Just a vague glimmer, perhaps not exactly even a thought, but something between a thought and a feeling. Still, it stayed with him—a code, a length of numbers, an equation, an algorithm that, added up, subtracted of the non-essentials, calculated and put into practice, amounted to two ambiguous meaningless words: The Program.

Daniel would give the words meaning. He would turn away from his sticky chest and sore chapped member, away even from before that, from the moment of awakening when he emerged haunted by a body on him like a lost nightmare—The Program would take him back past all that, back past the dream he had once, that prolonged dream, the dream still going on.

Now he works. Hunched over his screen like a toad on a lily pad. He's got the visor plugged into his monitor, is playing the keyboard, the hand-held keyer. People say it's boring, it's 0s and 1s. But Daniel knows the beauty of it, the simplicity, the infinity. 0. 1. He thinks of the Professor, the way his face is soft and juvenile, unreadable, a perpetual promise. His fingers wave over the equations. The Program is a kind of music; it's the feel of an electric moment.

They say it can't be beautiful. Daniel reaches out to touch it. A madness. A euphoria. What's it like?

It's beautiful.

The Program is the senses. The Program is passion, only you never have to lose control, you never have to be alone in love.

The urge never goes away.

What is The Program?

Try it for yourself.

He pauses. How long has he been here? He thinks ten days, but it might be longer or shorter. No one comes to look for him.

On the visor, a kind of symphony: metre and rhythm. But it doesn't sound right, he knows. Ten days. He's been in this room, naked, sweating—he's on the third floor of a hot brick house. Ten days. This is day ten. Ten years old, he thinks. Closes his eyes. If he closes his eyes, he'll lose it. It'll be gone. Keep going. Don't sleep. Don't think. Just keep going. He jars the keyer, stuns himself back into consciousness with a flash of pure blinding epileptic light. Blinks till he can see again, thinks to himself, There. It's there. I'm almost . . . there.

Onscreen, the numbers in a pattern. On the visor, the numbers again. Overlaid with their graphical counterparts, a series of spikes, the hills and valleys of horizontal indicators stretching for miles, ages, forevers. There is the point where the parallel lines meet. It's the connection. It's The Program. Not brain and computer. Not flesh and computer. Not flesh and brain. But computer and flesh and brain and something deeper than all of that, something that makes all of those nouns meaningless ironic stand-ins for infinity—there is the inner of language, that thing that goes beyond language, beyond the expressions of the body, beyond the only two words there really are, affirmative and negative, 1 and 0—there, Daniel thinks, there, he can see and be it and touch it, it's not outside but inside him, not a product of the computer but a function of the cybernetic loop truly closed for the first time, the final continuity the computer has always promised to deliver, there there and there—the instantaneousness of eternity; the solace of oblivion.

Not later, but now.

The images careen through his mind, turn into something else, reflect back at him. The Program works, he can feel it. The problem isn't mechanical or code related; it's him, his brain, an unresolved resistance to the liberating principle.

The Professor says they'll always be hated because they are the first to reveal what the rest have become. But isn't it also the other way around? Aren't they also becoming what the others have fought against? And who can blame them? Why *should* we seek eternity, hard-wired moments of perpetual memory, life projected on the miniature movie screen of an inner lens, loops and reels trapped and regurgitated? We take comfort in ignorance, in being able to forget. We love our bodies, drooping and extra, padded in all the right places, the couch, the potato chips, the toilet seat warmer, padded in all the places, why should we want to change that?

Daniel watches the numbers cross and shift. He is skinny and hard, escarpments and ragged cliffs. He has no padding, no soft spot to fall on. Look, Professor, I think it's—do you see?—the lines almost touching. But something is missing, something that will make the brain light up like a slot machine jackpot.

Professor, wait, it's not—

Daniel rocks back and forth gently, moving with the flow he can feel through him.

The Program, he'll tell them when he returns to the lab, doing his best to imitate the Professor's tone of authoritative pedagogy, The Program connects the dependent carnal capacity to the methodical autonomy of the digital will. It is the ultimate device of control but also a creature of perpetual psychoanalysis, a thing of minute introspection.

But what does it *do?* he imagines them whining, anxious for it all to be spelled out in the reports and synopses of the scholarly journal.

See for yourself, he'll say.

The Program. In his brain, in his smooth chest, in his taut tart belly, his wet groin, his long thighs. They ache, and when the lines touch, they will disappear and everything will be different, inescapable, permanent in the most fleeting way. When you go, he'll tell them, it goes. When you change, it changes with you. The ultimate reality mediator. Reflecting the world through you, providing intimate knowledge of the self on the brink of dissolution.

Daniel is twenty years old.

The Program is the self. It's me, it's you, in the same way, he'll explain, the music video *is* the song.

He's close. He knows he's close.

He swivels his chair. The graphs arcing, the numbers racing, each one a work, an image, a possibility, an infinite zero. The crack over the door, widening gulf, warm crevice, lost dream.

The house is hot. The crack sweats.

His heart beats. He works the keyer, adjusting the sequence. The flow through the machine, into his brain. They aren't colours; they are his thoughts, reflected back to him, mediated, hyper-attenuated, captured and returned. The Program does to thought what the visor's laser projection does to the visual world. It mediates and returns it. It stores it and adds it up and feeds it back.

Daniel stops rocking. He doesn't move. Doesn't even breathe. This is The Program. It comes to him in an avalanche tumble, all at once, blinding and suffocating. The Program is here. It happens. Impossible speeds, fragrances, notes, shades, that could never have existed before the moment.

The entire world: electronic truth: script, soundtrack, action.

Total control. There is nothing outside. There is nothing left.

Video.

Professor, I—

Look at it. Look at it, Daniel.

He's hard, sticking out, the crack closing. He is inside nothing. He thought he had it under control.

Didn't he have it under control?

Nothing.

The crack closing.

Tight fit, Daniel.

The visor. Hot. Searing the backs of his ears.

His brain. The brain.

Bone melting. Soft underneath.

His body jerks, slumps.

He shoots his stuff. Falls into a fetal curl.

In the pine hills three hours north of the city, what's left of the wolves howl a welcome warning.

The Professor, in his head:

Now we are far from ourselves. Far from our flesh. Far from our flesh machines. We are lost dreams spiralling into the night—stars reaching earth with their faint pulse a million years after they're deep into darkness. So it is with us, to reach forward into time, to believe in our reverberations, to be seen in the future, to be dreamed up—that is all we have now, Daniel, that is all we can expect—the poignant comfort of a cliché: stars fading in a mist of long-distance light.

So what are you doing here? What brings you to be lying in this hospital bed? Why, for instance, aren't you out at the pub, the girls in their tank tops, the

boys with their baseball cap smiles? Why, just hypo-
thetically, aren't you dead, Daniel? You should be
dead, do you know that? Why are you here, and not
somewhere else? Is it the past that pushes the future
around? Are we blinded by the dark overwhelming
night always behind us? Is it something or someone that
won't let you go? Or is it the future you have fallen into,
only to find that same dark yawning maw? Do you
like girls, Daniel? Daniel, you search for the future,
you seek restitution in the possibility and, like me, you
believe you can dissolve the body. You want to overcome your humanness—we are a deficient species, it's
true, and the past haunts us. But what gives us the
right? Who are we, to do this or that? Will you die for
it, Daniel? Will you give up the ultimate—humanity—
for something else, maybe death, maybe something
more perfect than death—the sum of the past, the
totality of the future?

Why aren't you dead, Daniel?

Why don't you wake up, Daniel?

He opens his eyes. Spasms. Startles. Not at where he
is—hospital—where else? But the plainness of everything. Its static naked obviousness. *So. Slow.* He tries
to move. He needs motion, craves the perpetual
expanse of cybernetic space. A line in his arm. Drip.
Watches the clear swollen solution snake through the
plastic.

Eternity.

Drip drip. Drip. Drip. drip drip.

———

He wakes up. To the song of his muscles mocking him. The tiniest gesture sings pain in a fusillade of triumphant notes. It's the kind of pain that makes you realize how many moving parts you have, how smart the human orchestra really is, how precisely each note prefigures the next.

And yet, easily reduced to dissonance.

I did this.

Wakes up. Vomiting.

Dream, Daniel. Dream.

The Professor. There in the room with him. Sitting. Perched in a vinyl armchair next to the window. The light is grey, an overcast early evening. The sound of traffic passing. A gentle noise like the hum of machinery or Jews praying in silent repetition on Erev Yom Kippur, tonight it begins, the time of atonement.

Daniel needs to say something. But he has no words. He is simply body: a lump, a log, a lie.

What does the Professor know?

I was never a boy.

Bullshit. He wants to tell the Professor the truth, how much of a child he really is, trapped in a lurid miniature fantasyland, the Professor too a mere infant, his passion, his belief, no more sensical than a toddler's tantrum.

It rains in the hospital room. Grainy and dim. The Professor is unshaven, face spotty with tufts of wispy adolescent hair. He talks. He talks on and on and on.

Daniel stretches out his hand. To grab a finger, stroke a cheek, see if anyone is really there.

Who's there? Professor—?

Daniel. Why didn't you come to me? I've gone through your programming, taken the liberty—well, in truth, I can tell you, Daniel, that I've been following you all along. I wouldn't intervene. I vowed not to intervene. But watching your progress. Peeking into your head. You're not surprised. You wanted me there. I congratulate you. Your use of the programming interface. Amazing. Admittedly, somewhat alarming. You're barely alive, Daniel, you've barely lived. But Daniel, I must tell you, I've examined the programming and it's really very exciting. Daniel, I have told them I'm your uncle, and they've accepted it, a freak with a family of freaks. It's quiet in here, isn't it? You expect hospitals to be loud, frenetic, involved with the anxious business of saving lives. But in truth human life is a dull monotonous business, isn't it? Daniel, I told them I'm your uncle. I'd like you to think of me like that, as an uncle. After all, we really are like family. Your program is closer to the true spirit of my work than anyone has ever come before. I'm flattered, really, Daniel. Flattered and jealous. I envision more like us one day, Daniel, each individual orbited by a community, billions of stars, single voices united in constellations. Can you imagine the extraordinary light! Your program is, in its way, what I've dreamed for and sensed all my life. But what is it? What does it mean? What does it—no, I won't ask you what it does, because of course we both know it doesn't do anything. A thing of beauty and mystery, the first epic poem written for the cyborg future. Quiet in here, isn't it? I won't visit again. Daniel, why don't you wake up? Why don't you die? I had a normal childhood, so to speak, if there is such a thing. I just couldn't abide being told what to do. Early on I invented an electronic warning system that alerted me to when my parents were approaching my bedroom. Ridiculous. You see, I never wanted to be out of control. My life, the project, it's about finding a way to grasp every aspect of the world all at once. But you know, better than anyone, you know how control can elude you. You arrived out of nowhere, a cyborg genius, your head already in the murky atmosphere of parallel worlds. But where do you live, Daniel? You arrive, I reach out to you, you endanger the lab with your obsessive scheme, your narcissistic program of self-expansion, self-destruction. I won't stop you. I won't get in your way. Daniel, you wanted to erase your body. You wanted to kill yourself and live on. You sought to obliterate the past and occupy only an endless future. Why didn't you do it, then? What prevented you? There are questions being asked, you know, Daniel. Your mother has been contacted, the university is close to calling for an inquiry. They will have different questions than mine, Daniel. They could shut us down. I deny any knowledge, of course. I'm just building a wearable computer system capable of instant continuous broadcast to the World Wide Web with the help of my dedicated team of students. I don't know anything about ten-day-long marathon naked coding epics to create a useless program that monitors and reflects brainwaves back at the wearer, I don't know about the black void where we float effortless and pretend we are free until it sucks us down, encompasses us. I'm an engineer, not a social worker. I can't guarantee that my laboratory is a pressure-free environment, but my door is always open for my students to come to me and whisper in my ear their mid-term terrors. Daniel, it might be better for everyone if you never wake up. But if you do wake up, Daniel, think of me as your uncle.

Blinks. Surprised. He doesn't know where he is. He sits upright, suddenly teeters to one side. Rails keep him from falling out. Tube in his arm. Becomes aware of his own struggling chest. *Breathe*. Breathe.

Grabs on to the rail, hoists himself up. Opens his eyes cautiously, slowly.

Hospital, he thinks.

He can hear the slow swoon of the city traffic. He can smell antiseptic and reheated food. Exhaust, exhaustion.

It's all so . . . familiar.

Turns his head to the window. Sees an orange vinyl armchair. There's something dark on the chair, catching the glint of the city lights through the shaded window. At first it seems like a pair of eyes. Wolf pup pupils shyly peering out into the hostile world. Then

Daniel blinks, sees it for what it is: his gear, jumbled pouch of wires, black transparent visor glasses.

Dull throb, deep tissue bruise the size and shape of a skullcap.

(Get out of my head, Professor.)

Wakes up. Becky holding back tears.

He's barely spoken to her since he left home. University on the other side of the continent. Sure, why not? Why shouldn't he? That's the way the kids are doing it these days. City of light and perpetual summer almost over.

Hospital, he thinks.

Mom, he thinks.

He starts to cough and it hurts deep inside.

Hey, his mother says. She touches his pale bony back. Strokes lightly. There. It's okay. Here. Here. She gives him a sip of water from a plastic orange cup.

He manages to swallow.

How are you feeling? she says.

She says it like she doesn't care, like dinner options and perfect strangers.

Mom?

Then she cries.

Wakes up. Remembers now. The hospital. And some of the things before that. Switch flipped. Dark. Then bright.

Very.

Bright.

———

Sun through the window. Mid-afternoon. His mom sitting primly on the orange armchair. Knit white sweater and black tights. Brown hair. Trim and neat. A petite woman. Beautiful. They were friends once, of a kind. She held on to him and the loudspeaker said: Last call for boarding.

Then her boy stepped onto the plane and disappeared.

A year almost gone by. She expected him to come home for the summer.

I've got a job here, Mom. I'm working in a computer lab.

Oh, she said. I thought it was psychology you were—

Well, it kinda is. It's like a combination project. Psychology and computers. It's very exciting research, he said.

Honey, that's—I mean—terrific. I mean—maybe we could—

When it was over, he heard the steady hum of the empty line.

Pinch yourself. Because nothing is real.

The line pinches when they gently slip it out of his arm. The doctor says: You'll be going home soon.

Home? Daniel thinks.

He's still very weak, the doctor says. To his mom.

He wakes up.

They don't talk much in the lonely hospital room with its damp city light and the incessant distant presence of traffic passing down below.

Just: Would you like some more juice? or Let me get you another pillow or Here, I'll help you. Take my arm. Slow and nice. Nice and slow.

Everything hurts. Everything she says sounds like a question. Let me help you? Take my arm? Would you like some of this Jell-O? Nice and slow?

He tries to go to the bathroom by himself and almost falls. She's there. Take my arm?

They don't talk much in the lonely hospital room. Questions. My mother. My beautiful mother.

They have him use a wheelchair, orderly in white gleaming under fluorescent light, his mother's quick steps at his side. She carries his bag, keeps up a nervous chatter: How do you feel? Is it too much for you? Let me know if you're feeling dizzy. We can stop, no rush, no hurry, nice and slow. And when we get you to the hotel, we'll lie you down and for dinner—room service, anything you want, honey, anything at all. No more of that horrible hospital food. Are you okay? Are you going to be sick?

He slams the door to the taxi. Just to show her he can. She pretends not to notice. He pretends not to wince. It's like a bruise that starts at the top of his head and goes all the way down. The driver frowns, one hand on the wheel, one hand on the cellphone, heavy foot on the gas. They drive away from the hospital.

Daniel doesn't speak. He's actually feeling much worse than he intends to let on.

He wants to sleep, die, puke. In that order. In any order. He's packed the visor in the bottom of his bag, covered it with socks and underwear. Everything is too bright. He keeps shutting his eyes and opening them.

An imprecise system. All or nothing. No way to choose what to exclude.

He longs to feel the rush of life in particle streams. What's left out of the video feed. The red blinking light in the upper corner. Cut, paste, delete. The commands don't change. The commands are the same.

She puts him to bed. Stands over him. His eyes flutter.

He wakes up.

Mom? he says. Is it true? Was I—did he—

She turns away.

He sits in the bed. His skull feels soft, you could poke a finger through it. Thought leaking out like yolk past a poached egg. Daniel remembers that he hasn't been back to his filthy room for some time. He remembers being naked, he remembers the pale blue hospital room. He sees his mother in a robe. He thinks to say her name. Rebecca. Rebecca Stern. Everyone calls her Becky. The robe she is wearing is thick and white. Has the crest of a hotel. A hotel, he thinks, and the moment comes to him.

Now then, he hears her say. Let's get you out of bed.

He allows her to dress him. To position him on the

edge of the bed. To stand him up. His arms slip into another white hotel robe and his mother ties the sash. He stands in place, his knees trembling, his skin in goosebump minefields.

Her hand cool on his arm, or sinking deep into the hot wet swamp of his forehead.

You're feverish, she says.

No, he says. I'm just—I'm—

Shh, she says.

She leads him into the adjacent room, neat little parlour with a couch, a television, an armchair, a baby refrigerator. She puts him on the couch, pillows behind his head. He stays there, breathing like it matters. It's all different now. After The Program. It moves so slowly. His thoughts creeping. Each invisible moment of consciousness divisible. Pieces. Fragments. Instants. To be seen and pondered.

She stands with her back to him. She takes his hand and presses it against her cheek. She is trim and beautiful. He was the kind of little boy who had to be constantly told the obvious—the kind who couldn't seem to remember anything.

They thought I was—

—stupid—

Danny, his mother says. Her back to him. Her shoulders shaking.

He sleeps again. Wakes up on the couch.

How long have I—

He will finish it. It's still there. Nothing is resolved.

He feels it, a cancer, a pregnancy, something growing inside him.

—it's still here, Professor. Wherever here is—

His mother returning, the door closing. The smell of coffee.

Well, hello there.

Daniel waves weakly. Shy smile.

How are you feeling?

Shrugs.

You must be hungry.

Shrugs. Nods.

What would you like?

He smiles at that. Says it out loud. His voice a whisper. Bubby's soup.

What's that, dear? But she heard him the first time.

Bubby's chicken soup. With kreplach.

Yeah, she says. Your grandmother's soup.

She turns away from him. Sighs. Picks up the phone. Room service? she says.

Afterwards, he tries to stand up. He holds on to the arm of the couch and eyes the door. He imagines the long hall and the elevator and the lobby and the street first wide then narrowing.

How long have I—

Narrowing.

Hey, she says, sitting down again. Wake up, sleepyhead. You've been asleep for two days.

He shakes his head. I don't—

Do you remember being in the hospital?

He shakes his head.

You were there for more than a week. Her voice is frightened, accusatory.

A week? What's— He coughs, realizes suddenly how dry and cracked his throat is. Water, he manages.

She gives him a small bottle from the mini fridge. Watches him struggle with the cap.

Drinks. The cold sluicing through him.

Thanks, he says.

Danny, she says. Her voice cracking. She turns away.

She feeds him, and even though he's pretty sure he can do it on his own, he lets her do it.

Afterwards, she sits next to him on the couch, tries not to ask him any questions.

He wakes up and she's there, putting a blanket over him.

My brain, he says. It overloaded.

Shhh, she says.

Finally it's the morning. He dresses in the outfit she bought him. They take the elevator down, and he presses the button over and over and over, counts to ten then twenty. So slow. Fakes a smile, toothy grin at the woman, his mother, standing next to him.

In the hotel restaurant with its meaningless name— Interiors or Horizons—he feels like people should be staring at him.

They hate us, the Professor says. Because they are us.

—stay out of my—

He orders a huge breakfast. It's the first morning. His mother laughs.

Mom, he says, leaning in over his coffee, I'm—I just want to—you know—I'm sorry for—

Danny, she says. She touches his hand.

He pulls away. Grabs the handle of the coffee cup.

One night, his mother says, when you were . . . delirious . . . you said something strange. Something about your brain.

Did I?

Yes. You said, my brain—my brain must have overloaded.

He laughs. Now, finally, drinks from the hot coffee. Hand shaking. I said that?

Yes.

She looks at him. He has his father's fake laugh, his father's nervous all-encompassing desire. But he's slight and fair like her.

Danny—

Yes—

I want to know what you meant. I want to know what you did to yourself. Danny, did you—I'm your mother, I have to ask—Danny, did you . . . were you trying to . . . hurt yourself?

Hurt myself?

You were hooked up to some . . . machine? And they said you were trying to . . . deliberately trying to . . .

He looks down at the fork in his hand. When will breakfast arrive? He's hungry. He can't believe how hungry he is.

No, he says, smiling. No, Mom, it wasn't about that. It wasn't like that.

It wasn't like that?

She doesn't believe him.

Mom— He says it louder than he means to.

The table next to them. Looking or not looking. No way to exclude. Daniel misses the freedom of barriers, black plastic shielding his face. Laser pinpoints accessorizing the sensory. Moments in fragments, broken down, break it down.

Mom, he says again, almost whispering now, I was just trying to, I mean, I was trying to . . . it was an experiment, that's all.

The waiter sidles up. Plates and side plates. Steam carrying the smell of hotel breakfast—musty and rich, like furs in closets. The plates, arranged. Daniel surveys his eggs Benedict, the bright yellow splash of hollandaise, the potatoes in those perfect hotel cubes. Then the side of bacon, crispy and beaded with sweat. Half-melon split open oozing cool dew. The coffee, refilled now. Glass of orange juice, freshly squeezed, looks like a tropical sunset.

Mom, I— He tries again.

Let's just eat, she says. She's trying to be cheerful.

Later, he'll tentatively ask her: Does . . . did you . . . does Dad know what happened?

Oh, she'll say. Your father. That same tone. Like it doesn't matter. Your father, she'll say again. He's off somewhere, saving the world.

———

The summer ends in heat waves and unhappiness. Air conditioners hoarding windows, dripping and buzzing. The streets stink. Garbage collectors on strike. Half the city on strike. Cars idling in traffic, the roads hazy and crowded, curbs lined with black plastic bags bulging and spilling over. Smog hangs in the air like mustard gas. It's trench warfare on the sidewalks.

The summer ends in heat warnings and smog advisories. Don't go out of the house. Don't breathe. Don't drive. Don't water your lawn.

Ambulances idle in alleys, filled with the very young or the very old, anyone who can't quite carve a chunk of sweating air out of the city's gelling chemical stew. The summer ends in wet armpits and T-shirts stained at the belly in permanent shadows. The summer ends in a protest or a riot or an act of civil disobedience. The summer ends, surely, the summer—with its great giant bottomless bowl of an upturned sun—must end.

Daniel's mother sleeps on the fold-out couch.

He pictures himself kissing her goodbye. He thinks about stealing her cash, her credit cards, her supply of traveller's cheques. He thinks about leaving her a note, teaching her a lesson.

Groping through the gloom, he finds the doorknob. He can hear her, rustling.

He adjusts his visor. Blinks twice, initiates.

Password. Sequence. Confirmation. Execute.

Execute.

Night bursts open in all directions. Spews everywhere. Then he's on the street. It's like nothing happened.

Nothing happened.

He knows it's there.

The Program.

He feels a presence. Settling his mind into the grooves of expanding darkness. The lurking omniscient shadow.

The Professor.

—Professor?—

His father is a foreign aid worker now. Daniel imagines him in some hot land, face tanned and ruddy, a desk in a banana leaf hut, an old rotary phone ringing constantly, brown men in khaki suits listening attentively as Maury instructs them on corporate insurgency and the dangerous corrupting allure of a predetermined world he helped invent and knows better than anyone.

Maybe he'll track him down, hop on a plane, plan a visit. Maybe Maury will ask him to stay. He'll shrug. Sure, why not?

But first he's got to—

Finish what you started, Daniel.

Professor?

He doesn't have to look for it. Knows exactly where it is. Goes there and touches it. Struggles to pull away. Feels so good, like scratching a poison ivy rash. He won't—not yet—if he's wrong, it'll— The Professor was there too, stopped by for a visit, his mental footprints all around, an animal circling the tent after the bonfire is out and everyone is slumbering in carefully engineered heat-retaining sacks.

The Professor—

In my mind—so what? Let him—

Watching, waiting, capturing memory like it's an exotic butterfly to be pinned and collected.

The heat is oppressive. Unbearable after the cloistered perfection of the hotel's air conditioning.

He feels around the edges, assesses the damage. He knows what he has to do. Just needs the courage. Needs to work up to it. The heat pressing down on the city like a giant iron smoothing out the wrinkles. If it happens again, he won't make it back. He slips in and out, his body moving down the street. He presses gingerly on the centre of that interior bruise. Winces. Tests again. Harder. The streets are empty. Piles of smouldering garbage. Nobody sees his hands flutter to his head. Chest heaving. Calm down, he tells himself. How eerily absent are the streets in the big city. Like a set in a movie. Daniel looking inward. Doesn't see.

He walks not to arrive but to remind himself of movement.

He's been still for so long.

He promised her he wouldn't hurt himself. She threatened to file a complaint, to go see the Professor.

Mom, he said, I'm not a little boy. I can take care of my— His mouth shutting. Her elfin face indented with disbelieving wrinkles.

Suddenly old.

It doesn't matter what he promised her.

———

Daniel stumbles. Pulls out of the vortex of colours and cascading currents. Looks around him. He's veered off the sidewalk. It's absolutely quiet. But the street is occupied. That's the word for it: Occupied.

He sees the police first. Rows and rows of them. Masked and armoured, wielding translucent shields and black billys.

Then the protestors, not in rows but in a sprawling clump. Their organic single mass shifting and bulging. An amoeba of bandanas and balaclavas, gas masks and garden gloves proffering placards bearing the sort of slogans no one really believes any more.

And Daniel, tripping out of the side street into the middle of this. Into no man's land. Into nothing. He doesn't move. No one moves. Then his hand in his pocket. Working the keyer. Doesn't think. Tries not to think. Works the keyer. Furiously inciting the sequence.

His face impassive and smooth. He doesn't even sweat.

Just like the Professor.

But underneath, his bruised brain churns, runs dark red, his skull swelling.

Program.

Set up.

Transmit live signal.

Interface.

Scramble.

Capturing.

0111011101011010101011010101010100101010101010101010101011110

Scrambling.

Capturing.

Interfacing.

Looping.

Looping.

Program.

In the endless darkness he sees the shadow glint of the Professor's impassive half-grin. He sees the yellow of a wolf's moonlit eye.

Then the heat hits him hard. Sweat not in beads but streaming down his face. The summer arrives, comes and goes like a stillborn, lives for a while in the belly, in the imagination, ejects itself, dead and sticky, slicking thighs. Rots like garbage.

He's in the space between the warring parties. Who are these people? Danny does not know what they want. He only feels their urgency. Shares it, in a way. The pause to feel it coming. That gathering storm.

His legs tremble and give way. He falls to his knees. He manages to get his hand in front of the visor. Wants to see himself. Can't see himself. Smoke too thick.

Tear gas. Rubber bullets. Molotov cocktails.

He isn't dead.

It didn't work, he thinks.

But those visiting a certain website just past midnight on a certain July evening—what do they see?

A hand fluttering like a burnt moth against a night dark with heat and smoke and spotlights.

An instantaneous portal to an infinite world where ideas and actions are the same, where desire signals humanity, and nobody can hurt anybody because we

are ethereal and eternal, our lives adiabatic reactions
that require no loss or gain.

Electronic utopia.

A fragile hand. Waving then falling.

All hell breaking loose.

Every standoff ends sometime. The summer surges like
a power overload on its way to that inevitable blackout.

Daniel, in the middle, lightning rod, unknowing
catalyst.

The protestors hurtle forward, one giant hungry
cell. They want to encompass this stranger in dark
glasses, this sweaty man-child. They believe they have
the program to save him, the agenda of correction to
help him out of his current plight, on his knees in the
hot zone of a war zone.

The police nervously eye the boy, floppy new clothes
of the most recent style and colour; doesn't seem like a
radical, but you never can tell, can't see his face, could
be on something, could be a recent convert, they're the
worst kind. What's with the glasses? Regardless,
enough is enough. This boy is the final straw.

Daniel hangs his head back, feels its weight. Above
him the tall office buildings and hotels sway to the
beckoning of billboards. A woman wearing nothing
but a nose piercing and a bikini clutches a bottle of
Jimmy Trad whisky to her billowy cleavage; two
filthy yet perfect kids in various states of undress
sprawl in a dirty gutter, their designer po'boy hats
colourfully tilted on their greasy heads; a giant monitor

displaying a globe spraying electronic arrows; summer almost over, fall lineup in bright explosions, sit-
com smiles and the latest in medical drama. Where
are the caring doctors now?—his head is hot and hard
to hold up.

It didn't work, he thinks.

He paws the keyer.

Why didn't it work?—

—Professor?—

Filling up with blood.

Whistles and radios and bullhorns.

Sequencing.

Scrambling.

Executin

XXXXXXXXXXXXXXXXXXXXXXXXXXXXXXXXXXXXXXXXXXXXXXXXXXXXXXX

<too late for that daniel>

—What?—

—Professor?—

Bodies filling the absent space. The cops and the
protestors and a night sky obliterated.

Daniel looks on like he isn't there. Hands grasp for
him, pull him one way then the other. His flesh a swaying requiem to the innocent possibility of the image—
new landscape, new way to make the heart beat or to
beat the heat, universal particulars, each rotation
orbiting novel complexities, the image is alive, is as
accurate as the latest laser surgery or laser strike.
Hands on him. Tearing now. The piece of the image.
The boy in the nowhere zone who could go either way.
His visor ripped away. Daniel feels his heart pumping

not information but a truer yield—knowledge sticky and confusing as blood.

It's gone. The switch flicked. The plug pulled.

Daniel is aloft, passed back and forth.

Sees hands below him, thinks, again, of the Professor, his sharp claws—

—he doesn't know—what I—

Easy there, son, a cop says, grabbing him by a fragile wrist.

Leave him alone, pig! a protestor yells, yanking hard on Daniel's flopping legs.

The lab is dark.

The Professor, under pressure from a spooked administration, no longer allows his students to work weekends.

He stands in the middle of the gloomy room. Doesn't turn the lights on. Breathes, the sound lost in the hum of empty terminals lined up on the counter like unseeing eyeballs.

In a rage, the Professor sweeps an arm across the long table, knocks keyboards and screens to the floor.

They are blind. They don't see.

Grabs a thick report arduously prepared at his behest and shreds the pages. Throws a stool at a mainframe, heaves a visor in progress at a workstation. Doesn't stop to watch the ensuing shower of glass and smoke. He whips a keyboard out of its socket, sends it careening into a rack of transducers. He is silent as the hardware rains down all around him. The machines hum and syncopate their electronic circumstances, plot their slow lumbering mindless plots.

—Daniel? Are you—?

Empty reverb. Nothing. Worse than nothing.

Daniel moves by habit. His legs jerk forward, robot-style. Unable to navigate the tall steps up into the building, he finds himself on his hands and knees. Crawling. Down the long empty hallway. Leaning against the wall for support. The door to the lab. Ajar. Open. Vulnerable. Daniel's brain wiped clean. Emptied. Downloaded but not saved.

Daniel's just flesh now. Shuffling along the floor. He reaches his workstation. His hands grab the edge of the counter. Pull his body up. Stands, quivering.

Daniel! The Professor's gaze a gleaming black diamond.

Daniel teeters, turning. His white milky eyes wet and empty.

The Professor approaches, arms open.

Daniel points behind him. At him.

The Professor opens his mouth. Prepares to deliver his final soliloquy.

Blood oozing out his student's pupils.

The Professor falls silent.

Daniel falls into the Professor's grasp.

The Professor's hands grope. Pull off his glasses.

He leans into the boy. Their foreheads touch, skin to skin.

You'll be released tomorrow.

I know.

They've explained the conditions?

Five hundred times.

Dr. Reivers smiled. She indicated the seat next to her. Two armchairs at familiar angles in a gloomy corner dwarfed by floor-to-ceiling bookshelves.

She'd always seen him in the sterile treatment centre. He'd never been in her office before.

He sat, his knees tucked.

How do you feel?

He didn't answer right away.

This isn't counselling, she said.

I know.

She leaned closer. He could smell her.

Starting tomorrow, Dr. Reivers said, you've got your whole life ahead of you.

And behind me.

That too.

I used to have an office, he said.

Would you like to again?

No. He tried to sound confident.

What would you like?

I— He looked away from her, focused on the desk, piled with reports and studies and directives from the state bureau of mental health and hygiene.

It's okay, she said. It isn't fair of me to ask you that. She took his hands in hers.

They were both leaning forward, their faces almost touching.

He rested his head on her shoulder.

The phone rang.

I'll be late for my next appointment, she finally said.

He didn't move.

We shouldn't be doing this, she said.

Who says? he whispered. Who says we shouldn't?

She let go of his hands, gently disengaged his head from her soft pillowed shoulder.

She looked at her watch. It's time to—

The phone ringing.

Did I ever tell you, he said, that you remind me of my ex-wife?

Why's that? Dr. Reivers sighed, withdrawing into her armchair.

I mean, in a positive way.

She didn't respond. The office an entombed vault. Walls lined with books.

It's quiet here.

Not usually.

Doctor, can I ask you something?

Yes.

Do you really—I mean—can someone . . . like me . . . really be—

Don't think of it like that.

————

Let me ask *you* something.

What do you want to ask me, doctor?

Did you touch them?

No.

You didn't touch them?

No.

I believe you.

Thank you.

Dr. Reivers started to get up.

He spoke suddenly, loudly. You want to know? You want to know what I did with them?

You don't have to—

I—

Go on.

I worshipped them.

MAURY PULLS INTO YET ANOTHER fast food parking lot.

—thirty percent—

But what choice does he have? There's nothing else for miles. This is it, a last outpost, final monument to a crumbling civilization he is in the process of leaving behind forever. Day fading into night. He thinks he's hungry. He gets out of the car. He stands under the golden arches breaking through the impenetrable sky. He feels the greasy drops of sleet on his cheeks. On the short walk to the fast food enclave, he stops in the empty outdoor playland plastered with wet napkins, discarded burger boxes and rotting leaves. He thought he was hungry.

He moves by habit, by what has been conferred on him.

At the counter, he is met by a teen with a spotty forehead. Thinks of his brother as a young man.

I'll have, uh . . . He scans the brightly lit overhead menu. He closes his eyes. A coffee.

Can I get you anything else tonight? the boy drones.
Maury pulls out change.

Driving again. Maury purses his lips, digs the cup
from between his legs. No cup holder, of course. His
old car. Coffee, cream and double sugar, which has
what relevance to our nutritional needs? Maury
knows about it. Maury's expounded on the lifestyle
accoutrements of a habit-encouraged populace. How
to foster. How to take advantage.

His fleshy lips suck in. His head tilts back. The
brown brew gushes. Hits his mouth. Maury splutters.
Burn rising. Perforations. Tongue. He drops the coffee,
which gurgles onto his lap, seeps past his suit pants.
This new pain Maury barely registers. Maury spits
coffee on the dashboard.

The road is curving. Maury's old car is not curving.

A guardrail. A ditch. Several adolescent trees struggling to make a life out of the hardscrabble off-the-
highway dirt.

Car ends up on its side, wheels spinning. Maury,
somehow, struggles out, stands in the wet night gasping for breath. Hot blisters in his mouth. He feels
warm liquid on his chin, on his crotch. His palms
locate the wet spots. He presses his hands down, but
he can't feel any kind of injury. Should be relieved.
Isn't. This is the end of the old car. Becky always hated
it. Old car lying on its side and making a noise like
gears needing to shift.

Maury looks behind him. In the diminishing light,

in the rain getting colder, he can barely find the trajectory of the incident. The way he came through the fringe of the woods. He is a novice at following paths, always considered himself a trailblazer.

The headlights of the car are still on. They reveal the rain: drops bloated with cold. He thinks, suddenly, of his wife, pregnant with their first and only child.

Danny.

He kicks the squashed car. Headlights blink, then flicker out, a fading memory. In the sudden darkness he kicks the car again, hard against the soft tip of his loafer.

Maury stands in front of the accident, frozen rain forming crystals in his hair. He can smell the sink of mud and decomposition.

Night of reckoning in a forest smelling of childhood. Somewhere in the darkness, somewhere past his overturned car, he'll find redemption. It will come in the form of a cluster of falling-down cabins, a cinderblock meeting hall, a wooden dining room—seems small, but when we were kids . . . a rotting dock buoyed on a silver lake.

Maury's trying to be reasonable. He's trying to picture it the way it is, not the way it was.

His long-lost brother sobbing in his old bunk, his tears blurring an old comic book or the wrinkled well-thumbed picture of a half-dressed girl. The musk of unwashed bodies, the chemical stink of green mosquito coils, the hot wet breath of twenty boys sighing into their polyester sleeping bags.

He feels the wet—a verdant puberty—in his nostrils.

He could die in these woods. Early frost. Or are the seasons further along than he imagined? Where has he been? What day is it? Maury has no idea. The rain gathering weight as it comes down ice. Exposure, panic, starvation, hypothermia. Maury doesn't think to trace his way back to the highway, to flag a ride to the nearest Hilton, to have himself a steak dinner and then resume operations in his office on the twenty-second floor in the third most prestigious advertising firm in the country, the continent, possibly the world.

He paces around the car. Claps his hands. Runs his fingers through his unruly mane of hair, the ice bits catching in the cracks between his fingers. And then another revolution around the car, on its side like the centrefold girls they used to keep in a cache under his mattress. Another few handclaps barely audible in the downpour of hail, another graze of fingers through hair. Maury lost in the moment of arrival.

He sings the camp song. *Gesher, Kadima Gesher! Gam ba layla, gam ba boger, Kadima Gesher!* It could be as close as behind that grove of debilitated trees or that thicket of angry drooping raspberry bushes.

The lake, he thinks of the lake, remarkable body of water always so warm when it rained.

They let us swim in the rain.

Gesher! Kadima Gesher!

He'll dive in, the water sluicing around him, cleaning him.

He can smell himself: sweat and beer and fast food and sex.

He can't go back.

Maury stops circling. He stands beside the car, still dragging his fingers through his hair. He doesn't know how cold he is. He's breathing heavily. Are these even the right woods? Take a deep breath. The rich biodegrade of fall turning into winter. His skin still exuding coffee and grease and hangover, but the odour getting fainter, the forest washing over him; that smell—it's so— Maury thinks about god, and fate, and destiny. He thinks:

That smell.

It's so!

Why not? They've called a chocolate bar the whichamacallit? They've sold beer via a bull terrier and tires via an imaginary white marshmallow creature. Willy Wolf available in over fifty countries.

That smell.

A slogan can come from anywhere. Like a lightning bolt. He hears a distant rumble. He cranes his head for a look at the sky through the skeletal fingers of the trees reaching upwards. Gets a face full of sleet for his troubles.

Close your eyes and picture the dirt road into camp, the sign even then faded paint peeling, tree boughs brushing the top of the school bus. As the bus sliced through the barely standing wood-and-rope archway, all the boys fell silent. Through the windows smeared with dirty nose grease they contemplated the impending summer—a gradual weight like diving to the murky bottom of the deep end and bringing up a fistful of reeds to show your friends.

Maury could never reach the bottom.

But the lake was clear, and you could see it down there, a calm plateau.

What is he waiting for? He's wet, soaked through.

The forest all around him.

Maury wants to cross over, wants to join his son, lost so he can be found.

He loves his wife.

She's so beautiful.

—and Danny—

Maury wants to see a light and move away, into the darkness where he thinks the truth might be hidden under a decrepit building: the old meeting hall where the counsellors got drunk and smoked pot and no campers were allowed, but you could hide under it until the time came for you to make a break for the flagpole, for Palestine, for liberation. The thing to do was watch for the light and then shrink down behind old cinder blocks and discarded chunks of lumber and Styrofoam. After the light went away, it was time to make your move.

Maury got caught every year. Until, finally, he graduated from oppressed to oppressor.

In this kind of darkness, you might see anything. You might be standing right next to something and not even notice.

He's cold. He needs to—

Maury sighs, steps away from the wreck. Wrestles his way into the woods.

He moves through dark crevices of absent foliage. Deeper and wetter. How long is the night? His legs tremble. He wipes the melt from his face. The rain goes hard, then drizzles. Maury trips over a desiccated log, scrapes his hands on a rock. Scrambles on his hands and knees like a crayfish. He's on the fringe of a clearing. An eight-foot boulder lurks in the centre. He hauls himself to his feet. Relieved for some reason, he moves to the rock, visible as a slightly darker mass in the dark night. He bumps gently into the rock, spreads his arms in an embrace. He closes his eyes, presses a cheek against the craggy surface. He recalls the way he could see every detail of the playland, illuminated by the halo of the fast food restaurant's familiar arches. He sees himself walking back to his car through the mostly empty garbage-strewn parking lot. If it doesn't matter, he thinks, it doesn't matter. He holds on to the rock. Imagines holding Dr. Reivers. His wife. His son. All of them. Holding on for dear life.

My brother—

He shivers.

Maury hurls around, careens like a digital fighter pilot shot out of the pixel sky courtesy of the uncanny reflexes of the average ten-year-old working the trigger of an arcade game console. The bog Maury has fallen in could be quicksand. He feels the way the wet is slowly pulling his thrashing legs under. He won't remember the feeling. He'll remember this place. This is the place where he'll find the lost boy. I'm sinking. Don't panic. He's a good boy, the kind of boy who knows and remembers the rules. Don't panic. Don't wander. Don't disappear. This isn't the jungle, he reasons. There isn't quicksand. Swamp lapping at his calves. He extricates his feet and legs. Pulls his body. Surveys the bog, a black expanse that could end a truck's length in front of him or go on forever, consuming men, brothers, boys, last decade's new model compact, last week's supercomputer. He jumps for it. Sinks to his ankles a few stumbles from shore.

You can be lost in your backyard, lost in the basement, lost in the space between the couch and the stereo cabinet.

He's here, Maury thinks. His heart in beats and night cricket flutters.

Maury sinks a little deeper, feels silty water clinging to his thighs. He wrenches a foot free of the grasping mud and tries to find a place to step. Loses his balance. Falls over.

Thrashes, gasps.

Forces himself to lie still, face in the mud.

He calmly sits up.

His heart beating.

Wipes the mud out of his eyes, gets more mud in his eyes. Sucks at the air, tastes dirt. Sits in the mud on the edge of the shore panting and dripping.

He gets on all fours, blunders and blinks to the bank, which isn't really a bank but a gradual hardening of the earth, a thickening of the damp brown vegetation. He pulls himself up an oozing weedy peninsula. Behind him, a row of stilted crooked trees. It's not the way he imagined. Being lost. Being alone.

Maury drips mud, has tentacles of brownish green slime striping his sports jacket.

He closes his eyes. Hears the icy rain against the wood of empty trees. A sound like kernels popping. Danny loves popcorn.

Imagine the hard rain. Imagine a soft-boned boy with a luminescent smile. Imagine where a boy like that would get to in a night like this.

When you're lost, you should shout for help every ten minutes. That way the rescuers will be able to pinpoint your location faster.

Maury smells something through the damp rich murk of mud. Whiff of smoke. Taste of rubber. Something burning.

There are all kinds of rodents in the woods. If a man could learn to find them and trap them, he could eat them raw or roasted and stave off starvation for a day or a week or a month.

Maury sniffs, his nostrils forward like a rat's snout. Looks around him. Everything is a variation on the theme of inky black.

Maury's not an outdoors man. He prefers a bargain to a bonfire.

He wants revenge, but on whom, and for what?

He pushes himself off a Precambrian boulder.

I'm looking for him, Ma. I'm doing just like you said.

The old lady's phone rings and rings. No one answers. The television blares on, oblivious, hypnotized by its own bright flickering variation.

Progress is slow. Maury can barely see two feet in front of him. He brings a forearm down hard, branches scattering like tiny brown mice. There's a pain in his chest now, a broken rib poking its jagged white point into the underside of the heart, where the muscle is vulnerable and overworked. He's near. He thinks he's near. He wants it to be over. He wants it to be like when he was a kid, when they wordlessly sat on the bus together and watched the forest advance.

The night, the smoke, the blunder through the trees. Maury doesn't bother trying to discern a path, a location, a direction. The rain picks up again, slaps his face with dense waves of sharp icy projectiles. He takes tentative faltering steps.

A boy gets lost and found almost every day. A rescue is hardly extraordinary. There could be wolves in these woods. Angry sulking creatures who gorge when they feed. Maury moves by instinct, by pain, by regret, by deduction from logic, by expertise, by divine light.

He follows the smell of smoke.

No one ever asked him, at all his lectures and appearances, Aren't you a fraud? Aren't you just lucky?

He doesn't think about it any more.

Once, he had a brother. Maury pictures a flannel shirt and leather vest, a burly man standing on an eternal hilltop, one boot balanced on a boulder. That rugged fellow contemplating the vast terrain before him, grimaced smile begrudging his been-there face. The caption: *Jim Franklin's Traditional Bourbon. Because the Good Things in Life Never Come Easy.*

A burst of hail.

Then it stops raining. The dripping night. In the sudden air, the smoke smells thicker. Unnatural, chemical, it burns thick and wet. Maury breathes it in. It doesn't matter—why should it matter? Maybe it doesn't matter. I'm here, he thinks. Aren't I here? He steps silently between trees, tracking the shadow ahead.

The frozen rain has stopped, but he feels colder and wetter.

He moves, his bones brittle and reluctant. He imagines the bunks and the dining hall and the meeting room, he can see the flagpole area where they sang the national anthems—of the holy land, of course, and of the Western country where they resided in a state of temporary permanence.

Fleeting clarity. But now he's—

He strains to see in front of him. It's darker now. Colder too. He thought by now he'd have arrived. He figured by now the sky would lighten, morning breaking like a Ritalin fog.

He forces a leg, then another. Trips into underbrush, somehow stays upright. He can't seem to think.

He can't seem to make a decision. Why isn't it morning? Danny in his coma haze. Is it like this? A slow ponder, a decision-making process that never leads to a decision? His soaked muscles cringing. Branches breaking and shaking. Cold sluicing down his back.

He holds a hand up to his face. He sees it there, a variation in the quality of the darkness.

His hand shaking. His fingers swollen and useless.

He hears a cellphone ring, the artificial sound eerily misplaced yet familiar. Paws at it. Keep walking. The bush, his phone ringing, the smell of fresh acrid smoke.

He doesn't have a cellphone.

He manages to get a bloated grip on the bleating machine. The ring echoes and penetrates, dispels bats and voles and a pack of sharp-teethed fishers. Night creatures emerging into wet.

The forest wired for cellular transmission.

He says: Maury Stern here, with all the confidence and authority of a man sitting at his lavish oak desk, taking in the view of the city from his perch on the twenty-second floor.

Maury! Hi! It's Dr. Goldstein calling.

Doctor, hello.

Hullo! Maury! Can you hear me?

I can hear you, doctor!

Maury, I can hear you too!

Doctor, how is—

Listen, Maury, I'm calling about that son of yours.

Danny—is he . . .

He's fine! Terrific!

Is he . . . out of . . . the . . .

Maury! Speak up! You're a thousand miles away! I can barely hear you!

I'm—I—never mind. Doctor, listen, Danny, is he— Maury shouts now. Is. He. Out. Of. Danger?

Danger? Maury, he's fine! He's great! He's terrific!

But what about . . . the . . . coma?

He's a great kid. Maury, you don't know how lucky you are. You should see some of the kids we get in here. Kids with attitudes. Kids in need of serious meds to adjust their flawed emotional construction.

He's so thin.

Maury! Better thin than fat. These days, kids are gigantic. *Titanic*. They spend all day microwaving snacks and doing who knows what on the computer.

Doctor—I—can you just tell me, is he . . .

Maury, you're a good man. You really are. A real gentleman. So here's what we do. Why don't we keep him here a few more days for observation? We'll run some tests and see how he's doing. How's that sound? Of course, it's an extra care issue, a precaution, so it isn't covered, Maury, I hate to bring this up, but, Maury, these kinds of cases are expensive. I know you want the best for your son.

What's wrong with him? *What* kind of cases?

Oh, about eight hundred a day should cover it.

No. I said— What's. Wrong. With. Him!

Okay, so, listen, if it's too much, we can look at other alternatives. We can ship him down to the state hospital if you prefer, no problem, I'll get the nurse to—

No, that's not what I—

Maury, before you decide, let me just hold the phone up to his— Can you say hello, Danny? Danny? Your dad's on the line—go ahead, Maury, talk to him, he's a little—shy—

Danny! Danny! Are you—

Maury's feet move. He looks around him. He's stopped shivering. In fact, he feels warm. Hot. He holds a branch in his fist. His fingers are loose now, supple and alive. He's yelling at the branch.

Why am I—?

He's so hot. He takes off his sports jacket. His fingers deftly unbutton the front of his shirt. He looks down at his feet. He's on a rutted road. The camp road, he thinks. He's hot, but it's a strange heat. He lets his fist go. Drops the stick.

His muscles on him like a coat.

Is it over?

He thinks it must be almost over.

The sun pale through branches.

Maury shivers, can't get warm.

The forest is alive, a breeze rustling the boughs of water-soaked grey-brown firs.

Maury slumped against a tree.

His lips cracked, tongue swollen.

In the end, all the mistakes in the world won't matter.

Struggles to stand, manages to hoist himself up, wrapping his arms around wet bark.

Wait, Maury mutters. I'm coming.

The morning breeze brings the aura of unnatural singeing, a burning easy to separate from the rich brown of the drying forest. The tree branches glisten with melt, go dark and brown, look like the limbs of slick animals caught in the rain.

Maury thinks of Danny. That march into the woods. The way the wolves paced below them, civilization peering through the murky darkness to catch a glimpse of its true nature.

He'll find his brother and tell him everything.

You did this, he'll say. You did this to me. *To us*.

Maury rounds the slow curve of the road. And there it is. Faded green plywood sign, white paint turned a dirty grey announcing: *Camp Gesher*.

Gesher means bridge, he once told his brother.

The gates sit open, partially collapsed, logs hollowed out from inside.

Maury stands in the sports field. Looks around him as if he's never seen a baseball diamond. As if he deserves some kind of explanation. A breeze through the brown grass dotted with patches of ice and muck. The diamond is smaller than he remembers. He played outfield in the grass studded with blooming clover. He worried, at the time, about bees stinging him as he ran to catch a fly ball.

The sky is huge.

He could be anywhere, he could be—

You could fall into the sky and never be heard of again.

His hands are shaking.

The sky, he thinks. Smoky detritus of an extinguished bonfire.

We were just boys.

He moves numbly down paths. His feet are swollen. It's like walking on two plastic balls. Through naked trees, the familiar buildings become visible. This old meeting hall, the new meeting hall, the dining room, the various bunks in various stages of permanent decay.

They all seem so small. This place, Maury thinks. I shouldn't have—

His mother dies alone.

His mother dies watched over by Becky, convert daughter-in-law.

Maury feels something. Can't be sure. A faint stabbing, though it could just be hunger. In one of those bunks his brother signed his name, thick cursive letters rendered Magic Marker permanent on a thin wood wall.

Pauses in the playground area. Rusted swing set, teeter-totter, a few crumbling picnic tables, a pole for tether ball. Another one of those faded green signs, white words bleached yellow by the elements: *Marx Park*.

The stench of smoulder is stronger now. Maury can see the plumes of grey dispersing. Log bridge leads him over a stream flowing down to the lake. The logs are wet, rotten, the ropes binding them frayed. Maury crosses, feeling the bridge squirm under him. He does not look back at the bridge. The camp as it was thirty years ago, only smaller and shabbier, its ideologies more evidently crude, like a corporate theme park, Maury thinks, Willy Wolf hugging the kiddies and handing out half-price passes for the castle tour.

He has this illusion about childhood. That they were happy. That what started started later, didn't have anything to do with him.

His brother is here. Where else could he be?

All the paths lead to the same place: the hill in the centre of the camp where the flagpole flies the flags, one for the supposed homeland of the Jewish people, one for the country good enough to keep them in cars, jobs, houses, hospitals, malls and private schools until they make the final pilgrimage. The flagpoles are gone, taken down for the season. The hill, more of a lump, looks barren. At the top of the hill, a smouldering fire.

Maury thinks he sees something else. Squints and peers. Is it a boy, naked flesh smudged with ash? Tiny life smeared against the vast blue sky.

Maury hurries down the wide path. All roads lead to the flagpole hill. He focuses on the deep aquamarine of the sky merging into the lake. He breathes evenly, mechanically. The air reeks of kerosene and melted plastic. As he draws closer, he can see that the night's giant bonfire is now just a smoking nest; partially melted clothing strewn around a smouldering pit: kid-sized running shoes soldered together, scorched jeans, smoking sweaters, parkas, baseball caps. A solitary pair of kid-sized underpants, half consumed, draped over the black edge of a fuming log.

A boy stands. His thighs, dappled grey, white bits flashing. The boy glows under the rising sun. He smiles at Maury. Waves. The bright morning pale and irrelevant.

Maury stops at the foot of the stunted hill, not nearly as tall and wide and impressive as he remembers it.

Some things don't change. The lake rolls, green and gentle, invites dramatic dives and painless drownings.

The wind shifts. Smoke in Maury's face. He closes then opens his eyes. Blinks, tries to see. Brushes away tears.

The boy is gone.

There isn't a boy.

With thanks to Darren Wershler-Henry and Emily Pohl-Weary for their valuable comments on the book as it progressed.

Thanks, also, to my parents Sam and Nina Niedzviecki for their enthusiasm and dedication.

An excerpt from this novel first appeared in *Descant* magazine's Speculative Literature issue. For some reason, they thought I was writing science fiction. I'm glad they did.

Gratitude to Rachel Greenbaum, for continuing to inspire me, for giving freely of her time to comment on this work, for reminding me to care.

Finally, respect and appreciation to my editor Anne Collins for her sharp mind, canny instincts, and ongoing support.